VIRGINIA GOLD

A NOVEL

VIRGINIA GOLD

A Perilous

Journey for an

Impossible Dream

WILLIAM THOMAS

WinePressPublishing
Your Book, Defined. Since 1991.

Unless otherwise noted, all Scriptures are taken from the *Holy Bible, New International Version®, NIV®*. Copyright © 1973, 1978, 1984 by Biblica, Inc.™ Used by permission of Zondervan. All rights reserved worldwide. WWW.ZONDERVAN.COM

Scripture references marked KJV are taken from the *King James Version* of the Bible.

Scripture references marked NASB are taken from the *New American Standard Bible*, © 1960, 1963, 1968, 1971, 1972, 1973, 1975, 1977 by The Lockman Foundation. Used by permission.

Hard Cover:
ISBN 13: 978-1-4141-1708-9
ISBN 10: 1-4141-1708-6

Soft Cover:
ISBN 13: 978-1-4141-1707-2
ISBN 10: 1-4141-1707-8

Library of Congress Catalog Card Number: 2009914231

To Jane Thomas Chandler.
Her love of history, and the preservation of the story of
John Thomas, the first Thomas to come to Jamestown in
1610, gave me the challenge to write this historical novel.
It is based on some historical facts and some imagination
of what could have happened during the years for which
we have no record of him.

CONTENTS

FOREWORD

I WAS A lad of nine when historical novels first captivated me. The stories that most captured my imagination were tales of an English lad who lived among the Blackfeet Indians of Montana in the mid-eighteen hundreds. In my imagination, I lived out the stories that author James Willard Schultz brought to life in his historical novels. Most of my childhood friends back in the thirties were just the opposite. My playmates were spellbound with the futuristic Buck Rogers. His space travels, then, were just a dream in some writer's mind.

Whether the past captures our imagination depends a great deal on how historical events are portrayed. I believe all of history is a story, consisting of many peoples' stories. But all too often we read them as lifeless facts.

A college history professor once asked, "Do men make history, or does history make men?" He was asking a basic question in life. Did the desire for independence from England make George Washington the great leader he became? Or, did George Washington, by his character and leadership, create the results of the struggle that made history?

By taking apart the word *history*, we actually have two words: *his* and *story*. It's when we combine them that something is lost. They become lifeless dates, events, and facts. The person in history is lost. "They are no longer living," we say. But does this make them irrelevant? Hardly, most historians would say.

Many famous people, both present and past, have acknowledged the importance of history. Pulitzer Prize-winning historian David McCullough asked some important questions regarding the value and importance of history in *Parade Magazine*, June 22, 2008. He asked, "How important is history in the United States? Why does history matter?" And finally, "What can we learn from the past?"

Many have heard the saying, "Those who never learn from history are doomed to repeat it." Winston Churchill once said, "The farther backward you can look, the farther forward you can see." And yet, according to a recent survey, less than half of high school youth know the dates of our Civil War. According to David McCullough, "Trying to plan for the future with no knowledge of the past is like attempting to grow cut flowers."

It has been said that Albert Einstein believed the only difference between the past and the future was a stubbornly held illusion, and Ralph Waldo Emerson once wrote, "There is properly no history, only biography."

The greatest historian of all, Almighty God, in His book, the Bible, inspired men and women to tell their stories of His love, truth, and compassion so as to teach us wisdom from the past, plus faith, trust, and hope for the future.

My historical novel is based in part upon those truths found in the book of books, the Bible, as well as some events that occurred in the earliest founding of our nation. My aim has been to make history come alive in the lives of real characters who lived out their story in this tale of historical fiction. Whether we believe it or not, all of us owe something in our character to those ancestors who lived out their stories, just as we are living ours.

Perhaps one of the greatest purposes and meaning of history is to take the best from the past, use it, and seek to enhance it, and then pass it on to posterity. When we do, history comes alive.

PROLOGUE

IN 1985 I stood on a bridge over Queen's creek, about three miles west of Williamsburg, Virginia, where I-32 crosses. This landmark evoked a special meaning for me. The place where I stood was originally part of a land patent granted to my Welsh ancestor, John Thomas, by the governor of the colony of Virginia. This patent was for five hundred acres and happened approximately four hundred years ago.

Today, this land belongs to the state of Virginia. But, in another sense, it still belongs to me as part of my heritage. My ancestor, about ten generations ago, lived here and hacked out a plantation from pine forests. He found gold here.

However, the gold he found was not the metallic kind. Rather it was "Virginia Gold," better known as tobacco. The introduction of tobacco growing in the colony began with John Rolfe, husband of the legendary Pocahontas. Rolfe sailed to the colony of Jamestown on the same ship, the *Sea Venture,* as my ancestor John Thomas in 1609.

The Persians, Spaniards, and later the Indians, in the Western Hemisphere, grew and harvested tobacco for many years prior to 1600. A market for this plant was developed in Europe in the fifteenth century, where it became popular with the populace.

Prior to leaving England, Rolfe secured some tobacco seeds from a Spanish trader. A few years later, after his arrival in the colony, he planted them just as an experiment. He didn't know the climate of Virginia would be so favorable to growing the plant. Results were amazing. The news spread, and soon growing and exporting this crop made the colony one of the most prosperous in the New World.

My ancestor, John Thomas, came to find wealth and status in Virginia. He became a gentleman farmer and grower of "Virginia Gold." I believe he realized his dream, and much more. He sired a family called Thomas, who, along with many others with different names, carried out similar dreams. They helped create these United States of America, the greatest nation on earth.

This novel is an attempt to understand more of my heritage, as well as the forces that motivated young people to risk the security of their homeland for the dangers, gamble, and promises of an unknown future. John Thomas's faith in his impossible dream, and in his God, enabled him to live the American dream of going from rags to riches.

ACKNOWLEDGMENTS

WHEN I TRY to remember those who have had a part in helping me write this novel, I could almost call it their book. Truly, I am indebted to many who helped educate me in the fine art and craft of writing. Some were published authors, others were novices like myself. Enough of it rubbed off to keep me at my computer until I finished my first draft.

A professor once told our class that everyone has at least one book in him or her. I'm delighted I believed him. The ministry was my first love, and only after retirement did I give in to this dormant desire that lurked just below the surface of my mind.

My wife, Donna, has been a constant source of encouragement and help by perusing my writing and offering constructive ideas and feedback.

Several writing class instructors gave me insights that helped to hone my latent talent and attempts at this craft. First among these is the late Wendy Haskett, who blended her critiques with warm smiles and her Irish wit. Avoneellee Kelsey was another teacher and first publisher of our classes' creative gems, and

Beth Sherman was a teacher who gave much time and talent to promote my interest in poetry as well as prose.

Members of these writing classes are honored as fellow travelers for their penetrating criticisms. Among these are two ladies, Mary Chandler and Barbara Ludwig, who were particularly helpful.

I especially want to thank my editor, Dr. Dennis Hensley, for all the hours he spent making sure I had a readable novel. Without his help, I could not have done it.

Last, and most of all, is a lady, Jane Thomas Chandler, who compiled a book titled *The Thomas Tree*. From her work I read a brief account of the indenture of John Thomas of Wales to Jamestown who was part of the *"Sea Venture* Saga." His story is the genesis for my novel.

Finally, I have written this novel in memory of my father, Willie Horace Thomas, for being my link to the novel's main character, John Thomas. Our ancestral chain led from Virginia to North Carolina, Kentucky, Tennessee, and finally to Oklahoma, where I was born.

My father migrated from his native state of Tennessee at the age of four. My mother, Augusta Hamilton Thomas, did the same from the state of Arkansas. Both parents embodied that westward migration spirit that eventually populated our great nation from sea to shining sea.

PART ONE

CHAPTER 1 ❧

OUTBOUND

JOHN NERVOUSLY FINGERED the rope shrouds that ran from chain plates on the hull of the ship to the mizzen topmast above the poop deck. These rope shrouds provided lateral support for the mast and were the only means of climbing to the stern lookout forty feet above the ship's tiller.

Ratlines crossing these shrouds provided ladder-like steps for John's ascent to the observation platform. With his new sea legs under him, he conjured up his nerve to climb the swaying rope ladder leading to the precarious perch. The thought of falling from there crossed his mind.

Standing next to John was second mate Tim Rogers. At the tiller, within earshot, a salty, old cockney grinned at John's nervousness.

"What do you think, laddie? Bet you've never climbed one like this."

"Right you are."

John turned and looked at Rogers, a swarthy, bearded man of heavy build, in his early thirties. Rogers had charge of the sails and other duties of the deck. He was also called the bosun.

With a hint of doubt in his voice, Rogers asked, "Are you ready? You can still back out."

"Yes," John said softly, "I am ready."

He followed the bosun and began climbing the swaying rope shrouds. Hand over hand he pulled himself up. His stomach began to churn. The muscles in his arms and legs tightened with each step. He told himself, "I will not look down."

His breath came in short gasps. Though it was only eight bells, he felt warm beads of sweat running into his eyes. He dared not release his grip on the ropes to wipe them away. Instead he blinked the sweat away as a cool breeze brushed his face.

The bosun was five feet above and climbing easily. The shrouds began to sway back and forth from their combined weight. John had never climbed anything like this.

"What if I should fall?" he wondered. The ship was seldom directly below. "Would I land in the water or on the deck?" John pushed these thoughts out of his mind and continued his climbing.

This reminded him of a bad experience he had as a child. Monkeylike, he had climbed a high chestnut tree in his parents' garden in Wales. Suddenly, his feet had slipped off the limb, and he had landed on his back across another limb ten feet below.

Finally, the bosun reached the yardarm and moved above it to the topmast mizzen shrouds. They were only halfway up. Cautiously, they climbed the remaining twenty feet to a solid platform where the lower and topmast were joined.

At this juncture John saw a cask securely fastened to this platform. At the bow of the ship, on the foremast, it was called a crow's nest. Here, it was called the stern lookout.

A wave of dizziness swept over John as he glanced down at the swaying ship forty feet below. The deck, first on his left and then his right, never appeared directly underneath.

The bosun signaled him to climb into the cask. The barrel, large and anchored securely to a small balcony, provided added safety for the lookout.

The big schooner rocked from starboard to port and then bow to stern as it sliced through the whitecaps. John gripped the sides of the gray cask with both hands and tried to adjust to the rhythmic motions. He mumbled under his breath, "Crazy, crazy to have volunteered for this task." He looked up as the bosun shouted over the wind.

"Keep your eyes on the last ship in the fleet. It belongs to Sir George Somers, our fleet admiral. This long glass will help you see all the vessels. That pinnace has been lagging behind all morning. They may have trouble." After a brief pause, the bosun continued his instructions. "They will signal with their cannon or by smoke if they need help. Blow this pipe if you see or hear their signal. I'll leave you now, but remember, look down when going to the deck. If you fall, you might miss the deck entirely. Stay until your relief shows."

John took the small black pipe and glass. He watched Rogers make his descent to the deck. Taking a deep breath, he put the pipe and glass in his pocket, then continued to grip the sides of the cask until the pain in his hands forced him to relax. Only then did he begin to breathe more easily and look around at the fleet.

The nine-ship fleet, known as the *Third Supply*, had been underway for about fifteen hours. The fleet had sailed on Friday, June 2, 1609, with the evening tide, and five hundred passengers were aboard. The sun was past midmorning. Their destination was Jamestown, the little colonial outpost across the Atlantic.

They were now slicing through six-foot swells off the French west coast. John, aged seventeen and only a passenger, had volunteered for this hazardous job after a crewman failed to report for duty at Plymouth, England. His job was to keep tabs on ships to their rear, and watch for any hostile vessels.

3

John's ship, the *Sea Venture*, carried a total of 150 passengers and crew. He adjusted his long glass and began to scan closely each of the other ships. All were flying the Red Cross of St. George on their mastheads, proud against the blue sky filled with fluffy, white clouds. A wave of excitement swept over him as he told himself, "I am part of this venture to establish a colony."

The fleet of tall ships sailed in a loose V-formation led by John's three-hundred-ton flagship. Two of the three pinnaces sailed within this V. The one in trouble tagged along at the bottom of the V.

The *Sea Venture* led the fleet by approximately four hundred yards. After surveying all the ships, John rested his glass again on the lagging pinnace.

"What a small vessel making such a long voyage," he thought. "The other pinnaces in the middle of the fleet are larger than this one."

He could see some men moving about the decks. He refocused his glass on the smallest ship. "What could be their trouble? Perhaps they just can't sail fast enough. Surely the admiral wouldn't have brought the vessel along on this hazardous journey unless he was sure it could keep up."

Such thoughts ran through John's mind as he kept his glass focused on the lagging ship. Moments later, he heard the distant boom of a cannon in their direction, a signal that all was not well.

CHAPTER 2

THE DECISION

JOHN SAW BLACK smoke at the rear of the fleet, near the small pinnace. A few seconds later, he heard another boom of its cannon. To make certain, he adjusted his long glass again. He was now sure this small vessel was in trouble. He heard a third boom from the cannon.

Taking the pipe from his pocket, he blew it several times. He heard another dull roar of a cannon coming from the same direction, but louder. It was probably from the larger ship closest to the pinnace. It was making certain the fleet admiral was alerted.

John looked down and saw Second Mate Rogers walk swiftly up to the quarterdeck. Cupping his hands around his mouth, John yelled down, "Bosun Rogers, smoke on deck of that smallest pinnace."

"Yes, we heard the cannon. Keep your glass on it and stay at your station till relieved."

"Right, sir."

Refocusing his long glass, he saw the small ship make a rendezvous with a larger vessel. Next, it slowly turned and headed back in the opposite direction, away from the fleet.

"They are returning to Plymouth," thought John. Looking down, he saw his relief climbing the ratlines.

As they exchanged places, his relief asked, "What happened?"

"The small ship at the rear of our fleet is in trouble. I saw it heading back toward Plymouth. Here's the pipe and glass. We will know what happened when the other ship passes along the information to our captain. By the way, I'm John Thomas from Wales."

"Pleased to meet you. My name is Kenneth Smith. I'm one of the crew. I joined the fleet at Plymouth." Smith, thin and a head taller than John, was not much older.

"Will you be my regular relief?"

"Not sure," said Smith. "Our duties are rotated."

John nodded, then turned and began his descent.

Upon reaching the deck, he suddenly felt nauseated. His mouth watered and he felt dizzy as he ran to the aft rail. Leaning over as far as possible, he heaved. Almost immediately he felt better. He wondered what would have happened if he had gotten seasick while in the stern nest. Perhaps the old cockney at the helm wouldn't be smiling now.

"Feel sick, lad?" the helmsman asked.

"A little," said John, thankful this time the old seaman had not called him laddie. He still felt a bit queasy as he made his way toward the waist of the ship. He paused again and tried to catch a final glimpse of land. It was too late; fog obscured the coastline.

He turned and looked across the quarterdeck. On the starboard side he saw the ship's captain, Christopher Newport. The captain, approximately forty-five years of age, muscular, and bearded, stood about six feet tall. He had a metal hook in place of his left hand. John thought, "I wonder how that happened. Maybe Bosun Rogers knows."

Captain Newport spoke to a sailor John had earlier identified as Master Mate Ravens. Ravens moved quickly over and spoke to the helmsman.

Immediately, the *Sea Venture* began to turn slowly from lead position and trim its sails. Newport pointed to the last ship in the fleet coming up the middle of the formation. "They will tell us what happened," he said.

A short time later, the *Falcon* overtook the *Sea Venture*. Her captain shouted through a trumpet, "Captain Newport, pinnace has bad leak. Turned back to Plymouth."

Captain Newport acknowledged this bad news. He next ordered the *Sea Venture* to retake the lead. John continued watching Captain Newport. He turned to his right and spoke to the fleet's admiral, Sir George Somers, standing close by.

Somers was taller than Newport, and John guessed him to be ten years older. He had a darker complexion and wore a goatee. Both men were experienced navigators, and both were admirals in the British navy. However, Somers outranked Newport.

John had learned from his sponsor, Sergeant William Sharpe, that Somers had gotten his rank through battles. Newport earned his by explorations for the Crown. Sir George Somers was known as one of the top navigators in the British navy. He had been knighted for his part in a raid on Cadiz, led by the Second Earl of Essex in 1596.

Newport had made earlier voyages to the West Indies, plus two trips to the coast of America to establish plantations. Thus, he was the leading voyager for planting new colonies. In addition, he invested heavily in the Virginia Company.

The top-ranking gentleman aboard the *Sea Venture* was Sir Thomas Gates, lieutenant governor of the new colony of Jamestown. Gates was approximately the same age as Somers, though taller and heavier. He was part of the stock company granted a charter by King James I for the Virginia plantation.

Earlier, John had seen Gates strolling along the quarterdeck with his wife, and later he saw him deep in conversation with Captain Newport. Occasionally, from his perch in the stern nest, John could hear Somers and Gates arguing. He only caught snatches of their conversation but sensed it had something to do with authority at sea.

John turned back to the rail to watch the swirling ripples around the prow of the ship as it smashed through the blue-green waves. He gripped the square, oaken rail of the schooner's upper deck, worn smooth by countless hands of crew and passengers. Pausing near the ladder leading down to the waist deck, he found a cooler spot in the shade of the sails. Seabirds had left droppings on the edges of the ship's rail, and he cleaned a portion of the rail with a piece of deck rope.

As he gripped the rail, his mind wandered back home to Dorothy, the girl he'd left behind. Would he ever see her again? Dismissing the thought, he climbed down the port ladder to the waist deck. Spying six of his fellow passengers from his hometown, he walked over and said, "Mind if I join you?"

His friends were engaged in a card game and barely looked up. Gambling aboard was prohibited, so no money was in evidence. However, there were ways in which the crew and passengers could gamble with something that could be wagered. Sometimes, it was an item of clothing or something else desired by the winner. John never got interested in the game and thus had never won or lost anything of value. Gambling had never interested him for some reason. Yet, here he was, betting his life that this venture he was on would reward him handsomely.

The nagging question he kept asking himself was why he had indentured himself to travel thousands of miles and become a slave for five years, just to fulfill a dream. Perhaps, by the time the voyage was over, he would figure out his real motive. Just then the supper bell sounded, and soon all were scrambling to the tables for the evening meal.

CHAPTER 3 ❧

A SHIP IN TROUBLE

THE FLEET HEADED south along the western coast of France, one week into its voyage. Admiral Somers hoped to reach Jamestown, sometimes called James City, in about two months. The Virginia Company, a recently formed stock venture in London, backed this commercial enterprise.

John's mind was not on the Virginia Company as he climbed to his watch in the rear lookout. It was on Dorothy, his parents, and Carmarthen, Wales, his hometown. He climbed into the cask, made himself comfortable, and began to daydream.

John and Dorothy had made a promise to wait for each other, but would she wait? She was a beautiful, blue-eyed lassie of sixteen, with fair skin and brown hair that hung halfway to her waist. Closing his eyes, he could picture her now.

John, seventeen, of ruddy complexion and just shy of six feet, had brown eyes and dark brown hair. They made a handsome couple. He was fortunate to have her promise. If only he had some means to earn a livelihood to support them.

Then, the unexpected had happened. Just a fortnight ago, John and twenty other young men of his area had met with John Rolfe, a recruiter from the Virginia Company. This gentleman from London, in his smartly tailored waistcoat and finely crafted boots, spoke very convincingly. He told of wealth and land to be had in a new colony across the sea.

Rolfe explained how this was possible. It would require five years of indentured service. Each colonist would be given land to gain wealth; perhaps even gold and jewels might be found, something almost impossible where they currently lived.

"Rolfe is a good salesman," John had thought at the time. "What future do I have here? How could I ever hope to find a job or even an apprenticeship that could provide more than a meager living for Dorothy and me?"

What this recruiter was saying began to sound more and more interesting. John had listened carefully to the questions and Rolfe's answers.

"Sir, how long is the journey?" one of the older men in the group had asked.

Rolfe had replied, "I am told it takes eight to ten weeks, though I have never made the voyage."

"And how much will we be repaying?" another young man seated next to John had questioned.

"You will owe for your passage over, plus room and board for the time required to repay the debt. It will require five years of service to the colony."

"How might we acquire land after we repay our debt?" John had asked.

"You will be given a land patent from the governor of the colony."

"How much land?"

"At least fifty acres each, maybe more. But, to take advantage of this opportunity you will have to sail five thousand miles and be willing to work hard."

When all questions had been answered, John and nine other young men from his hometown had signed a contract to go. They would board ship at Plymouth for the journey in two weeks. For John the hardest part would be leaving his parents and Dorothy.

By prior agreement, John and his group had walked seventy-five miles to Plymouth. It took three days. It was there that they had met their sponsor, Sergeant William Sharpe, and boarded the flagship of the fleet sailing for the colony. In addition, fifty more men and four women had boarded the *Sea Venture*. The following evening, the fleet had moved slowly out with the tide and headed southwest.

Now, everything was gone: his homeland, his parents, his friends, and his sweetheart. He had never felt so alone. It was just he against the world. "Can I really pull this off? Will I ever see any of them again?"

The following day during John's watch, the fleet ran into a sudden squall. Rain and wind rocked the ship, and John's perch became very precarious. A small stool within the stern's nest gave him the choice of sitting. He hunkered down to be less exposed to the rain. Due to his optimism about the weather, he had failed to bring along some oilskins. Soon, the rain soaked his clothes and began to fill the bottom of the barrel.

While in this uncomfortable state, John wondered what caused him to sign on this venture so quickly. Was it a recurring dream during the past year? Or, was it his ambition to become a country gentleman, part of the landed gentry? John Rolfe had certainly projected the image of a country gentleman as he persuaded the group.

John recalled the first time he had had his recurring dream. Shortly before Christmas, seven months ago, he dreamed he was on a boat sailing on some unfamiliar river. When the boat landed, he found himself among strange-looking people who couldn't understand his words, nor he theirs. This made him very uncomfortable. But, soon, he was able to speak with them. These strangers became his friends. That's when he awoke, only to fall asleep again and dream the same dream with only a slight variation.

Every month or so, John would dream some variation of this dream. He couldn't figure out what it meant. Since he considered himself a practical man and not a dreamer, he had put these dreams out of his mind. Then he had heard that a representative of the Virginia Company was coming to his village. John Rolfe had indeed spoken very convincingly of wealth to be gained in a distant land about which John knew nothing.

John's dream of someday owning land and rising higher than his father's meager estate had definitely figured in his decision. No doubt Rolfe had stoked the fires of that dream. He recalled the first time he told himself, "One day I shall become a country gentleman."

It had started when he attained his first job as stable boy for one of the wealthy farmers near his village. As he cleaned stalls and occasionally exercised riding horses, he pictured himself as a country gentleman farmer owning his own land, horses, and cattle.

He could almost see himself coming back to his hometown in ten or fifteen years. He would have enough wealth to buy some land and become one of those gentleman farmers, or at least buy a business. He often wondered why his parents could be content with their meager resources. Maybe their religious faith had something to do with the sense of peace and contentment they expressed in their lives.

His mother used to quote from the Bible, "Contentment with godliness is great gain." They certainly reflected that idea in their lives. And, what was that other verse she would quote to him? "But seek ye first the kingdom of God and His righteousness; and all these things shall be added unto you."

When John asked what this meant, she said simply, "John, if you will keep God first in your life, He will bless you. Put first things first."

Still, they didn't discourage John from following his dream. They were very saddened by his decision to leave his home and face the dangers and risks involved in this venture. However, they didn't try to talk him out of it.

When John told Dorothy his decision to sign on this trip, he saw the hurt look in her eyes. She began to cry and say she wished she could go with him, but they both knew she couldn't leave her parents, especially her ill mother with younger children who needed her help. She was needed now more than ever, at least for the next few years.

Over the next several days John asked himself where he ever got the courage to undertake such a perilous journey. He had always been quite aggressive, but not reckless.

John was not averse to hard work. In fact, he enjoyed manual labor. Yet, he tried to find the easiest and quickest solution to any given task. He had been blessed with a quick mind, and he sought to use it to the best advantage. He had no inkling what this venture might hold for him. Still, he believed he could meet any challenge with enough courage and grit to succeed. Volunteering for this task of rear lookout had proven this.

He was under no illusions that tougher tasks and challenges lay ahead. He knew he must not become overconfident. His old rector had told him more than once, "John, you can do all things through the strength and courage your faith in Christ will give you." John believed that. He had been confirmed in the same faith as his parents. He was a Christian. Yet, he sensed this commitment to go to Jamestown would test his faith in God, and in himself, as never before.

CHAPTER 4 ～∂

RACHEL

JOHN'S DUAL ROLE as a passenger and substitute crewman had its advantages. He began to learn more interesting things about the ship's operation and navigation. From his observation post above the helm, he could see and hear the activities that affected the way a big sailing vessel was operated.

He had wondered how ships were sailed across vast stretches of the ocean without landmarks. Since coming aboard, he heard the expression that a ship's navigation was sometimes "by guess and by God." Yet, he knew Captain Newport and Admiral Somers had additional means by which to pilot vessels and fleets safely to their destinations. He observed them using the compass and consulting their charts, as well as taking sightings on the sun and other celestial bodies. They did this with something that was called a cross-staff and a back-staff to determine the ship's location. How that information got translated into a specific latitude and longitude to fix a ship's location on a chart, much less the ocean, was still a mystery to him.

Often John would linger awhile after his watch and talk with the helmsman, who was glad for his company when not engaged by one of the ship's officers. Still, even the helmsman didn't know the answers to John's questions on navigation. Only the ship's captain and the ship's master mate knew the answers to John's questions. Perhaps, before the voyage was over, he would ask these pilots of the sea how they did it.

Captain Newport, Sir George Somers, Sir Thomas Gates, and William Strachey spent most of their time huddled on the starboard side of the quarterdeck, discussing this latest voyage of the Virginia Company. John picked up snatches of their conversation from his perch.

From the bits of conversation John gleaned, he learned that in 1606, King James granted charters to two companies to explore and set up plantations in the New World, between latitudes thirty and forty-five degrees north: the London Virginia Company, and the Plymouth Virginia Company. Both companies were to be managed by a Virginia Council in London. The London Virginia Company had the southern half of these latitudes, while the Plymouth Virginia Company, the northern.

Jamestown, where they were headed now, was the offspring of the Virginia Company in 1607. It was made up of wealthy London merchants. Among its principal stockholders were gentlemen such as Admiral Somers, Sir Thomas Gates, Captain Newport, William Strachey, John Rolfe, and a few others aboard the *Sea Venture*, plus other ships of the fleet.

On this journey, these officers and gentlemen, plus the ladies with their husbands, were served their meals in the captain's galley. Four of the single lassies took turns assisting the steward in serving the captain's galley; the other two were exempted.

The single lassies, when not busy serving meals in the captain's galley, spent their time visiting on the deck or in their cabins. Occasionally, four of them would come out along the port side of the quarterdeck. The cabins on the quarterdeck faced inward. The starboard side of the deck was reserved for the captain, officers, gentlemen, and Mistress Horton.

John noticed that one of the younger lassies was quite attractive. She reminded him of Dorothy, with her curly tresses hanging down her back beneath her bonnet. One morning, when John was on duty, she came out of the galley and strolled along the port side of the quarterdeck.

The helmsman tried to engage her in a conversation, but she only lingered briefly then moved on. She stopped and leaned against the port rail, looking back at the ships of the fleet. Removing her bonnet and running her hands through her hair, she then tossed her head to one side, letting her dark tresses fall gracefully down her back.

Facing the wind, she stood for a few minutes before replacing her bonnet. Then, glancing upward at the stern lookout, she noticed John watching her. He waved without saying anything. She smiled and waved back.

Until then, he hadn't noticed how petite and lovely she was without her bonnet. Also, she reminded him of how much he missed contact with the opposite sex. Just a simple wave quickened his pulse.

Feelings of homesickness swept over him. If he were home, he would be spending time with Dorothy. They had never discussed marriage, per se, but John always felt that she would be the wife for him as soon as he could offer her something more than the poverty that pervaded their section of Wales.

That night John dreamed of Dorothy again. It was always the same dream, with her waving goodbye to her parents and boarding a ship to come to him. Each time, the next scene in the dream would fade. Strange that he would have this recurring dream. What did it mean?

John began to notice that the young lassie who reminded him of Dorothy would come out each morning about midway through his watch. Sometimes she brought a stool and sat on the deck next to the wall of the cabins, enjoying the sunshine and reading from a small book. Usually, she would remove her bonnet and her dark hair would glisten in the sun. Often her friends would join her. When alone, she would look up and wave to him. John always waved and smiled back.

One morning, after finishing his watch, John climbed down his ladder to the quarterdeck. He walked over to the port ladder leading down to the waist deck and paused at the rail. There, reading from her little book, was the lassie sitting on her stool. John turned and looked at her. She looked up at him, and his heart began to beat faster. He cleared his throat and then spoke:

"Greetings! I'm John Thomas from Wales."

She nodded. "I'm Rachel Jones."

"Where are you from?" asked John, as he moved closer and leaned against the port rail.

"I am from London. Have you ever been there?"

"No, I've never been out of Wales, except three weeks ago when I boarded this ship at Plymouth. Have you ever been to Wales?"

"No, I've barely been out of London. Where are you from in Wales?"

"Carmarthen. It's about sixty miles from Plymouth. How do you like sailing?"

"This is my first long journey. I'm fearful of the sea. It's so vast and powerful. I'm not sure I made the right choice to go to Jamestown."

John noticed her deep blue eyes, with just of hint of freckles across her cheeks, and slightly upturned nose.

"Why, then, did you decide to come?"

"My brother, Larry, went to Jamestown two years ago. He wrote and wrote asking me to come. So here I am."

"Plantation life will be far different than London," quipped John.

"Yes, I know. My brother told me it would be very difficult, and I must not come if I didn't think I could accept it. I wrote and told him I would like to try. I could always go home if I found I could not stand it. So, I decided to try it."

"I admire you," said John. "Are your friends, the other lassies, from London?"

"Yes, they have relatives in Jamestown, like me. So we try to cheer each other as best we can. Captain Newport and the other gentlemen have been very encouraging. They said the Virginia Company was very happy to have single ladies to help establish the colony."

John found himself beginning to feel slightly uncomfortable with the enjoyment he felt in the company of this attractive young lady. She, too, was smiling and obviously enjoying their conversation.

He wondered if she had left someone behind, a suitor. Also, thoughts of Dorothy kept coming to mind. Being a rather sensitive person, John was aware of just a tinge of guilt that maybe he was enjoying Rachel's company more than he should.

What would Dorothy think? But, what if their roles were reversed? Wouldn't she enjoy talking to some young man, as he had with Rachel? Troubling thoughts like these tried to interrupt the flow of his conversation with Rachel. He kept pushing them to the back of his mind. After all, what harm was there in just being friendly? Wasn't it just that? Finally, John begin to listen a little less to his conscience and to work up enough nerve to ask Rachel if she had left a suitor back home in London.

She looked slightly embarrassed by the question, and John noted the blush of her cheeks. Putting on her bonnet, she said,

"Yes, John. I had a suitor, but he found another lassie and married her."

"I should not have asked. I am sorry, but I was just curious that an attractive young lassie like you would be going off alone to such a place as James City."

"Well, I ask myself that question almost every night. But, I think maybe the trip will help me decide more clearly what I want in life. And, like I said before, I can always go home." She paused. "Tell me, did you leave someone at home in Wales?"

Now it was John's turn to be uncomfortable.

"Well, yes, I did. One I think about a lot. We are close friends. And she may come over to Jamestown one of these years."

Now that John had gotten that truth off his chest, he felt more honest and open with Rachel and less uncomfortable in meeting her and talking. Just then, the sounding of the bells for dinner interrupted their conversation.

Rachel excused herself, saying she enjoyed getting to meet and talk with him. He nodded as she extended her hand. When their hands touched, John felt an excitement not unlike his feelings when near Dorothy. As he made his way to the waist deck, John wondered, could he still love Dorothy and feel this excitement around Rachel? Later, he would have to figure that one out.

One day, not long after his meeting Rachel, John learned that Captain Newport had been in charge of the first small fleet of three vessels that had sailed across two years earlier to establish the colony. Rachel's brother was probably on one of them. He also learned that Sir Thomas Gates, the governor designate of the Jamestown settlement, had orders to take command of the colony until the new governor arrived. No doubt the success of the *Third Supply's* mission, and perhaps even the survival of the colony, depended upon Captain Newport, Admiral Somers, and Sir Thomas Gates. John had overheard Admiral Somers discussing with Captain Newport the five hundred new colonists and hundreds of tons of fresh supplies and livestock that were aboard their eight vessels.

Periodically, during John's duty at his post, he would look back at the other seven vessels and wave at some of their passengers. The ships were staggered in their V-formation behind the *Sea Venture*, each about a quarter-mile apart.

The two small pinnaces—a fifty-ton, the *Virginia*, and a thirty-ton, the *Catch*—kept their places in the middle of the fleet. Hopefully, all would make it to James City. Still, what if they hit a big storm? Would they be able to stay together? John was not the worrying kind, but he couldn't help wondering what would happen to the fleet if it did hit a big tempest. He was not afraid of water, but this was nothing like the streams, rivers, or lakes at home in Wales.

He had taught himself to swim at a fairly young age, but he recalled the stark terror he felt as a young child of four when his father, holding him in his arms, waded into a small lake near their home.

That experience instilled a healthy respect—or was it a fear—for large bodies of water. This body of water was no lake. He hoped he would never experience such fear again, especially here of all places.

Gradually, John had outgrown this fear of water and began to enjoy swimming in the same small lake near his village. He had even swum across that lake on several occasions with several of his young friends during the warm summer months.

However, swimming was not a priority with him. Besides, as he got older, his interest turned to exercising horses on the farm of a wealthy landed gentleman a short distance outside his village. This part-time job taught John some valuable lessons about the difference between work and play. Riding horses was play. Mucking stables was not.

John was beginning to feel that his commitment to indenture himself and travel to Jamestown would teach him a new meaning of work, a meaning he had yet to experience. In fact, he was now just a slave to his sponsor and to the Virginia Company. His freedom to choose had been taken from him when he signed that paper.

CHAPTER 5

SMOOTH SAILING

THE FIRST TWO weeks of the voyage were uneventful. John's duty in the stern nest helped keep his mind off Dorothy and home. His perch was directly above the helm, the steering mechanism for the ship.

One of the helmsmen told John that the helm was just a wooden rod, called a whipstaff, fastened to the rudder by means of a yoke. Movements on the whipstaff could change the direction of the ship as much as five degrees either way.

John observed that the quarterdeck, in addition to being the control center, contained seven cabins. Three were on each side, and a larger one across the stern housed the captain's galley. Captain Newport, the ship's officers, and official guests occupied the six cabins. The quarterdeck was reached by ladders on the port and starboard sides of the waist of the ship.

Gradually, John got more adept at climbing up and down the shrouds. At times, he felt like a bird on a tree limb, swaying back and forth in his perch. However, most of the time, he enjoyed his unique view. His station gave him the opportunity to hear some of the happenings on the quarterdeck that floated up from below. Often, his thoughts returned to his decision to take this journey.

He prayed he hadn't made the wrong choice. John wasn't a religious man. He was barely grown. Yet his parents had instilled in him the basics of the Christian faith, and a belief in prayer was one such tenet. However, could prayer guarantee a safe trip across this perilous sea? Would it help repay his indentured debt and make possible the fulfillment of his dream?

Why did his dreams have the power to motivate him to leave home, friends, and comforts, plus the love of his life? How could his dreams have enticed him to face the unknown, to risk everything, perhaps even his own life? Was it merely a dream for wealth and land, to become one of the landed gentry? Or, was it a desire to explore the unknown, to test his courage and skills to their limits, to test his manhood? Perhaps it was all of these.

John recalled his mother, Sarah, telling him the story of Joseph and his dream from the Bible. What was that verse she made him memorize? "Your old men shall dream dreams and your young men shall see visions."

Was his a dream, or a vision? Was he just an old man in a young man's body? Whether it was a vision or dream, for a young man, John had a fairly strong picture of what he hoped to accomplish in the next few years. He would either live or die by his dreams.

The smell of food drifting up from the captain's galley directly below brought John back to an awareness of his stomach. His duty for today was over. The bosun had told John he could eat with the crewmen whenever he wished, since he was doing some of their work. They ate in the fo'c'sle galley, located above the bow of the ship.

The ship had a third galley. It was the main galley, located one deck below the waist deck, near where John and most of the passengers were housed. These three galleys fed the passengers, the crew, and the officers. Each group was housed near its respective galley.

Just as John reached the waist deck, Bosun Rogers was making his way toward the crew's galley.

"Thomas, come and eat with the crew. I want you to meet them."

"Thanks, Bosun. I've been planning to do that."

He followed Rogers into the fo'c'sle galley, where most of the crew members were standing around talking and waiting for the steward's helpers to finish placing food on the tables. Rogers took his place at one end and motioned for the crew to sit. John seated himself on the bosun's left and watched him signal for silence.

"Mates," he said, "this is John Thomas, who volunteered to help us with the stern watch. He's got a good pair of eyes and is helping our captain keep track of the rest of the fleet. He has my permission to eat with you mates whenever he wishes. So don't short him his rations. Understood?"

"Right, Bosun," chorused the group.

With that, the men fell upon their victuals like a pack of hungry dogs. John's table manners were excellent compared with those of these men of the sea. He ate quickly, as did most of the crew, then filed out of the galley with those who went to relieve others.

John was not used to sleeping in a hammock. The only advantage was that its gently swaying motion helped rock him to sleep. But due to the hot sultry weather, crowded sleeping conditions below deck, and the stale air below, he preferred sleeping on the main deck under the stars.

Here, John's thoughts and dreams invariably drifted back home. At first, the brightness of the moon kept him awake. Sometimes, he would just sit upon a hatch cover and look at the moonlight's silvery path across the waves. He would watch the silent ghostlike ships, with their tall masts in the moonlight, flanking the flagship. When he could stay awake no longer, he would return to his pallet and soon be dreaming.

In one such dream, John saw Dorothy waving goodbye to her parents and boarding a ship at Plymouth for Jamestown to become his bride. It was so real that he tried to keep on dreaming, even while he was waking up.

He was hoping to see Dorothy come off the ship in the colony. But that dream, like the morning fog, drifted away. His recurring dream of the boat on the river hadn't occurred since leaving home.

Most of the 150 passengers aboard the *Sea Venture* were men. Of the nine women aboard, three were married: Mrs. Thomas Gates, Mrs. John Rolfe, and Mrs. Edward Eason. The Easons, a young couple, were friends of the Rolfes and were expecting their first child.

John knew nothing about the six single lassies, except Rachel. He observed that they were about his age. Two of the younger lassies were servants. One worked for Mrs. Rolfe, who was beginning to show signs of her pregnancy. The other, Elizabeth Persons, was a maidservant to Mistress Horton, a wealthy stockholder in the London Virginia Company.

The six cabins on the quarterdeck housed the three married couples, along with Captain Newport; Sir George Somers and his German police dog, Lady; and Reverend Richard Bucke, the ship's chaplain.

Beneath the quarterdeck were ten other cabins. William Strachey, who was the secretary-elect and recorder of the Virginia Company, and several other gentlemen stockholders occupied five of these. Lady Horton and her maidservant were housed in this area, and the single lassies also occupied three cabins in this section of the ship.

The tenth cabin was given to two Indians, Matchumps and Namantuck, who were returning to their native land. Rumor had it that Captain John Smith had persuaded them to come to England the previous year for promotion purposes to King James and the royal court. John noted that they kept mostly to themselves on deck and at mealtimes.

Reverend Bucke conducted two services daily for the passengers and crew: morning prayers and evening prayers. Worship was compulsory, unless one was on duty. The morning service was held in the main galley, following breakfast. Evening prayer was held on deck before supper, except in bad weather, when it was held in the main galley. John attended the evening prayer, since he was on duty most mornings.

Chaplain Bucke was a personable young cleric whom John figured to be in his late twenties. When not in his cabin preparing his homilies, he could be found visiting with the passengers on deck. John's sponsor, Sergeant Sharpe, had told him that Chaplain Bucke was a replacement for the former cleric in Jamestown, Richard Hakluyt, who had died.

CHAPTER 6

SCUTTLEBUTT

LIFE ABOARD THE *Sea Venture* settled into a daily routine with the thirty members of the crew standing their watches and sailing the ship. The passengers mostly clustered in small groups on the waist deck near two scuttles. These were fifty-gallon barrels of drinking water placed on opposite sides of the ship.

Rumors, storytelling, gossip, card-playing, and other trivial pursuits took place around these scuttles. John was glad he had a job to occupy some of his time. Otherwise, life aboard would get boring with just "scuttlebutt" to listen to.

Each day, after his duty in the stern nest and after dinner, John would find some of his group of nine from his hometown sprawled somewhere on the waist, or in the shade of a sail, near one of the scuttles. They would be playing cards or napping. Usually, they would be napping. He would join them and soon be snoring.

One day after his watch, three weeks into the voyage, he found his hometown group sleeping on the waist deck. John joined them. Upon awakening, he spoke to William Wooley, who was shuffling a deck of cards.

John was better acquainted with William than with the rest of the group. In their hometown, Wooley's father was a local merchant who employed John's father. Wooley was about John's age, though heavier. He was munching an apple.

"How was your duty today?" William asked around a bite of apple. "Doesn't it get boring up there?"

"Yes, at times. So far I've managed to stay awake and not fall out. I watch the ships of our fleet with the long glass of the bosun's. Sometimes I focus on the crew or passengers aboard other ships."

"See anything interesting?"

"No."

"How does the ship's crew treat you?" asked William.

"Fine. I've eaten in their galley a couple of times. They're a pretty close group. I just listen to their 'scuttlebutt' and sometimes ask about their jobs. I don't think I would like to become a sailor. They have a very rough life."

Lewis Jones, the eldest of their group from a village near John's hometown spoke up. "How come Sergeant Sharpe asked you to help the crew? Did you know him before?"

"No. I met Sergeant Sharpe the same day you did. You will have to ask him that question."

"Just curious," said Jones. "I wish I had something to do besides helping the steward prepare meals and clean up tables."

"You only do that one day a week, right?"

"Yes," sighed Jones, "but that's enough."

Each of the nine had galley duty one day per week. John was spared this chore due to his bird's nest assignment. The small talk continued for another hour or so until Chaplain Bucke arrived and announced the evening prayers.

This service was shortened when a sudden squall drove them to take cover below deck on benches around the tables in the main galley.

Certain other passengers could be seen assisting the ship's steward with preparations for the evening meal. The passenger dining area was dimly lit with lanterns that swayed from the rocking motion of the ship.

This galley could only accommodate about half of them at one time. Usually, John ate at the second serving, unless he decided to eat with the crew. The smell of the cooking fish drifted in the galley, prompting William to ask, "Does anyone know if we're getting sea pie tonight?"

Willie Cooke, youngest of the nine, seemed to know in advance when the steward would surprise them with this special dish. It consisted of layers of meat, vegetables, and fish, with crusts of bread, or broken sea biscuits in between.

"I think this is the night," he said. "Yesterday the steward said he wanted to start serving it at least twice a week to avoid throwing out vegetables that might spoil."

The *Sea Venture* had an excellent steward. Mr. Summers loved his job. Sea pie was a favorite dish of the crew, but he only served it once per week to the passengers.

At that moment bells for supper sounded, and passengers began filing in and filling up the tables as servers brought in large bowls and platters of steaming, savory food. This evening, John decided to remain and eat with his friends.

Four ladders led down from the waist deck into the main dining area for the passengers. However, only about half of the one hundred passengers could eat at one serving. John was in the first group to be seated. Those of the first group ate quickly and retired to their bunks or went back up on deck.

Usually, John went back up on deck and slept there with some of his friends rather than in the stuffy quarters off the dining area. Good weather was another reason to stay on deck as late as possible.

CHAPTER 7

DEVIL'S ISLANDS

A MONTH AFTER leaving Plymouth, Sir George Somers gave a brief talk in the waist galley. He explained to the passengers how far they had come on their journey, and how they would cross the Atlantic.

"Men," he said, "we have been sailing along the French and Spanish coasts for a while. Soon we will turn southwest to the Azores Islands. Afterwards we will turn west by northwest, pick up the trade winds, and take a circular route across the Atlantic to Jamestown. Any questions?"

"Yes, sir," one of the men replied. "How long will it take to get there?"

"About six more weeks, if we have good trade winds and hit no tempests."

After answering a few more questions, the admiral made his way back to the quarterdeck. In the days that followed the admiral's talk, John tried not to think of storms or violent weather. In fact, their sailing had been mostly smooth and uneventful as they passed the French and Spanish coasts.

Occasionally, a French or Spanish galleon was sighted heading eastward.

Passing the Azores Islands on the starboard sides, the fleet turned westward and picked up the trade winds blowing from their stern. The ships put on every bit of canvas and clipped along.

A school of dolphins danced and dived off the starboard side of John's ship. This gave him a chance to observe them closely with his spyglass from his vantage point in the stern lookout. A pod of orca tried to stalk the dolphins, but the dolphins were too quick and agile for them. This little show reminded John that in spite of the tranquil appearance of the sea, it was a place of danger and death for the unwary.

In the mouth of his knapsack, John had a highly valued book given to him by his old rector, Father Williams. It was a small copy, titled *Book of Psalms*. Father Williams had given him one of his precious books as a farewell gift. In addition, it was a gift of thanks for John's faithful devotion to his church and for helping the old sexton when he was too ill to keep up his church duties.

John had placed it in his knapsack along with the rest of his belongings. He tried to read a couple psalms each day. Since there were 150, it provided him more than enough readings to last the trip. So far, he had read over a hundred of them.

One evening, approximately a month after Admiral Somers had given his talk, John was sitting on the starboard side of the waist, below the quarterdeck, thinking about home. Directly above, Captain Newport and Admiral Somers were discussing the weather.

"George," said Captain Newport, "I think we're about ten days out of James City. We've had some damn good trade winds pushing us along this time. I am surprised we haven't had more foul weather. On my first trip two years ago, when we first established the colony, we had fair sailing with our three smaller ships.

"However, we left London in January, and it took us four months to cross. This time, we will do it in about two months. Those trade winds out of the southeast in the summer make the difference. They push us right along, but they also bring storms. Those clouds are beginning to look more threatening."

"I agree, Christopher," said Somers. "Do you think we've passed Devil's Islands yet?"

"I'm not sure," replied Newport. "I would not like to be near them in any foul weather. Might end up on a reef. I hear that has happened to more than one ship. As near as I can tell, we are in the twenty-seventh latitude and the sixty-seventh longitude, give or take a minute or two. Devil's Islands should be on our starboard side in twenty or more leagues."

The two men moved away from the rail of the starboard quarterdeck and out of earshot. John was left with his thoughts. What was this about Devil's Islands? Doesn't sound like a place he would care to see. He wondered how it got its name....

There was just enough daylight left for John to read from his book. Books were scarce, especially the Bible. John was very careful with his leather-bound *Book of Psalms*. He took it from his pocket and opened it to his mark, Psalm 107.

Partway through the psalm, he read, "Those who go down to the sea in ships who do business on great waters, they see the works of the Lord, and His wonders in the deep." John could attest to that. He had been awestruck with the power and vastness of the ocean.

He read on, his curiosity growing. "For He commands and raises the stormy wind that lifts up the waves of the sea. They

mount up to the heavens, they go down again to the depths."
So far, thought John, they had fairly smooth sailing, except for
that one short gale off the coast of France during their first week.

His eyes wandered back to his book. "Their soul melts
because of trouble. They reel to and fro and stagger like drunken
men and are at their wits' end." Is this what he and the others
would face if they hit a bad one?

Once again his eyes were drawn back to the print. "Then
they cry out to the Lord in their trouble, and He brings them
out of their distresses. He calms the storm, so that its waves are
still. Then they are glad because they are quiet; so He guides
them to their desired haven."

Wow, thought John, what a description. Is this what they
could expect if they hit a mighty tempest? He prayed they
wouldn't experience one. His meditation was interrupted by
the approach of his friend William Wooley.

"Hello, John."

Turning slightly he said, "Greetings, friend." He was getting
to know Wooley better.

"Have you heard when we will reach James City?"

"Yes, I heard we should reach it in about ten days, unless we
hit a storm. Have you ever heard of Devil's Islands?"

"No. Where are they located?"

"The captain thinks they're up ahead and on our right. He
sounded worried about them being close and the weather looking
more threatening. Said something about ending up on a reef if
a bad storm develops and our ships are too close."

"Let's hope our good luck holds for a few more days," said
Wooley. Turning, he said, "I am going to see who is winning
that card game."

At that moment, the second mate strolled by on his way aft.
Seeing John, he stopped a moment to talk. Supper was over, and
the heat of the July day was subsiding. Small groups of men were
standing and seated on the waist deck engaged in games and

small talk. The wind had increased out of the southeast, and black clouds were beginning to form to their rear.

"How do you like the stern's nest watch, John?"

"Fine, Bosun Rogers. Looks like we may get some bad weather before morning."

"Not sure, John. Know what the sailors say about the weather?"

"No, what?"

"They say, 'red sky in the morning, sailors take warning. Red sky at night, sailor's delight.'"

"All day, the sky in the east and the west has been covered by clouds. So then, how do you tell?"

"Anybody's guess, I suppose. But, if I was betting, I would bet we get a nice gale before morning."

"Bosun, I have another question that maybe you could help me with. Have you ever heard of Devil's Islands?"

"Why yes, I have. We sail by them on our way. In fact we are not too far from them now. Where did you hear of them?"

"I overheard the captain mentioning them. Where did they get their name?"

"I can't tell you, but I think there have been several ships wrecked on their reefs, so ships try to give them a wide berth. That may have something to do with their name."*

And with that, the bosun resumed his walk toward the quarterdeck.

---

* Juan Bermudez, a Spanish sea captain, discovered the islands in 1515. Later, they were named Somers Islands, after British Admiral Sir George Somers. Sometime later, they were renamed the Bermuda Islands.

CHAPTER 8 ❧

THE TEMPEST

SOMETIME DURING THE night, John was awakened by the increased swinging of his hammock. He thought someone might have brushed against it. Instead of the gentle rocking motion he had grown used to, it was now a more vigorous motion, and not simply from side-to-side, but end-to-end.

He could hear loud creaking and groaning from the ship's timbers in the belly of the ship. This was new and alarming. Swinging his feet out of the hammock, he stood for a moment, trying to adjust his balance to the swaying and rocking of the ship. He felt a sense of nausea and knew he had to reach the main deck before he lost his supper. Holding onto a horizontal beam that supported one end of the hammocks, he made his way quickly along the dimly lit hallway toward a ladder. This led up through a hatch onto the waist deck. Sensing this way was longer, he reversed, and headed for the ladder in the main galley.

A dim lantern swung by its handle over the tables, casting ghostly shadows about the dining area. The lantern provided just enough light for John to see the ladder in the corner leading to the waist deck.

Reaching the top of the steps, he looked up and could see a tiny star through the shifting clouds. Slowly, he regained his sense of balance, and the nausea passed. Outside, the wind was blowing with gale force.

As he stuck his head out the opening, rain and salty spray from the storm stung his face. It was a good thing they had been warned to sleep below deck tonight, otherwise he would have been drenched.

The big ship was now moving faster through the mounting waves, pushed from behind by winds that howled in the rigging and sails. Against the white background of the foremast sails, members of the crew ran back and forth, climbing the yards, and shouting to each other as they reefed in the topmost sails on all three masts.

John didn't know much about ships in storms, but he had heard that too many sails in a heavy storm could break the masts that supported the sails. With them gone, the ship would be at the mercy of the waves.

Though his nausea was gone, John felt a rising fear in his gut, as the winds continued to shriek. Taking another step up the ladder, he could see more of the crew in wet rain gear, scrambling about cross bars, reefing in sails, battening down the hatches, and securing equipment left on the decks.

Swinging ship lanterns cast eerie shadows through the rain as Captain Newport, the officers, and the crew worked fast to make the ship run before the storm. This was no little gale. It began to feel more and more like the tempest Captain Newport and Admiral Somers had feared. How close were they now to Devil's Islands? John scrambled back down to the galley.

There, one of the crew thrust a ship's lantern into John's hands and told him to awaken all the passengers in his section. When John entered with the lantern, the whole compartment was awake and the buzz of conversation was growing. Men began to rise from their hammocks and dress into suitable clothing for whatever this night might hold. For sure, no one would sleep tonight in this storm.

John sensed from the noise level in the ship that this storm was getting worse by the hour. He breathed a silent prayer for all aboard, and especially the crew, who were up there on deck battling this monster.

Quickly, he dressed into the rain gear loaned to him by the bosun and walked into the main galley. Wooley, and others of his group, were gathering at a corner table near the stairway. Knots of passengers were gathering in the galley around various tables. All were waiting for some word from the ship's officers concerning this storm. Two more ship's lanterns were lit, making the galley a bit more hospitable.

The ship's rolling and pitching continued to increase. Now, even with the four hatches closed in the corners of the galley, the sounds of the wind and the waves crashing on the waist deck began to drown out the conversations in the room.

From the passageway leading to the stern quarterdeck, Reverend Richard Bucke strode into the galley. He raised his hand for silence. "Men," he began, "come closer, if you can't hear me. We have hit a bad storm as you all can tell. Captain Newport and Admiral Somers are busy with the crew, trying to keep our ship running before this storm. The first thing I want to do is call you to prayer for the officers, crew, and all of us aboard this ship and the other ships in our fleet. Pray that God will grant us His grace and help in this time of need. Would you join me in the Lord's Prayer?"

The chaplain led the assembled passengers. Then he said if any were needed to help the crew, they should be dressed and ready to respond. While he was still speaking, Ken Smith, one of the crew, came in and walked up to Reverend Bucke. The chaplain stopped a moment and conversed with Smith. Then, raising his voice, he asked for four volunteers to help the helmsman control the ship's rudder.

John lifted his hand and was one of the four to follow Smith toward the rear of the ship along the middle passageway. Smith led them down the hallway, past the passenger sleeping quarters, on past a room on each side of the hall, and into a tack room against the stern end of the ship.

The tack room, two levels below the quarterdeck, held ropes, canvas, and other supplies. However, its main purpose was to house the device that connected the rudder to the helm on the quarterdeck. This was done by means of a whipstaff. The whipstaff was fastened to the upper extension of the ship's rudder, called a tiller.

Smith explained to them that the violence of the waves and storm on the rudder exerted such pressure that even two crewmen above could not keep it steady. It would drag them from side to side. So he asked them to stand, two on each side of the waist-high tiller, and to brace it so it wouldn't flap back and forth. They would be guided in their pressure by instructions shouted down a tube from the helmsman. When he yelled to the right, they should exert their pressure right, and if left, then left. This would force the rudder in the appropriate direction.

John could hear giant waves smashing against the rear of the ship as he and the others took up positions on each side of the tiller. John asked Smith before he left them if this tempest was as bad as it sounded.

"Worse," Smith replied. "I've never seen one like this before." He explained what would happen if the ship was pooped. This meant the ship would be inundated by a giant wave from the rear, sweeping over the entire ship, and possibly swamping it.

Losing the ability to steer would make this more likely, thus the need for the four of them to help the helmsmen. With that, he moved up a ladder in the corner of the room and headed for the quarterdeck.

The noise level in the room grew worse. The four could barely hear each other speak. A ship's lantern provided the only light in the room. It swung mostly in a circle now, just another indication of how intense the storm had become. John wondered how long they would have this duty. He knew no one would be assigned any nest duty in this weather. At that moment, Smith reentered the tack room for a large coil of rope.

He said they were going to use it to throw a line to the *Catch*, the smaller of the two pinnaces. The storm had broken its main mast, and the *Sea Venture* was going to try to tow it, he said.

Several hours went by before Smith again came through the door with four fresh volunteers to relieve John and his crew. The four said they had eaten breakfast, but could barely hold their plates on the table.

Smith told John's crew to eat and get some rest, if they could; he would call them to the tack room in about four hours.

Following a breakfast of cold porridge, John fell into his swinging hammock, fully dressed, and tried to relax. He was so tired from lack of sleep and the duty in the tack room that he fell into a fitful sleep and dreamed the ship was about to crash upon a rocky shoreline.

He awoke with a start to hear someone yelling for all the passengers to assemble in the main galley. Bosun Rogers was standing on one of the tables in the middle of the galley, shouting above the roar of the storm. His head almost touched the overhead beams.

"Hear me, men," he shouted. "We have sprung a leak some-where in the hold of the ship and we need six of you immediately to man the pumps down there. If we don't find this leak and get it plugged, it will be bad for us in this kind of weather. The crew is searching the hold to locate the leak. Let's pray they find it. I need six volunteers to go with me now for the first hour of duty. We will need six fresh ones each hour until we get the water out. Smith here will divide the rest of you in six-man teams to take your turns. He will give each team a number. We will rotate the teams by number. That's all for now."

Gathering up his six men, he motioned for them to follow him to the ladder that led down into the hold of the ship. Ken Smith began to divide the remaining passengers in the room into groups of six, with the exception of John's four.

John's group would continue in the tack room every four hours until the storm abated, or... John pushed that thought out of his mind. Is it possible they would not make it? Ships sank all the time in violent storms.

John had heard in his hometown of Carmarthan of ships that never made it back. He just never dreamed one day he might be on one so ill-fated. Maybe, just maybe, they would all make it to Jamestown. He wondered how the rest of the fleet was doing by now and where they were in relation to Devil's Islands.

He found William Wooley and some of his hometown group clustered at the end of a table and sat down. Wooley's eyes looked tired even though he had gotten more rest last night than John.

"What is your group's number?" asked John.

"Number two," answered Wooley. "Our turn is next. It will be good to get it over with before supper. I am not sure we will have any hot food. The mess steward said he may not be able to keep a fire contained in his hearths with all the rolling and pitching of the ship. He said the last thing we need is a fire aboard ship."

Just then, Reverend Bucke entered the galley for evening prayer. He had come by way of the tack room and ladders leading down from the quarterdeck. Usually, he came by way of the waist deck, but with the storm and hatches battened down, this was the safest way.

The men gathered about the chaplain, and he began his service. The psalm he used for his meditation was not the scheduled one in the *Book of Common Prayer* for St. James Day, July 25. Reverend Bucke used Psalm 107, the same one John had read just two nights before, concerning a storm at sea, how men cry out to God, and how God delivers them. Chaplain Bucke announced this would probably be their last service until the hurricane was past.

The chaplain glanced at the faces of the men before him and noted an earnestness and attentiveness, as well as fear, not seen before. The storms in life could quickly change a man's attitude toward spiritual matters. The sudden lurching of the ship sideways seemed to add an extra "Amen" to the reverend's closing prayer.

The service was concluding when Smith came in to notify John and his group to relieve the four in the tack room. Waving to Wooley, who was just leaving, John made his way toward the stern of the ship for four more hours of duty.

He could hardly keep his balance in the passageway. The stress of the past twenty-four hours was beginning to take its toll.

CHAPTER 9 ❧

ADMIRAL SOMERS

THE TEMPEST KEPT up its relentless pounding of the ship, its crew, and the passengers. The full fury of the storm broke on the morning of Tuesday, July 25, St. James Day. In fact, it blotted out all signs of daylight, which made it seem like a twenty-four-hour night. Only the night was darker than ever.

Captain Newport and the crew were able to hoist enough canvas to keep the ship running before the storm. Yet the crew had to monitor it constantly. Smith told John's crew in the tack room that if the ship didn't keep ahead of the waves from the rear, it would make the rudder useless.

If this occurred, the ship could not be steered and would be pushed sideways by the monstrous waves, perhaps capsizing it. This was why just enough sails were needed to keep the ship running ahead of the mountainous waves and permit some steerage.

John asked Smith what Admiral Somers was doing since the fleet had been scattered. Smith said the admiral was working with Captain Newport near the helm. Each was taking turns out in the storm, trying to keep the ship moving in the right direction. Additionally, Admiral Somers was navigating by guess and by God from his cabin.

John asked how this was possible. Smith could not explain it.

For three days and nights, the tempest raged on, giving no indication that it was lessening in strength. John and his crew fell asleep standing at their station, awakened only when a shout or command came down the tube from the helmsman.

Admiral Somers sat hunched over a small table in one corner of his cabin, staring at the sea charts showing Devil's Islands. The admiral had taken readings from the sun and stars on the day before the tempest struck. By reckoning their speed and direction, he still had a fairly accurate idea of the ship's location in relation to Devil's Islands with their deadly reefs. By watching his compass, and estimating the location of the ship in the storm, the admiral kept plotting the ship's approximate location on his chart. However, now with both sun and stars blotted out, he had no way to verify his latitude and longitude.

The only light in the room came from a ship's lantern, swinging slowly in a circle from its hook in the ceiling. Shadows danced across the chart beneath the admiral's bowed head. His eyes were closed, as if in prayer, when Captain Newport rushed into the cabin.

"George," Newport said. "We had to let go the tow rope on the *Catch*. Without a doubt she will capsize. We couldn't stay enough ahead to keep her from slamming into our rudder. If the storm hadn't gotten worse, we might have been able to tow a while longer. Now, it's every ship for herself."

"You're right. How's the leak in our hold coming? Have you found the cause?"

"No, and it's getting worse. If we can't fix it, we will probably go down."

"We can't let that word get out to our people," said Somers. "We must keep on fighting and doing all we can to stay afloat. If we get near enough to Devil's Islands, we might be able to run her into some cove, or get close enough to save ourselves."

Newport nodded.

"I'll put more people to bailing. Some of our barrels of bread broke open. The pumps appear to be stopping up due to bread. The bucket brigades may be our only hope if pumps fail."

"Right you are. It appears from my calculations and the changing direction of this compass that we are moving slowly in a large circle. How big a circle, I don't know. I am not sure where we are in relation to Devil's Islands. We need to keep a sharp lookout up high as possible on the bow."

"We have a man there now," said Captain Newport with a sigh. He rose slowly to his feet as if shouldering a heavy load. Then he left the cabin. Somers cradled his head in his hands and began to pray for God's help.

Admiral Somers had been in dangerous places before, but never where he felt so helpless. Always before he had options, choices that could influence the outcome, but now, in spite of all his skills and reputation in seamanship and navigation, he was at the mercy of this vast storm, over which only God had control. Or did He?

Somers didn't consider himself a saintly sort. He came from honest, hard-working stock, devoted servants of the Crown. He was Anglican in faith. He had played an important role in helping the king prepare for the Spanish Armada that had attacked England in 1588.

Lyme Regis was his hometown and birthplace. It was a port city on the English Channel in the county of Dorset. Each major port had been called upon to furnish a fleet of ships, to respond to the call, when the Spanish arrived.

He never went to sea with the fleet during the great conflict, but that soon changed after the Spanish fleet was destroyed. Following the defeat of the Spanish, and the increasing dominion of the seas by the British, the admiral became directly involved in many of the major sea battles between the British and the Spaniards. He came out of these battles with a proven reputation as an excellent seaman and military leader. His sea battles in the Azores and Venezuela gave him much wealth and notoriety. From 1595 to the early 1600s, his reputation as a navigator and privateer provided him with eager sponsors for his voyages. Financial backers were convinced that he could never get lost, could navigate to any location, and would never return empty-handed. But never had George Somers been caught in such a mighty tempest as this. So he did what most people do when they have done their best to control their destiny and yet feel helpless. He prayed. Then, exhausted, he slipped into a troubled sleep.

It was Friday morning when Captain Newport breathlessly entered the admiral's cabin and shook his shoulder. The admiral looked up through glazed eyes and mumbled, "I must have drifted off, Christopher."

"Can't blame you, George. I've got bad news. We are not keeping ahead of the rising water in the hold. I believe we are going down. The pumps are stopped up and useless. The crew and the passengers know this. They have given up."

The admiral, through bloodshot eyes, sensed his captain had correctly assessed the true condition of their ship. They had been fighting this battle to save the ship for four days. Neither had slept nor changed clothes. They were exhausted. Both had served in the bucket brigade, lifting water out of the hold along with passengers and crew. After all, there was a limit to any man's endurance, theirs as well as the crew's and passengers.

Maybe he had reached the end of his life and now was the time to resign himself to God's will. Yet, down deep in his breast,

George Somers felt if they could just keep fighting a little longer, they would sight those Devil's Islands.

Hanging up on a reef would tear the ship apart, but perhaps some of them could make it to land. With these thoughts still running through his head, he heard the captain speak, "George, some of the crew broke open the casks of brandy and rum. They are getting drunk to ease their fears of going down. I say it's hopeless."

"I agree, but let's keep those bailing who have not given up. Maybe, just maybe, we will sight those blasted islands."

Admiral Somers arose and left the cabin with Captain Newport. From the poop deck, they could see the ship was riding deeper than ever in the water, as the water level in the hold kept rising. With this added weight of water, the ship was more sluggish and moved more slowly through the waves.

All possible supplies and baggage were thrown overboard to lighten the ship, including some of the cannons. All that remained now were prayer and hope.

However, the storm appeared to be quieting down. Even the clouds were starting to lighten up, with small patches of sky becoming visible. "If only we could stay afloat a little longer," the admiral thought.

Just then, the lookout in the forward crow's nest shouted down, "Land, ho!"

Captain Newport and Admiral Somers scrambled down the ladder to the waist, and ran forward to the forecastle. They rushed around the crew's quarters to the bow of the ship for a look. There, just a few miles ahead, they could see waves breaking over reefs. It was indeed the precious land they had prayed for.

It had to be Devil's Islands. The captain and admiral turned, and with tears streaming down their faces, they gave each other a bear hug amid the cheers of joy and yells from crew and passengers.

"Land, ho! Land, ho!"

"Land, ho! Land, ho!" echoed throughout the ship as crew and passengers took up the chorus, hugging and crying with tears of joy.

This was all that was needed to put new spirit into everyone. Captain Newport ordered renewed bailing. Additional canvas was quickly hoisted to the yards. The ship veered sluggishly to starboard in search of a sheltered cove.

All possible canvas was hoisted for speed, now needed to avoid sinking offshore. Singing and shouting could be heard throughout the ship, as stormclouds slowly drifted away, and people bailed with all their might.

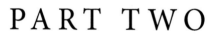

PART TWO

CHAPTER 10

PARADISE

ADMIRAL SOMERS AND Captain Newport worked side by side to locate a safe harbor. A sheltered cove was needed to anchor the stricken vessel. All hands were instructed to keep bailing until they could find a safe haven.

It was a race now to see if the sinking ship could be kept afloat. John joined the other passengers on deck from his station in the tack room. The rudder no longer needed their power for steerage. He sighted Wooley in the bucket brigade and joined him. As he passed along the small barrels of water to him, John said, "Isn't this great? Looks like we are going to make land soon."

"Right," gasped Wooley. "If we make it to Jamestown, I don't think I'll ever sail again."

Catching his breath, John replied, "If we hadn't run into that storm we would already be in Jamestown."

The *Sea Venture* continued to turn starboard and began to circle the islands.

Soundings were made to keep the ship off the jagged reefs. Carefully, Captain Newport sailed the half-sunken vessel parallel to the coast for several miles. The ship slowly turned portside as it rounded the eastern end of the Islands.

A small, wooded hill on his left dominated the skyline. Ahead, the waves were less boisterous. After a couple more miles of sailing, he turned to Admiral Somers and pointed ahead north toward land.

"George, I see a beach and cove that will allow us to get close to shore. Do you see it?"

"Yes, I see it. Go for it."

Barely afloat, the *Sea Venture* turned portside again and headed for the harbor. The lookout at the bow of the ship suddenly yelled, "Sir, two large rocks just below the surface!" We will run aground unless we turn."

Realizing they might not make it any closer to shore, Captain Newport made his decision. He would ram the bow of the ship upon the rocks. This arrangement would allow the ship to stay afloat longer. Now, all aboard could be safely landed in the longboat. It was still lashed to the waist deck. Also, they would be able to take ashore supplies not ruined by the storm. This all seemed like a miracle too good to be true.

"Steady, she goes," Newport instructed the helmsman.

The ship shuddered violently as it ground to a halt upon the rocks. She would eventually sink, but not before some of her timbers could be salvaged. Perhaps from these and the trees on the island, they could build smaller vessels.

"This is indeed a miracle."

"Fine job," replied Admiral Somers.

It was Friday morning, July 28, when they first sighted the islands. By eight bells of the afternoon watch, all aboard were safely on land. The stores and supplies that had not been jettisoned in the tempest were next ferried to land.

Food and shelter were their most immediate concerns. But tonight they would lie on mother earth and thank God for this paradise. What did John overhear Admiral Somers call these islands? "A Garden of Eden?"

John was among the last to leave the ship. He gathered his few belongings from the tack room and made his way to the longboat. All during the terrible storm, he had not let his mind dwell on their dangerous state.

True, he had been affected by the cries of anguish around him. And he had been scared as much as the others. However, he'd refused to give in to his fears. Instead, he'd prayed silently that God would spare them and that they would come through this horrible nightmare. Thank God, they had. Whoever said faith was not important must have never tried it.

Later, after all had landed safely, Chaplain Bucke conducted a brief worship service. Passengers and crew stretched ropes between trees. Sheets of canvas from the ship were placed over these. These primitive tents provided sleeping quarters and shelter for the coming night. Separate tents were erected for the couples, the lassies, and the ship's officers. Next, they lit campfires.

Somehow, the ship's steward, Mr. Summers, pulled together a meal. The crew had salvaged barrels of food from the ship that were undamaged by the water. Some of the men volunteered to begin fishing. They had seen an abundance of fish in the waters of the cove.

Things were fairly chaotic that first evening. A state of euphoria and festivity was in the air. People were still partially drunken—some from the spirits they had drunk when all seemed hopeless, others by the fact they were still alive.

John and his friends soon found each other. They staked out an area for sleeping in one of the makeshift tents. They would try the next day to salvage their hammocks from the ship. It would beat sleeping on the ground. But no complaints were heard as the exhausted survivors filled the night air with their snores.

The next morning Sir Thomas Gates called a general meeting. When all were seated on the ground, he began his remarks. John listened carefully.

"Gentlemen, ladies, passengers, and crew, as governor elect of Jamestown, I am also in charge during our brief stay here. Through the providence of God we have safely landed on these islands. I salute those of you who worked hard and did your best to help us stay afloat. I want to especially praise Admiral Somers and Captain Newport for their heroic efforts in sailing the ship to these wonderful islands."

John glanced at the gently blowing limbs of a large cedar tree above the balding head and bearded face of Sir Thomas. The lieutenant governor, dressed in his finery, made a commanding presence.

Seated near the front, John noted the broad, ruffled collar of lace that capped his leather-belted tunic, silken stockings, and tailored shoes. A wide leather sash studded with silver buttons crossed his chest to the broad belt at his waist.

"He wasted little time in asserting his authority," thought John. "This man would demand their respect and loyalty." John sensed Sir Thomas's job would be more difficult on these Devil's

Islands than had Somers' aboard the *Sea Venture*. Here, people were less confined and more inclined to roam or explore. John glanced out toward the half-sunken ship in the bay and breathed a prayer of thanks as Sir Thomas continued.

"We have a lot of work to do before we reach Jamestown. We shall begin by segregating into three working groups. One group shall be under my command. A second will be under Admiral Somers. The crew will continue to be under Captain Newport. Further salvaging of the ship will be the first order of business. The ship cannot be saved. However, we will salvage it. Its timbers will aid us if we have to build smaller vessels."

Again, John gazed at the harbor and noticed the stricken vessel was lower in the water. He wondered if it would stay afloat long enough for them to retrieve their hammocks. He looked up again as Sir Thomas spoke again.

"Admiral Somers and some of the crew will explore the islands and find out what other sources of food are available. Until they do, let us conserve our food supplies. I plan to dispatch the longboat with Master Mate Ravens and a crew to Jamestown as soon as possible. They will send ships for us. Water seems to be a bit scarce, but I'm sure we shall find enough to survive. Further meetings will be called as necessary. Don't go wandering off to explore these islands. Only Admiral Somers, Captain Newport, or I can permit that. These gentlemen will be answerable to me, and you will be answerable to them. I trust these orders will be sufficient."

John's head was starting to nod when he heard Sir Thomas conclude the meeting. The governor told all to remain seated until they were assigned their group. John hoped he would serve in Admiral Somers's group. The admiral was a man John much admired. He had watched him in the midst of the tempest giving orders, advice, and encouragement by example and leadership. Somers had worked alongside the people in the bucket brigades, then continued at his post as chief navigator, along with Captain Newport. Yes, this admiral was a true leader. John would be proud to be part of his team.

John had his wish. He and his friends from Carmarthan were placed under Admiral Somers. He was glad for this bit of luck. Actually, it was due more to Sergeant Sharpe. Sharpe had served with the admiral previously and had been selected by him as one of his subordinates.

Quickly, the passengers were divided into three groups. Sergeant Sharpe called John and the rest of his detail together to brief them. "Our first job," said the sergeant, "will be to build a more permanent encampment. We need one that will protect us from the weather. Also, we need to provide the cook, Mr. Summers, with a good kitchen. We will use standing trees, when possible, and our canvas and ropes. We need to look for suitable level ground. We want rain to drain away from the sleeping and living quarters. So, follow me as we scout out the surrounding areas."

He set off leading his group of ten men. They reconnoitered the high ground above the beaches. By walking about a mile up through cedar trees, they reached the highest spot on their island. From here they could see more islands to the south and west. Cumulus clouds drifted lazily, pushed by gentle winds. Birds flitted from tree to tree, singing their rhapsodies. The weather was cool, but comfortable. A chorus of tiny, high-pitched squeaks rose from the flora and fauna that covered the ground. The noise came from tiny frogs that infested the islands, whose sounds intensified after a rain. The island where John's group landed was the northeastern one in a chain stretching as far west as they could see.

After an hour of exploration, they found the ideal location for their camp. It was in a level meadow among the trees. The beach where they first landed was nearby. The meadow was large, and it gently sloped toward the ocean.

It had enough open space to build a circular camp. Tents could be placed in rows among the trees. The cook's tent would occupy the middle of the clearing. Next to it would be a place where all the camp could assemble. The trees would provide good protection from the winds and gales.

For several days, John and his friends worked long hours to turn the meadow into a camp. They hoped it would withstand nature's onslaughts, especially another hurricane. However, it appeared this northeastern end of the islands was more protected. The camp was completed in five days.

One week later, Sir Thomas dispatched a small crew in the longboat for Jamestown. Master Mate Henry Ravens and eight others volunteered. They rigged up the boat with a deck and mainsail then left for the colony.

Sir Thomas was most anxious to let the colony know their whereabouts. He requested rescue ships be sent. Admiral Somers and Captain Newport gave little hope for the longboat to make it to Jamestown. This would be especially true if they hit a bad storm.

The next day John watched Admiral Somers and the ship's crew begin to build two small boats. A week later they were finished and began their first island exploration. The admiral took along his German police dog, Lady, plus two four-man crews, including Matchumps and Namuntuck. Their first task was to locate food sources.

Six days later, they returned. Somers reported an abundance of fish in all the coastal waters. Wild boar, giant turtles, and many edible birds and their eggs were found.

The hunting skill of the two Indians was highly praised by Admiral Somers.

Sergeant Sharpe told John and his crew that many cedar trees suitable for ship construction had been found. Indeed, the islands seemed to be a veritable paradise. Somers told the assembled camp the islands could sustain them all indefinitely.

Somers and the ship's crew began a series of short trips to map the chain of islands in late August. The first trip took just a week. When they returned, he reported the islands stretched for at least twenty miles to the west, and were about three miles wide.

John had noticed Rachel and the other lassies since first landing on the islands. His group had built them three small tents, along with tents for couples, for Admiral Somers, Captain Newport, Governor Gates, and other gentlemen.

However, building the permanent camp kept John very busy. He had not tried to converse with Rachel to any length. They had passed each other in the camp, smiled, and exchanged greetings. But that was it. He wanted to talk with her but the time was never quite right.

A few days after the camp was completed, John's chance came. Rachel was carrying a pail of water from a nearby cave. John happened to cross the path that led to the camp. Rachel was resting for a moment in the shade of a large cedar. John asked how she was doing.

"Very well, thank you. We lassies are helping Mr. Summers prepare food for the officers, the ladies, and their husbands. Mrs. Eason is expecting her baby very soon. We are doing some sewing to make a few garments for the new child. It's all very exciting. What have you been doing?"

"Well, after we built the camp, Sergeant Sharpe had us look for more suitable trees. We may have to begin building a couple of boats to get us to Jamestown. That could be our next big task. However, I don't think it will start soon. If Jamestown gets word of our plight and sends a ship, we won't need to."

John noted anxiety in Rachel's voice as she asked, "Do you think the longboat with Mr. Ravens and his crew will reach Jamestown and a ship will arrive to rescue us?"

"I think our chances are good. We will eventually reach Jamestown. Admiral Somers and Captain Newport are excellent navigators, and once we build a couple of pinnaces, we shouldn't have any trouble getting there. I overheard Sergeant Sharpe talking with Admiral Somers about this today."

"I hope you are right, John. I cannot imagine what it would be like to never leave these islands. Yet, they are wonderful and beautiful. I have to go now, or one of the other lassies will be coming to find me. I have enjoyed our talk."

"Me too, Rachel."

He watched her go toward the camp, walking gracefully up the trail. John sensed something in the way Rachel looked at him and smiled. She was as lonesome as he for more of a relationship. He felt himself slowly being drawn into a desire to know her better. Now that he knew some of her work habits, he would try to arrange to see her more often.

John felt a bit of guilt after his conversation with Rachel. He had given his word to Dorothy that he would wait for her and come back for her. However, that promise shouldn't preclude just friendly conversation with Rachel, should it? After all, just being friendly with another lassie didn't have to lead to anything else. Dorothy was still his first love.

CHAPTER 11

REBELLION

ADMIRAL SOMERS AND his sailors were busy the first month building two boats to replace the longboat taken by Ravens and his crew. Next, they began making thorough explorations of the islands. They were on one of their mapping trips when the first serious challenge to Gates' authority took place.

One evening, while lying in his bunk, John overheard a few men talking in the next tent. They were speaking about staying on these islands. After near death at sea, they didn't care if they ever reached Jamestown. John dismissed it as idle talk.

However, Henry Hawkins, one of the aides to the governor, who bunked in the same tent as these men, also overheard them and told the governor the next morning. Gates swore under his breath, then ordered Hawkins to sound the bell for a camp assembly.

Rows of logs next to the cook's tent made up the location for these meetings. John took his seat and watched the governor pace nervously back and forth until all the stragglers arrived. Gates centered himself before the group. He began in a loud, sonorous voice. "If you are wondering why I have called this meeting, it is because I have heard that some of you are talking about staying in the islands. I can understand you preferring this to going on to Jamestown. But, our destination has not changed. We need to reach Jamestown, and all possible haste and effort will be taken to reach it. I especially need to reach it."

John watched as a bird landed on a branch slightly above the governor's head. When Gates resumed his speech, the bird began to squawk loudly. This brought muffled laughter. Gates, irritated, paused and waved his hand at this distraction until the bird flew off. Regaining his composure, he continued.

"Jamestown needs my leadership. Lord Delaware, the appointed governor, will not arrive until next year. In the meantime, any challenges to my plans on this island will not be tolerated. This includes idle talk about remaining here. Those who disobey this order will be punished. You are dismissed."

After the meeting John joined Sergeant Sharpe's tree-cutting group. During the rest of the day no one discussed the meeting with Governor Gates. None in John's group had ever talked about staying on the islands. They were almost as anxious as the governor to reach Jamestown. However, gossip had it that Nicholas Bennet and Christopher Carter were the ones fomenting this rebellion. The potential ease of living on these islands was too much of a temptation. They succeeded in convincing a number of others to join them in their plan to challenge Gates' order about staying on the islands.

One week after Gates had laid down his order, John awoke before dawn to the sound of pounding rain on his tent. For a moment, he was back on the ship in the midst of the tempest. He shuddered at the memory of those terror-filled days and nights.

The wind and rain continued to beat a steady staccato on the canvas as John snuggled deeper into his hammock. He was glad it had been salvaged. The ship's carpenter had built supports for the hammocks inside all the tents. This provided more comfort than the hard ground.

The storm soon lulled John back to sleep. Sometime later, he awoke to the sound of occasional dripping on the canvas. The storm had blown over. This time, he sat up, rubbing sleep from his eyes. He had slept through breakfast.

He heard voices behind his row of tents. Curious, he got up. Through the door of the tent, he could see Bennet and Carter. Moving slightly to his right, he saw eight other men. All were standing in front of Governor Gates' headquarters tent.

John heard one of Sir Thomas's aides ask Carter what he wanted.

"We wish to speak with Sir Thomas."

"What do you wish to speak about?"

"A private matter," said Carter.

The aide motioned all except Carter to sit on a log next to the tent. He signaled Carter to follow him. The two entered the tent while another guard, with musket, watched the seated ones.

John was not close enough to hear what Carter said. But all at once he heard the governor yell from inside the tent, "Hell, no!"

The governor walked briskly out of the tent, followed by Carter and the aide. Gates told Carter to join the other men on the log. The governor, now with guards on each side, spoke to all the men.

"You men have challenged my order and my authority. Twice I have said to you that our destination is Jamestown. But, since you wish to stay here, I will give you your wish. Do you see that small island over there?" He pointed southeastern, to a small island a half mile away. That shall be your island home."

Turning, he summoned several more guards. He ordered them to ferry the ten men to their island prison. They were allowed to take nothing with them but their clothes. About two thirds of the camp witnessed the governor's swift punishment of Carter and his men.

This action left little doubt as to the governor's ability to enforce his orders. That morning, John and Wooley were kitchen helpers and talked of little else.

"It looks as if the governor is a man of his word," said John.

"Indeed. We had better watch what we say. Personally, I don't want to stay here any longer than we have to. How about you?"

"I'm with you," said John.

Carter's rebellion, as it was called, lasted about two weeks. The rebels ate nothing but raw foods and had no shelter but trees. They soon realized life on their island prison would be difficult, if not impossible. They needed tools and other supplies in order to survive. One of the ten, Jeffrey Breare, tried to swim back to plead their case with the governor. He drowned during the attempt. His body washed up on the shore the following day. Chaplain Bucke gave him a Christian burial. The governor and several of his aides were in attendance.

About a week later, another prisoner, who took a more circuitous and less dangerous route made it to camp to plead the plight of his friends. Their request was to simply be allowed to return to the main camp. They promised to obey Gates' orders like all the rest. The governor said he would consider their request. Two days later, he sent a boat to bring the remaining men back. All were happy to be back, except Carter and Bennet, who complained they had been unfairly treated.

Gates began to realize that ruling this small island paradise would be more difficult than imagined. A few days later, he met with Captain Newport and Admiral Somers. Gates began by asking, "What did you know about this rebellion before it occurred?"

Captain Newport deferred to Admiral Somers. The admiral cleared his throat before he spoke. "My crew and I have been busy building the small boats and scouting these islands. I didn't get wind of anything like this until it happened." He paused a moment, then said, "I did hear some men talking. They called these islands a heavenly paradise. And I agree. So, I can understand why some might prefer to stay here."

Gates nodded his head, but said nothing for a few moments. Then he turned to Captain Newport.

"I've also heard a few rumblings," Newport began. "But I didn't think it would lead to open rebellion. I suppose we have underestimated the attractiveness of these islands. We went through hell in that tempest. Landing in this beautiful place has blinded some of the men. They have lost sight of our mission. I think we may have more problems with them."

"I agree," said Gates. "I've already taken extra security measures to guard our storehouse and supplies. However, I would appreciate any word from you regarding future rebellions. I plan to maintain tight control to prevent mutiny. A rescue vessel with Ravens and his crew would solve our problem."

The admiral lifted his hand as if to say it was useless. "Thomas, I don't believe we are going to see Ravens or his crew again. Christopher and I both doubt they made it to Jamestown. That longboat was a big gamble. It's been about two months since they left. I suggest we begin building two pinnaces. This will focus everyone's attention on reaching Jamestown. I would be happy to begin the construction of one. I can use the ship's crew, plus Sergeant Sharpe and his small group. Christopher could be in charge of the other. He could use Mr. Frobisher, our carpenter, and the rest of the men."

Newport spoke up. "I agree with George. I don't believe Jamestown is aware we survived the tempest. And we don't know how many of the fleet survived or even reached the colony."

"Well," said Gates, "I appreciate your counsel and suggestions. I will decide on these matters as soon as I'm sure Ravens and his party have been lost."

The next morning, Sergeant Sharpe called his group together at the edge of the camp. His steel-gray helmet glistened in the morning rays of the sun. He laid his musket against a log and loosened his belt a notch.

"Men," he began, "the admiral has informed me of a meeting with Governor Gates, and it appears we are going to need to cut a lot more trees for ship construction. We could begin building within a fortnight. The governor will soon decide this matter. Ravens and his men have now been gone two months. That is more than enough time to reach Jamestown and dispatch a ship. So, it looks as if we will be quite busy building pinnaces. I also want to ask you about the recent rebellion by Carter, Bennet, and the other men. Have any of you been approached to join that band?"

William Wooley spoke up. "I was approached by Chris Carter. He said several more men were talking about staying on the islands. He said when the time was right they would talk again to Governor Gates. He asked if I would like to join their group. I told him I am more interested in getting to Jamestown."

John and the others said they had not been approached. Finally, Sharpe asked the group to inform him of any more talk about staying on the islands. The conversation turned to boat-building and Jamestown as Sharpe led his men into the woods.

One week after the Carter rebels were granted amnesty, John heard another rumor of rebellion. This time it was from Stephen Hopkins. He had not been part of the first rebellion. He began to talk covertly to a few friends about staying on the islands. Some of these friends could not keep Hopkins' secret. Thomas Powell passed it along to John.

Hopkins was an educated gentleman with a degree in education. He was also an assistant to Chaplain Bucke. He had status among some of the passengers as a teacher. The next day, John was not surprised when Hopkins approached him. He told of his desire to stay on the islands and make it into a colony.

That evening, Thomas Powell, who was the admiral's servant, let slip to the admiral what Hopkins was up to. However, he hinted he thought it was all just talk. The admiral nodded, but said nothing.

Later that evening, Powell joined John and several others around a campfire. The evening was cool, and the wind moaned softly through the tops of the birch trees. The fire crackled and popped out sparks as resin in the birch logs exploded from the heat.

Gradually, the flames diminished and red coals mesmerized the group into silence. Heads started to nod. Powell waited until all except John had left for their hammocks. Then he turned and told of his talk with the admiral regarding Hopkins.

"Do you think Sir George believed it was just talk?" John asked.

"I'm not sure. I wouldn't want Hopkins to get into trouble. I believe Hopkins thinks Sir Thomas wouldn't discipline him as he did the others."

CHAPTER 12 ∾

LADY GATES

FROM THE BEGINNING of the voyage, the relationship had been rocky between Sir Thomas Gates and Sir George Somers. Weeks before the hurricane struck, Lady Gates had frequently heard them arguing. She felt her presence on the voyage kept the conflict more subdued between them.

"Thomas, Sir George is fleet admiral," she would often say. "You must support his position and not argue so much with him."

Thomas would just look at her and say, "I know. Don't remind me."

There was no doubt Somers was in charge at sea. As admiral of the fleet, he had final authority. She heard he was a lion at sea, but a lamb on shore. So, once the *Sea Venture* made land in Devil's Islands, the situation changed. Sir Thomas wasted little time asserting his authority over the entire group, including Somers. Admiral Somers, in order to keep the peace, accepted Gates' authority. Also, he attempted to support him.

Physically, Lady Gates was frail and not up to the rigors encountered on the voyage. She had grown up in a sheltered home where all of the amenities of life were provided. Her father was part of a growing mercantile class and had inherited his wealth from his father. He was delighted with his daughter's marriage to the dashing young Lieutenant Gates. Young Gates had hitched his wagon to such rising stars as Sir Francis Drake and, later, to the Second Earl of Essex, Robert Devereux.

She remembered her husband's excitement in being part of Drake's expeditions in 1585–1587. The first one had focused on a raid of the Spanish in the West Indies. Later, homeward bound, they helped remove settlers from the aborted attempt to colonize Roanoke Island.

In 1587, Thomas was with Drake in a raid on the Spanish port of Cadiz. This set back for a year the plans of Spain to sail its armada against the English. She was proud of him. This battle had given England more time to prepare for the dreaded invasion. Then, in 1596, Gates was knighted for his part in a second raid on Cadiz, led by the Second Earl of Essex, Sir Robert.

That's when she began proudly to wear her new title, Lady Gates. During those heady years when her husband was making his mark, Lady Gates was lonely and depressed. However, her parents and her two children gave her little time to feel sorry for herself. Over the past twenty-five years, with mostly an absentee husband, Lady Gates had provided a comfortable home for her children and for Thomas, when he was not at sea.

When her father died in 1605, she inherited some of his wealth. Thomas persuaded her to invest in the Virginia Company. In 1606, he was one of a group granted a charter by King James I for the colonizing of Virginia.

Gates was no stranger to attempts by England to colonize. Thus, when he was appointed governor designate of the Jamestown Colony for one year, Lady Gates decided to accompany him. This would allow her to see the wisdom of their investments and to spend more time with her husband.

She anticipated a one-year trip to the colony, and then home again. Little did she realize the risk and danger that would come during the voyage.

The first part of the voyage was pleasant enough. The small cabin they shared on the quarterdeck was cramped, but endurable. Thomas felt they deserved Captain Newport's cabin. This led to an argument between her husband and Admiral Somers.

"Sir George has the authority to give us the larger cabin," Thomas had said to her. "After all, I am governor designate of Jamestown. I take this as an affront to my position and authority with our company."

"Thomas, my father used to say, 'All things come to him who waits.' I believe, in time, you will be not governor designate, but governor of the colony."

She sensed his hunger for more power and authority. It was difficult for him, with his newly acquired title as governor designate, to take a lesser role aboard ship. At times, he tried to usurp the authority of the fleet's admiral, but Somers had quietly but firmly let him know they were still at sea.

Also, she sensed a bit of jealousy in her husband over the superiority of both Captain Newport and Admiral Somers in navigation and seamanship. Gates had never attained the title of admiral, nor commanded a fleet of ships.

By the grace of God, they had survived the terrible tempest and landed on these beautiful islands. But Florence Gates had not been surprised when her husband immediately, and without any consultation with Somers or Gates, made his announcement to govern all.

Being a dutiful wife, she never challenged the authoritarian decisions by Thomas that left her feeling used and depressed. She retreated from these encounters into silence, headaches, and her bed. She felt trapped, lonely, separated by more than just the sea from her widowed mother. Her mother had been her confidante over the years. Lady Gates missed her grown children and relatives back home. She feared she would never see any of them again. As the weeks passed with no word from Master Mate Ravens and his crew, her fears increased. Would they ever be rescued?

Lady Gates had no close friends among the other ladies. Mrs. Eason, who was about to give birth to her first child, was the closest to being her friend. Yet, due to their age differences, Edna Eason was more like a daughter than one in whom she might fully confide.

As the acting governor's wife, she wasn't sure of her role in the life of the camp. Thus, she tended to withdraw into herself.

Early in October, she found herself growing listless and weak. Her appetite faded, and the camp's living conditions became harder for her to accept. The food staples salvaged from the ship were rationed, and a steady diet of pork, fish, and only a small portion of fruit and vegetables grew monotonous.

Lady Gates spent more and more time walking along the beach or just sitting quietly on a rock, staring out into the ocean, mesmerized by the gentle sound of the waves as they rolled gravel, seaweed, and flotsam onto the sand, then out again. During those moments her mind would wander back to London and her spacious home filled with all the comforts she had grown to expect and enjoy from her marriage to Sir Thomas. The thought that she might never see her home again depressed her greatly.

Her husband didn't understand her fears and resented her lack of spirit and energy. She tried to listen to his concerns about the men who were fomenting rebellion, but often she found herself unable to focus on his problems. Instead, she was listening to her own thoughts and fears. Had she dreamed she might end up on this uninhabited island, in the middle of a wild and dangerous sea, she would never have made her fateful decision to come along. Such thoughts made her feel guilty and thankless for their miraculous fortune in just being alive. Was their good fortune a miracle, or just another consignment to a slow death?

When she heard that one of the rebels had drowned trying to swim back to their island, she felt a wave of sadness and compassion that wasn't shared by Sir Thomas. Though she couldn't place the face of the man, she identified with Jeffrey Breare's attempt to gain release from his prison, a prison somewhat like her own.

One morning, after Thomas had scolded her for spending so much time in her bed, she shared some of her fears with him.

"Thomas, I'm sorry I have so little energy. I get tired just walking to the beach. I have very little appetite. I get very little rest because I can't fall asleep. I just lie there and think of home, mother, and the children."

"Florence, I should never have allowed you to come along. I knew the voyage would tax your strength, but I never thought the trip would end this way."

"I know you didn't. Neither did I, or I would have stayed at home. Do you think we will ever be rescued?"

"Yes, but we must be patient and not give in to our fears."

Lady Gates continued to grow weaker. Thoughts of dying began to occupy her mind. One morning, she found herself unable to rise from her makeshift bed. Chaplain Bucke's visits and prayers over the past few weeks hadn't seemed to make any difference. She had given in to her fears. She developed a fever, then a hacking cough.

Pneumonia slowly filled her lungs, and as her breathing became more difficult, dreams of drowning in the tempest filled her restless sleep. When awake, she thought such a fate would have been preferable to this slow death. Mrs. Eason and the other ladies took turns nursing her. All the camp began to realize that Sir Thomas's wife was not long for this world. Her battle with pneumonia lasted about ten days with no break in a burning fever and cough. She died during the first week in October.

Chaplain Bucke, followed by the pallbearers and Sir Thomas, led the funeral procession westward through the woods from the main camp. After they had gone several hundred yards, they rounded a small hill to the final resting place for Lady Gates.

John Breare's body had been buried there one month earlier. John and Wooley were near the end of the procession, which included almost everyone in camp. No one anticipated deaths on this lovely island, but two funerals within the same month sobered the camp. The hostility of the island, in spite of its peaceful setting, was a paradox they hadn't anticipated.

The small burial ground west of the camp was nestled in a quiet vale among trees overlooking a beautiful lagoon with an inlet from the opposite side of their island. A small detail of men stood near a freshly dug grave.

Chaplain Bucke motioned for the camp to form a half-circle around the grave. John and Wooley moved nearer to hear the chaplain's opening remarks. After leading everyone in the Lord's Prayer, he said, "Governor Gates, your beloved wife, Lady Florence Gates, was a heroic soul who braved the wiles of the sea to come on this venture to Jamestown. She fought a good fight, and though not granted to reach her goal, kept the faith of all true disciples of Christ, up to the end of her life. We commend her spirit to God, even as we commit her body to its resting place. May her soul rest in peace. And may God save the king and bless you, Sir Thomas, as you lead us on to Jamestown."

The chaplain then recited the Twenty-Third Psalm and closed with a benediction. After the closing prayer, most of the crowd ambled slowly down the little vale toward the lagoon.

A longer and alternate path led back to the main camp along the inlet shore.

Some, like John and Wooley, lingered to watch the detail of men lower the birch box into the grave and fill in the hole. A stone marker was finally placed at the head of the grave.

Now there were two stone markers standing silently, like sentinels guarding the departed spirits of Lady Gates and Jeffrey Breare. As John and his friend made their way back to camp, he looked back and wondered how many more markers would dot this peaceful vale.

CHAPTER 13 〜

BERMUDAS

EDNA EASON WAS a young bride of eighteen when Edward married her. Ed Eason was the son of Sir Robert Devereux's wife by a former marriage. His real father died when Ed was an infant. The only father he had ever known was Sir Robert, Second Earl of Essex.

Sir Robert had invested quite a sum in the Virginia Company and had decided to send his stepson and new bride over to Jamestown for a firsthand assessment of his stock venture.

The young Mrs. Eason was four months pregnant when the *Sea Venture* left Plymouth. She and Ed had been assigned one of the small cabins off the ship's waist beneath the quarterdeck. The sailing seemed to agree with her pregnancy, and nothing much bothered her until the tempest struck. During those horrendous four days, she thought she might lose the baby or have a premature birth. She thanked God that Mistress Horton and her maidservant, Elizabeth Persons, helped her through those terror-filled days and nights.

Elizabeth Persons was about Edna's age. She and her mistress had occupied the cabin across the passageway from the Easons. When Ed was unable to help, or she had some question regarding her pregnancy, she could always knock on their cabin door.

Jane Horton had been a midwife in her younger days, and she understood what Edna was experiencing. She was as close to being a doctor as any aboard. Her age, experience, and being the daughter of a country doctor had made her wise in the treatment of the sick. Edna consulted her more often now that the baby's birth was imminent. By the middle of October, she was too uncomfortable to walk the distance to attend Lady Gates' funeral. She had been unable to help the other ladies with nursing care for the governor's wife. She told herself that if she could just carry her baby to term, she would be doing her best.

Ed hovered over her like a mother hen when he was not working with the other men laying the keel of the *Deliverance* that would carry them to Jamestown. He watched her for any signs of trouble.

During the day, Rachel looked in on Edna and did little chores to make things easier. "Do you think we shall ever reach Jamestown?" Edna asked Rachel one morning in the third week of October.

"Yes, Edna, I believe we shall, eventually. We must be patient, though."

"That's one thing I'm learning," sighed Edna.

"Did you ever consider not coming along with your husband?"

"Oh, no. Ed and I are so in love that I couldn't think of staying behind. And he felt the same. When we first sailed, I didn't know I was that far along. When the baby comes, it should be easier on both of us."

"Do you want it to be a boy?"

"Edward would be happy to have a boy. I just want a healthy baby, boy or girl."

Edna shifted the conversation away from her and the baby.

"Rachel, have you gotten acquainted with any of the young men during our trip?"

"Well, yes and no. I enjoy talking to John Thomas. He is quite lonely. He left his lassie behind in Wales, and I think they had thoughts of marriage. He is quite shy, though. I think he likes me, but feels a little guilty."

"What made you decide to come on this dangerous voyage?"

"I have been trying to answer that question myself, and I don't really know why." Edna smiled as Rachel continued. "The man I was in love with married my best friend. So all I wanted to do was just disappear. I saw this notice on our town's bulletin board wanting young lassies to go to Jamestown, all expenses paid, so I thought I would try it for a year. That was all that was required. Plus, I have a brother who is there, and he wrote me to come."

Just then, Edna lifted her hand. She leaned forward and her face contorted in pain.

"Would you run and get Mistress Horton?" she said to Rachel. "I believe my birth pains have started."

Rachel rose quickly and left the tent.

Mistress Horton, assisted by Elizabeth, helped deliver the Easons' baby, who was named Bermudas in honor of the Spanish sea captain, Juan Bermudez who discovered the islands. The new baby boy was the first known child to be born there.

Three weeks after the baby's birth, the Easons consulted Chaplain Bucke about christening their healthy son. Since arriving in the islands, the Chaplain had conducted his daily evening worship outdoors under a large birch tree at the edge of the encampment.

The following Sunday, one-month-old Bermudas Edward Eason was christened during a special morning worship attended by most of the camp, with Sir Thomas Gates as godfather.

CHAPTER 14

THE ENGAGEMENT

FROM THE MOMENT Thomas Powell had first seen Elizabeth Persons, he had been struck with her beauty. It had happened as Thomas, personal servant and aide to Sir George Somers, was standing near the rail on the quarterdeck of the *Sea Venture*. He noticed her as she walked up the gangplank at Plymouth, prior to the departure. She was with a handsome lady, and she was also struggling with a large bag. He rushed down and asked if he could carry her luggage. She blushed, but didn't object, so Thomas followed her to their cabin, where he introduced himself.

The elegant-looking lady with Elizabeth said, "I am Jane Horton, and this is my maidservant, Elizabeth Persons. She has been with me since she was fourteen."

Elizabeth, slightly blushing, added, "My parents were killed in a fire. I have no family, so Mistress Horton became my guardian."

Mistress Horton, smiling, said, "Yes, Elizabeth and I have been together about six years, and she has been more like a daughter than a maidservant. You see, I never married or had children of my own."

Thomas noted the elegance of Jane Horton's dress and mannerisms. He knew she must be a lady of some means. He wondered what had brought this pair of beautiful women on such a hazardous voyage.

As if reading his mind, Mistress Horton continued. "I own stock in the Virginia Company, so I thought it would be prudent to come on this voyage and see for myself whether to invest further in the company."

Thomas nodded. "I'm the fleet admiral's personal servant. Sir George Somers is an excellent navigator, and I believe you both will have a safe and delightful voyage."

Over the following seven weeks of the voyage, Thomas had used every opportunity and excuse to talk to Elizabeth Persons. They met on deck and snatched brief moments to get more acquainted. When Elizabeth and Mistress Horton were on deck together, she was very attentive to her mistress and only exchanged pleasantries with Thomas. However, she couldn't hide her delight in seeing Thomas from the observant eyes of her mistress. One day, Mistress Horton, noting the extra color that came into Elizabeth's cheeks upon seeing Thomas, made mention of it. "Elizabeth, I think you are enjoying young Thomas's attention."

"Yes, Mistress. He is so polite and respectful to me. I have never met another young man like him. Do you mind my talking with him?"

"Oh no, my child. I have talked with the admiral regarding his servant, and he thinks highly of Thomas. However, you must be discreet in your contacts with him."

"Yes, Mistress. We are always on deck when we engage in our talks."

That evening the weather had turned blustery, and within twenty-four hours the ship was caught in the giant tempest, which had put a temporary end to Thomas's courtship of Elizabeth. Both were busy and fearful it might be the last of a growing relationship between them.

After they had landed safely on Devil's Islands following the terrible ordeal, Thomas wasted little time in resuming their budding romance. He used every opportunity to ingratiate himself to Mistress Horton, seeing that her needs received the attention of the admiral when other remedies failed.

On the tenth of October, Thomas asked Elizabeth to marry him. This was no surprise, for she had been dreaming of becoming his wife.

"Oh Thomas, I would love to become your wife, but I must ask my mistress for permission. She has been like a mother to me, so I feel she will not object."

"I, too, will need to ask for Admiral Somers' blessing. And, we will need Chaplain Bucke's agreement to perform the ritual, and the permission of Governor Gates."

"Do you think they all will agree?"

"Why not, Elizabeth? We are both of age. As long as we continue to work out our indebtedness they should not object. Shall we talk to them this evening?"

"Yes, Thomas."

The next morning, Thomas met a smiling Elizabeth at the camp spring, filling her bucket.

"What's the good word, dearest Elizabeth?"

"I talked with Mistress Horton, and she said she has been expecting this for some time. We had a long talk, and she agreed to it. She said she would ask Chaplain Bucke to perform the ritual."

"Wonderful. I talked with Admiral Somers and Governor Gates and both thought it would be fine. They said it would give the camp something to celebrate."

"Oh Thomas, I'm so happy. We will need to set the date for our wedding. Would the fourth Sabbath of this month be about right?"

"That would be fine with me, Elizabeth."

"Do you think Sir George would mind giving me away?"

"I will ask him today. I'm sure he will do it. He thinks you are a fine lassie. He told me I would be fortunate if you became my bride."

"My mistress thinks you are a fine young lad and will make a good husband."

"You and I are fortunate to have the blessings of such fine masters."

The next two weeks were busy with preparations by Mistress Horton and Elizabeth. Several of the wives offered to help Elizabeth create a wedding dress out of their limited materials.

CHAPTER 15

THE WEDDING

ON SATURDAY AFTERNOON, October 28, Sir George Somers escorted Elizabeth Persons to the front of a gathering of the camp and stood before Chaplain Bucke. Thomas Powell, along with his best man, John Thomas, faced the chaplain on his left. Elizabeth and her maid of honor faced the chaplain on his right.

John glanced back at those seated. His eyes found and held Rachel's for a brief moment. He smiled and received her warm smile and nod. She was seated next to two of the other single lassies.

After the chaplain began with a brief prayer, John turned and looked at Thomas. Though the weather was cloudy and cool, the groom was perspiring slightly.

Chaplain Bucke made the announcement of the couple's intent to be married according to the laws of the Church of England, with the permission of Sir Thomas Gates, acting governor, and with the blessings of their sponsors.

Elizabeth was dressed in a white silk dress, with a veil. She was holding a bouquet of crimson wildflowers. Thomas wore his finest suit of knee-length britches and waistcoat, with shoes and socks borrowed from Admiral Somers.

Following the prayer and the statement of intent, the chaplain gave a shorter than usual homily, then proceeded with the wedding ritual after the giving away of the bride by Admiral Somers. John's feet were getting a little tired from standing when the chaplain finally introduced the new couple to the camp as Mr. and Mrs. Thomas Powell.

The camp held a feast in their honor and presented small gifts to help the couple set up their own private tent and begin housekeeping. During the afternoon's festivities, John and Rachel took their plates of food to a comfortable spot and began to talk.

"Wasn't that a beautiful wedding, John?"

"Yes. How did Elizabeth manage to get such a beautiful wedding dress?"

"Some of the married ladies had silk garments and gave them as a present to Elizabeth. Mistress Horton, being a fine seamstress, had little trouble making it."

"I noticed a tear or two on your face during the wedding. Were you sad, Rachel?"

"Yes and no. I thought about my best friend marrying the man I had hoped to marry. But then, I noted the radiance and joy in Elizabeth, so I just put the other thoughts out of my mind. Life goes on, John. Doesn't it?"

"It does, indeed. I am happy I met you, Rachel. I'm glad God spared all our lives so that we could have such a beautiful afternoon together on this paradise of an island."

"John, you say such fitting words. You lift my spirit. I hope when we reach Jamestown, we can continue with our friendship."

"Me too, Rachel. Would you like to take a walk along the inlet shore?"

"Yes. Let me tell Mary and Caroline I will join them later."

While John waited for Rachel to join him, he watched Thomas and Elizabeth Powell thank Chaplain Bucke, collect their wedding gifts, and walk toward their new home, nestled under a large cedar tree beyond the edge of the camp.

Before the day of the wedding, John had helped Thomas erect a new tent apart from the rest of the encampment. This allowed the couple more privacy and seclusion on their first days of marital bliss.

So ended the third month of occupation of Devil's Islands by the passengers and crew of the ill-fated *Sea Venture*. Two deaths, a birth, and a wedding seemed to suggest that a new name for the islands was needed to replace the old, superstitious one.

CHAPTER 16 ❧

MASTER MATE HENRY RAVENS

HENRY RAVENS, MASTER mate to Captain Newport, was an expert seaman who had accompanied Newport on his first voyage in December 1606 to set up a British outpost on the North American continent. Earlier in 1606, charters had been granted by King James I to set up permanent settlements along the American coast, between latitudes thirty and forty-five. The charter for the southern latitudes was granted to the London Virginia Company. The charter for the northern latitudes was given to the Plymouth Virginia Company. A Virginia Council in London was designated as the overseer for both.

The northern group, the Plymouth Virginia Company, mounted expeditions first to establish a settlement. However, their attempts proved futile until 1620 when the Massachusetts Bay colony was established.

Captain Newport, a stockholder in the London Virginia Company, was chosen to lead the first voyage. His prior experience in explorations, and his skill in seamanship, made him the logical choice by the Crown, as well as the company.

Three ships were in that first convoy, which finally reached a likely spot to build a small fortress. The site was on a river about fifteen miles inland from a large bay, later called Chesapeake. A small fort was located here at Point Comfort, and later named Fort Algernon.

They named the river James after their own King James. Approximately sixty miles up this river, the fortress, Jamestown, or James City, as it was sometimes called, was built on a peninsula jutting out from the north bank of the James.

They chose this inland site for the colony, rather than a coastal one, for defensive purposes from Spanish frigates that were exploring farther and farther north along the eastern coasts from their Caribbean outposts.

King James wanted to lay claim to this new territory and keep Spain from expanding its empire any farther north in the New World. Also, he thought a northern shortcut passage to India might be found. The finding of gold, precious minerals, and jewels was an additional motive for granting the charter. With these goals in mind, Captain Newport and his small flotilla set sail.

On May 13, 1607, those three frail barks, with 105 colonists, tied up to some trees on a small finger of land, approximately sixty acres in size, that stuck out into the James River.

Those first three years were extremely hard for the settlers. Disease, starvation, and attacks by Indians were constant challenges. By the time Henry Ravens and his crew were dispatched to Jamestown from Devil's Islands, near the first of August 1609, approximately five hundred colonists had arrived. Of those five hundred, only about three hundred fifty were alive. However, three hundred fifty of these were from the ships of the *Third Supply* who survived the great tempest. Henry Ravens and his crew were not among the *Third Supply* survivors. Another tempest was believed to have destroyed the longboat and all those aboard.

Word of the fate of the *Sea Venture* never reached Jamestown, nor England and the Virginia council in London, until after May 1610. Ten months would elapse before the survivors of the *Sea Venture* would finally reach Jamestown. By then, May 21, 1610, only sixty souls were found alive in the fort. Most had died from malnutrition, starvation, and disease. Of those who emigrated to Jamestown, prior to the arrival of the *Sea Venture*, approximately 90 percent perished during those first three years.

CHAPTER 17

DELIVERANCE

EARLY IN AUGUST, Governor Gates had estimated it would take Henry Ravens and his eight volunteers at least a month to reach Jamestown and to secure the sending of a vessel back for their rescue.

However, by the middle of October, it had been more than two months since the dispatch of Ravens, and still no word. The predictions of Admiral Somers and Captain Newport appeared to have come all too true.

After the death of Lady Gates, Governor Gates called a meeting with Admiral Somers and Captain Newport. "Gentlemen, I didn't want to believe your doubts about Ravens and his men ever reaching Jamestown, but now I must admit that you were right. And, even if wrong, we can't wait any longer to begin building two vessels large enough to get us safely to Jamestown. Do you agree?"

"Yes," said the admiral, and the captain nodded his assent.

"This is what I'm proposing: I want each of you to gather a crew to build a pinnace large enough for half our people, plus supplies. Captain Newport, I want you to begin your construction as soon as possible. Admiral Somers, I want you to delay your work for about a month, just in case Ravens or someone else shows up. Also, by delaying your construction, we may avoid any problems Captain Newport and his crew encounter in their task."

"Right," said Admiral Somers.

"What do you want me to call this first one, Sir Thomas?"

"Let's call her *Deliverance*."

"That sounds fine by me. I'll begin to gather my men tomorrow."

"One other suggestion, Captain Newport."

"Yes?"

"Our ship's carpenter, Mr. Frobisher, should be on your team. I hear he has experience with ship-building."

"Right. I heard the same from some of my *Sea Venture* crew."

"Sir George, I want you to select your team from the *Sea Venture*'s crew for your main helpers. You each will have to pick your spots for construction."

"That's fine by me," said the admiral.

"One final thing. Each of you must select your own men. I assume by now you know some of them pretty well. If you have any problems with any men, send them to me."

With that, the three arose and walked to their mess tent, where supper was being served by some of the single lassies. Two mess tents had been built, one for the common passengers and crew, the other for those with rank and status: the officers, couples, ladies, and gentlemen.

Status and rank separated the encampment in matters of food and living arrangements almost as it had aboard ship. Even the *Sea Venture*'s crew tended to bunk in close proximity to each other, though they ate with the rest of the common passengers.

The next day, Captain Newport began to assemble his team for building the *Deliverance*. The name had the sound of hope, and as word got around, the captain had more than enough volunteers. This pleased him, because it allowed him some discretion in choosing the more expert and experienced.

Captain Newport chose the ship's carpenter, Richard Frobisher, to be his lead man. Frobisher helped Newport screen the volunteers for those experienced in working with wood. They found about twenty who knew how to use saw and adze and prepare treenails. All were told they would work under close supervision of Mr. Frobisher, who suggested they build in the cove near camp on the eastern shore of the island. Their building site was partially sheltered, not buffeted by high breakers. Captain Newport called his site Frobisher's Cove.

Timbers salvaged from the *Sea Venture*, and large birch trees, already cut, were dragged to the site, where the men sawed them into planks for scaffolding to hold the keel in place. The keel was cut from two of the largest trees. Soon the cove took on the sound and appearance of shipbuilding. This was the first real project that took a goodly share of the men, following the construction of a campsite.

The food-gathering party under Admiral Somers required about ten men to keep the camp supplied with fresh fish, sea turtles, pork from the wild hogs, and other edible items on the islands. Spanish explorers must have placed the hogs on the islands at one time. Bread, corn, and food salvaged from the *Sea Venture* they carefully rationed in order to make them last as long as possible.

Another ten men under Sergeant Sharpe, John's group, were kept busy finding suitable trees for the *Deliverance* and a second pinnace, to be built later by Admiral Somers and his crew. Thus about two-thirds of the camp were kept busy with specific tasks. The rest had daily chores assisting the cook, serving meals, standing guard, and performing other miscellaneous duties.

With food so plentiful and the living so easy, Governor Gates began once more to hear talk of people wanting to stay on the islands and forget going on to Jamestown. However, he would have no such talk. Once again, he made it plain to all that as soon as the pinnaces were constructed and seaworthy, the camp would embark for Jamestown.

CHAPTER 18 ❧

PATIENCE

IN THE MIDDLE of November, one month after the keel of the *Deliverance* was laid, Sir George assembled his crew. The second pinnace would be named *Patience*. The construction site selected was a mile from the camp, near the northeast corner of the island. It was more sheltered than Frobisher's Cove. In fact, Sir George's crew decided to pitch tents near the site and to have food from the main camp brought over each day. Sir Thomas thought this a good idea, since it allowed the men to work more hours each day. Additional men were now required to keep both building sites supplied with timbers.

In fact, a little rivalry began between the two building teams to see who could be the first to finish the ship. Most believed the *Deliverance* would be the first completed since that crew had a head start. However, an event occurred that made the race more even. No sooner was the keel of the *Deliverance* in place, and most planking nailed to the spars, than another tempest skirted the eastern end of Devil's Island. Large breakers blew in from the southeast and swept up the eastern end of the island chain. The keel of the *Deliverance* was laid closer to the high tide mark than prudent. Given the breakers' reach, and lack of sufficient protection by Frobisher's Cove, the construction site was pounded by the huge waves.

A tug of war between the angry seas and all available men of the encampment quickly ensued. They tied ropes to both ends of the keel and then to the trees closest to the shoreline. As the tide and waves rose higher, the keel looked as if it would be yanked out into the cove. The breakers thrashed it fiercely for over a day.

In addition to the tempest and almost losing the keel, another tragedy occurred. One of the crew, Richard Lewis, was on the ropes nearest the keel, when suddenly he fell into the pounding surf. Several of the men rushed down to drag him to higher ground. John was one of the men who carried Lewis to the shelter of the trees, where a crowd quickly gathered about Lewis. They laid him on the ground beneath one of the rope-lashed trees. Rain pushed by high winds pelted his face. Mistress Horton knelt down to shield him from the worst of it and to examine him.

Sir Thomas, nearby, asked, "How is he, Lady Horton?"

"I can't feel a heartbeat, and he doesn't seem to be breathing."

Lewis's face was ashen, and there was no movement of his chest or stomach. He looked more dead than alive. Mistress Horton knelt lower and placed her head on his chest, then held a small leaf before his nostrils, sheltered from the wind by her hands. Seeing no movement, she said, "I'm afraid he is dead, Sir Thomas. I suggest we carry him to the sick tent out of this weather and see if he will come around. I will stay with him until we know."

John and several other men gently picked up Lewis, carried him to the encampment, and placed him in a lone tent designated for those who were ill or in need of special attention.

He never moved, groaned, or made any indication of being alive to John or the others who carried him. Yet, no one could pronounce him dead. Only time would tell. This was the first time John had been this close to a dead person. It made him uneasy. He realized how very tenuous life was.

That evening the worst of the storm was over and the breakers began to abate. By then the keel had lost much of its planking. The rest was filled with water and debris from the storm. Mother Nature had taught the novice shipbuilders a valuable lesson. The keel's proximity to the water was not to be taken lightly. When the storm finally ceased, Captain Newport's crew wasted little time pulling what was left of the keel higher up on the beach, safe from the clutching fingers of the sea.

The next morning, the work on the *Deliverance* began again, almost from scratch. Three weeks of work had been swept away. However, the keel, the ribs, and some of the planking remained.

The destruction of much of the ship was another lesson in survival and fortitude for the people of the ill-fated *Sea Venture*. They might be knocked down, but not out, thought John. Only God's providence could account for this.

Now the race between the two building crews could begin in earnest. However, the funeral of Richard Lewis would occupy their attention for the next day.

A simple graveside service was held the following morning for Richard Lewis, who had boarded the *Sea Venture* in London near the end of May as a single, middle-aged man with parents still living on the outskirts of London. Chaplain Bucke delivered a short eulogy, praising Richard for his work on the *Deliverance*

and his efforts to save as much of the vessel's structure as possible from the tempest.

The service was held in the little glen with the two grave markers. John was standing close enough to read the names of Lady Gates and Jeffrey Breare on the grave markers next to the open grave. Soon, someone would chisel Lewis's name on a third marker and would set it at the head of his final resting place, three feet wide, six feet long, and four feet deep.

John wondered how long it would take the news of Lewis's death to reach his parents. What if this was his funeral, instead of Lewis's? How would his parents and Dorothy ever hear, or react?

Given the uncertainty of ever getting off the island, his family might never hear of him again. What a depressing thought. Life was so precious, and yet so uncertain. How could one hope for a future?

It was this hope that Chaplain Bucke spoke about in his eulogy. He was saying that faith in the risen Christ gives us hope in a future. To John, given the risks one faced in life, it seemed almost a waste of time to plan one's future. Still, he felt he had a bright future, if he could somehow reach Jamestown and pay off his indentured debt.

This must be where his faith in God did play a role in his life. Believing he had a future brought a resurgence of hope to him, even in the face of death. As the chaplain concluded the service, John offered a silent prayer for Lewis and his parents. He prayed that God would help the camp to build the two ships to complete the journey.

CHAPTER 19 ∼

THE ROLFES

DURING THE STORM that almost destroyed the keel of the *Deliverance*, several tents were blown down. Among those was one that housed John and Virginia Rolfe. This was a matter of concern for the Rolfe's, for Virginia's pregnancy was in its seventh month. However, the problem was quickly solved, and life for the expectant parents returned to normal.

The Rolfes had only been married for two years when they sailed on the *Third Supply* for Jamestown. He was baptized May 6, 1585 in Norfolk County, on the northeastern coast of England. John Rolfe's parents owned a large farm in the rolling hills of Norfolk County. His whole life had been devoted to raising farm produce and animals. His parents were leading citizens in their part of the county and owned stock in the Virginia Company.

After his marriage to Virginia in 1605, they continued to live on his parents' large farm, which he expected to inherit someday. In January of 1608, the Virginia Company contracted with Rolfe to recruit settlers for the new colony of Jamestown. He spent over a year traveling throughout southern England and

Wales, signing up men and women. By then, he had decided to accompany the *Third Supply* to the new colony, along with Virginia, who was about two months pregnant.

As a wealthy planter, Rolfe was interested in a new product that was fast becoming the craze of Europe and England. Captain Newport, a friend of Rolfe, had told him about this new product that was raised extensively on Caribbean plantations. The product was tobacco, whose source for England was multiple sources from France and Spain. Newport had given Rolfe some tobacco seeds he had brought back from one of his cruises to the West Indies. He had suggested that perhaps the new colony of Virginia might be a suitable place for growing the plants. Rolfe had placed these seeds in glass bottles and packed them carefully in his luggage aboard the *Sea Venture*. He was able to save his luggage when the ship was lightened during the tempest.

He looked at them on several occasions and thought Captain Newport just might be right. He would find out how right, if they ever got to Jamestown. In the meantime, his seed he had planted within his wife was mostly on his mind. She appeared to have come through the recent stress-filled events in good order and was beginning to show evidence of her pregnancy. If they didn't get off this island in the next few months, their baby would be born here, perhaps by February. Lady Horton, as midwife, would be needed again. She was the next best thing to a doctor.

Rolfe, as his parents' heir and representative of their stock investments in the company, had special standing among the *Third Supply* leadership. It was young men like him the Virginia Company needed for planting this new colony.

Rolfe's wife never complained about living in a tent. The climate was mild, the food plentiful and easy to acquire. Her pregnancy took their minds off themselves and their personal discomfort.

"John, do you think we will have a boy or a girl?"

"I will be happy with either, Virginia, just so it is healthy."

"Me too. I have spoken to Mistress Horton about attending me when my time comes. She is such a nice lady. We are fortunate to have her with us, right?"

"Are you fearful about having the baby here without your mother and family?"

"I would be more fearful were it not for Mistress Horton. She has been a midwife to a number of women over the years, for which I am grateful. Her experience will give me more confidence and peace."

"It looks like it will be several more months before we can finish building the two pinnaces. So, I'm sure the baby will be born here. Have you thought of a name for it, Virginia?"

"I have thought about the name of the Spanish explorer who discovered these islands. I believe it was Juan Bermudez. The Easons named their boy, Bermudas. So we could use Bermuda if it is a girl and a new name if it is a boy. We have a couple more months to come up with a boy's name.

"Yes, that would be fine, Virginia."

CHAPTER 20 ∼

NAMANTUCK

BY THE FIRST of December, the keel of the *Deliverance* was securely anchored well above the high tide mark, but close enough for launching when the time came. They would dig a deep trench from the water's edge up to the keel, bringing in enough of the ocean water to help launch the pinnance.

The men fastened new planking to the ribs with treenails and pounded rope caulking into the seams along the bottom and sides of the ship. Each vessel could hold about seventy-five people for the ten-day trip to Jamestown.

It would be several more months, the following year, before both ships would be seaworthy enough for their first trial voyages around the islands. Cutting down trees, sawing them into planks and other pieces of lumber, then transporting these to the construction site kept the construction moving at a snail's pace. Often, the men doing the building had to wait several days for enough lumber to arrive before they could continue their work, but no one complained. Even Sir Thomas understood that it would probably take about twice the time estimated to complete both ships.

Early in January, 1610, one of the two Indians in the camp came up missing. Matchumps and Namantuck were part of the detail charged with food gathering on the islands. Since they were skilled in hunting and tracking animals, they were given free reign to roam the islands. They reported back to the main body of hunters when and where to find their quarry.

No one noticed that Namantuck was missing for several days after Matchumps ambled into camp alone. When asked by Sir Thomas the whereabouts of his friend, Matchump explained, "I left him at other end of islands."

"Why?"

"He want to go by self down other side of island to find more pigs."

Sir Thomas decided to send a search party for Namantuck. It left the next day and was gone several days. Upon returning, the party reported to Sir Thomas it had circled the entire island chain, some twenty-two miles long, but found no sign of Namuntuck.

The following week, the search party left again and re-circled the islands from the opposite direction, but still found no sign of the missing Indian. Sir Thomas again questioned Matchumps, but his story remained the same.

Inasmuch as the islands contained several caves with underground caverns filled with fresh rainwater, it was surmised that perhaps Namantuck might have explored one of these and become lost or disoriented in the process. Sir Thomas instructed all hunting parties to look into some of these caves for signs of Namantuck. He also gave the camp a new order that no one was to wander around alone on the islands. Those who disobeyed his order would be disciplined. Namantuck and his mysterious disappearance was the topic of conversation for many weeks. Many suspected that not all had been well between the two Indians. Perhaps an old feud that had gone unresolved was at the basis of Namantuck's mysterious disappearance.

Each group that had business on other parts of the islands continued to look for some sign of him, but all to no avail. He seemingly had disappeared without a single trace. The mystery would not be solved for several years.

Several weeks after Namantuck's disappearance, Matchumps let slip a clue that may have figured in the loss of his friend. In a conversation with Sergeant Sharpe, Matchumps confessed that there had been bad blood between him and Namumtuck. It was over the stealing of one of Matchumps' wives by Namuntuck.

This story circulated within the sergeant's own group, but never went any higher to Governor Gates.

CHAPTER 21

BERMUDA

BY THE FIRST of February, Virginia Rolfe was heavy with child. By the tenth, she told John to stay nearby. She felt she could deliver almost any day. Mistress Horten was also alerted and prepared the special sick tent for the delivery.

The construction of both ships was about half completed. Both crews worked as rapidly as materials were made available. The race was on to see which team would be first to launch a vessel.

The admiral's crew members were growing restless and beginning to fight among themselves, in spite of the best leadership skills of the admiral. Each evening he would gather them around the campfire and engage them in conversation about their families and plans for when they reached Jamestown. This helped take the crew's minds off the daily slow work on the *Patience*. However, patience seemed to be the one thing his crew was lacking. These men were sailors, not shipwrights. They were square pegs in round holes, almost like the wooden nails they were pounding into the hull of the ship. Admiral Somers began to hear rumors of a mutiny by some of the men. He knew so little of their plan that he was afraid to take action, though he knew enough to believe it was not directed against him, but rather against Sir Thomas.

He would be patient and learn all he could, then alert the governor. He had faced mutinous crews before at sea and knew premature action would not suffice. One waited until he knew the names of the leaders of the rebellion and the approximate time of the mutiny. In some ways it was like waiting and watching for a boil to develop a head, then lancing and draining out the poison. This would require patience, much patience, just like the construction of their ship.

February eleventh dawned clear and mild. The islands' latitude brought mild winter weather unlike England's. Virginia Rolfe awoke with a sharp pain that lasted a few moments, then went away. Mistress Horton had told her what to expect when her time for delivery was imminent, so when the pains returned a short while later, she awoke John, who was sleeping in the hammock at her side.

"John, I think my time for delivery is here. Would you go bring Mistress Horton?"

"Yes. I may have to awaken her. Are you sure you are that near?"

"Yes, John. I need to talk with her about these pains."

"Right. I will go as soon as I dress."

He dressed quickly, then walked swiftly across the open area in the midst of the camp to a group of four tents where the single lassies were housed. Mistress Horton's tent was nearest to the tents of Sir Thomas and other senior officials.

Dawn's early light was just beginning to penetrate the shadows of the trees from a full moon that hung over the western end of the Islands. The only ones awake, besides Rolfe, were a couple of grunting hogs in a makeshift pen, awaiting the cook's hungry knife.

Pausing briefly to catch his breath, in a low voice Rolfe called, "Mistress Horton!" Not hearing a response, he raised his voice a bit louder. "Mistress Horton!" That time he heard a stirring within the tent. "Mistress Horton, it's John Rolfe. My wife believes she is very close to giving birth and would like for you to come as soon as possible. Can you hear me?"

"Yes, John. I heard you. I will come as soon as I can dress."

"Thank you."

The sun was just rising when Mistress Horton and Rachel Jones, her new helper, arrived at the Rolfes' tent. Virginia's water had broken, and the pains were coming more frequently and with more intensity. Quickly sizing up the situation, Mistress Horton ordered warm water brought from the cook's kitchen and a pallet of blankets spread on the canvas floor of the tent. An additional lantern was lit, and Virginia was moved to the pallet where Mistress Horton could assist more easily with the delivery. Virginia's husband excused himself, saying he would be in the dining tent if needed.

Several hours later, after an intense struggle by Mistress Horton, Virginia had a breach birth. The infant girl labored in her breathing. Rachel went to find Rolfe to tell him the news of his new daughter. When they returned, Mistress Horton broke the bad news that little Bermuda might not survive.

Virginia wept as she tried to nurse her baby. Rolfe wiped her tears and kissed her cheeks, trying to console her. After Chaplain Bucke came and offered prayers for both child and parents, they felt more hopeful. But within twenty-four hours, Mistress Horton's prediction came true. The struggle to be born for little Bermuda had been too much. The second child to be born on the islands simply quit breathing. A fourth grave marker would now be added to the others in the little burial glen.

In his eulogy, Chaplain Bucke spoke of God as the God of all comfort... even in this death of the Rolfes' first child. He concluded by saying that time and prayer would bring healing to their wounded hearts.

CHAPTER 22

A SECOND MUTINY

NICHOLAS BENNET HAD led a rebellion two months after the *Sea Venture* landed in the islands. The second mutiny was a one-man affair by Stephen Hopkins.

Shortly after the first attempt by Bennet and Carter, Hopkins had talked to several, including Thomas Powell, aide to Sir George, about staying on the islands. Powell had told John about Hopkins' ideas, and had said that Hopkins might approach him with his scheme. John had mentioned it to Rachel and others. Sir George had told Sir Thomas the substance of Hopkins' ideas. Sir Thomas dismissed it as idle talk and did not take Hopkins seriously. Furthermore, as long as it was just talk and no action, Sir Thomas was too busy with other concerns to worry.

However, in mid-February, Hopkins, who was Chaplain Bucke's assistant, began trying to enlist several others to petition Sir Thomas. His request was to stay on the islands, even after the ships were completed.

This renewed affair by Hopkins came to the attention of the governor, and this time he decided to act. He called Hopkins in and ordered him shot. He purposely waited one week to execute his order to allow the news to spread and see what effect it would have. Several of Hopkins' friends came to see the governor and to plead that Hopkins be spared. They said they had never felt the request to stay on the islands would be granted and would not be a party to it.

The governor took this under advisement and decided his order to execute Hopkins had achieved the desired effect. He immediately canceled it, allowing Hopkins to live. The news of the Hopkins affair spread throughout the camp and was the subject of conversation in Sir George's crew on the *Patience*. Sir George hoped this latest action by the governor would diminish the rumbles he had heard about a mutiny within his own crew. For several weeks, it seemed to have that effect. But, around the middle of March, an incident took place that ignited the flames of a third and more serious rebellion.

CHAPTER 23

A THIRD MUTINY

SIR GEORGE'S CREW worked steadily building the *Patience*. She would be about thirty feet long, with a fifteen-and-a-half-foot beam, and would weigh thirty tons. Their work site was approximately a mile north of the construction on the *Deliverance*. Their sheltered cove kept them out of sight from Newport's team.

Sir George had selected most of the *Sea Venture*'s crew, approximately twenty men, plus a supplement of ten others from among the passengers. John Thomas worked with Sergeant Sharpe's detail of about forty men supplying timber to both building sites.

The *Patience*'s crew worked, slept, and ate at the work site. Thus, the main camp was divided. Although this allowed more hours for construction by the crew of the *Patience*, it tended to diminish the authority of Sir Thomas over the entire encampment and fostered a spirit of mutiny and rebellion that had been smoldering ever since the first attempt by Bennet and Carter.

Admiral Somers had sailed too many ships and worked too many crews not to be able to smell a mutiny before it happened.

107

He wondered if some in the main camp, in addition to his camp, were jointly planning something. What would be their plan this time? Time was running out. Soon, both pinnaces would be finished, and all would be compelled to leave the islands. Whatever was brewing appeared to be more ominous.

Did it involve killing him or Sir Thomas, seizing the storehouse, and making off with necessary tools and food? The majority of conspirators had to be among his crew, and possibly a few others in the main camp.

These thoughts troubled Sir George. He wished he knew just what his men were planning. It was possible a few of these mutineers might be in Sergeant Sharpe's detail. He would ask the sergeant what he could find out. Something was definitely in the wind. He could feel it in his bones.

In Sergeant Sharpe's detail, John noticed that three particular men always stayed together when cutting trees and that they would quit talking whenever he worked next to them. Since these men didn't bunk together, John wondered about their togetherness on the job.

One morning, he was relieving his bladder behind a tree near the three, when he overheard the one named Joe speaking to the others: "Henry, when do we strike and kill the bastard?"

Henry was silent for a moment. He slowly looked around. Not seeing anyone, he lowered his voice and said, just loud enough for John to overhear, "Carter has not said definitely, but he told me in about two weeks."

"Middle of April, huh?"

"That sounds about right."

John froze. His bladder was empty. He dared not move. He just stood still, hidden by the trees and heavy underbrush. They had quit talking and were busy chopping, intent on bringing down the large birch tree.

As quietly as possible, John turned and slipped back behind more trees, careful to stay out of sight of the three men. When a safe distance away, John looked for Sergeant Sharpe.

This was too important to let pass. This did not sound like idle talk. Who could they mean by the "bastard"? It had to be Sir George or Sir Thomas.

Sergeant Sharpe was in a knot of men, cutting a large birch. As soon as it fell, John motioned to him. Walking out of earshot from the others, John quickly related what he had just overheard, and identified Henry Paine as the spokesman with the other two.

Sergeant Sharpe frowned. "I will take this information to Somers as quickly as possible. He asked me yesterday to keep my ear to the ground for rumors of a possible mutiny. This will definitely pin it down. Carter was part of that first rebellion and is one of the main ones in his crew. He no doubt is one of the ringleaders."

"When will you inform Sir Thomas?"

"I will let Sir George decide. It appears most of the mutineers are in his camp. Don't breathe a word of what you told me to anyone. Not even Wooley or any of your other friends."

"You have my word," said John.

CHAPTER 24 ∼

APRIL 15

ON THE FIRST of April, Sir Thomas, accompanied by two of his armed aides walked into the cove where the *Patience* was nearing completion. He came to see the progress on the ship and a possible completion date. However, his main motive was to confer with Sir George regarding the message of a possible mutiny. After looking the vessel over, Sir George invited Sir Thomas into his tent. Making sure they could not be overheard, Sir Thomas asked for details of the planned mutiny.

The admiral quietly told the governor what John Thomas, one of Sergeant Sharpe's men, had overheard. Henry Paine and his friend Carter were planning a murder. Either the governor or himself, or both, could be the target. Their killing might be part of a mutiny by men in both camps.

This sounded ominous. Governor Gates swore under his breath, then was silent for a moment. Finally, he spoke: "George, I have a plan as we approach April fifteenth. I will assign Paine to several days of guard duty. That should prevent him from carrying out his plan of murder."

"Sounds wise to me. I will alert Sergeant Sharpe to bring a detail of his men up here to my work site to help with the construction, but mainly to keep an eye on Carter and some of his conspirators."

Gates nodded his approval. "This should enable us both to keep the lid on this development. I will alert Captain Newport, and with the number of loyal men he and I have, we should be able to handle anything they attempt."

"Right," said the admiral.

"Keep me informed if you hear anything else."

"I will."

With that, the two left Sir George's tent and walked back to the ship's construction site.

As the governor was leaving, Admiral Somers said, "At the present rate of progress, the *Patience* should be ready to sail around the first of May, unless ...?"

Sir Thomas nodded, then with his two aides walked swiftly down the trail toward the main camp.

The two weeks dragged following the talk of mutiny between Somers and Gates. Sergeant Sharpe moved ten of his detail of tree cutters into Somers' camp.

John was part of this detail. Sharpe had designated John as his liaison with this squad of men. John requested that Wooley also be part of this team, which Sharpe permitted.

None in John's group appeared to be part of any conspiracy, past or present. He was certain of Wooley, and almost as sure of the others. The *Sea Venture* crew was the other close-knit group at Somers' work site. Chris Carter was among this group of approximately twenty.

John had said nothing to Wooley about being privy to the planned murder. However, one day when the two were alone sawing up a tree, he brought up the subject of past attempts by some of the men to rebel against the governor.

"William, we've had a couple of attempts by some in our camp to rebel against the governor. Have you heard any recent talk by the men you know of any rebellion?"

"No, John, I haven't heard any such talk, nor has anyone tried to approach me with any such foolishness."

"Sergeant Sharpe asked me to pass along any rumors of rebellion. So let me know if you hear any."

"I will, John."

CHAPTER 25 ❧

THE EXECUTION

THE TWO PREVIOUS attempts at mutiny by a few malcontents had only resulted thus far in the death of one man, Jeffrey Breare, by drowning. But this was soon to change. A third and more serious attempt began to unfold due to the revelation of a plan overheard by John Thomas around the middle of March. Other than those involved in the plot, only Governor Gates, Captain Newport, and Admiral Somers, plus a select few in the camp, knew something was brewing.

On April 14, Henry Paine walked slowly to the governor's headquarters tent. A helmeted guard asked him his business.

"I want to see Governor Gates about my guard duty."

"Follow me," said the guard, motioning.

Governor Gates was seated at a small desk flanked by flags of the Red Cross of St. George on seven-foot supports.

"State your business."

"Sir, I have had two days of guard duty and request I be relieved."

"What did the sergeant at arms tell you?"

"He said I must serve two more days."

"Then why have you come to me?"

"Sir, the other men only serve two days in a row, then they are off for two."

"Mr. Paine, you have not served any guard duty until now, correct?"

"Correct, sir."

"Then I see no reason to relieve you from further guard duty. You are dismissed."

With a frown on his face, Paine turned and left the governor's tent. The sergeant of the guard was waiting outside. He ushered Paine back to his guard post, where he would be under careful surveillance for the next forty-eight hours.

The next day, Paine refused further guard duty. This was the date John had overheard of a murder being planned by Paine and others. The governor, being privy to this, ordered Paine arrested and held in a makeshift brig under two guards.

The following day, after a brief trial by the governor, with John's testimony being one of several witnesses of Paine's conspiracy, the prisoner was ordered to be hanged. Since he was a gentleman, Paine asked to be shot and was given this option.

William Strachey, secretary to the governor and the Virginia Company, wrote in his minutes this brief final disposition of the matter: "Henry Paine had his desire, the sun and his life setting together."

Word of Paine's execution spread like wildfire. In Admiral Somers' camp, Carter and twenty of the crew, thinking that Paine had implicated them in the plot, decided to run off into the woods to another island. However, before leaving, Carter approached Admiral Somers.

"Sir," he began, "we heard about Paine being shot. The rest of our crew is leaving this camp. We don't trust Governor Gates. We don't blame you for Paine's death. Would you spare us some food and supplies?"

Somers studied Carter's face for a few moments. He realized he could not reason with him or the others. He decided to go along with his request. Later, he would try to get them to reconsider their rash actions and return. "Mr. Carter, I will grant you the request. If you need more food, send one of your men to me, and I will see what I can do for you."

Smiling, Carter saluted Admiral Somers. "Sir, thank you for your help. The crew will not forget this."

Somers led him and two of the crew to the storehouse and gave them the requested items. He watched as Carter and twenty of his crew left the camp. The remaining crew of ten decided to stay in the camp with Somers and remain loyal to the governor.

As soon as the rebels had left, Admiral Somers sent a runner to Governor Gates with a message of the mutiny and his reasons for giving the rebels food and supplies. He instructed the runner to wait for the governor's response.

It was soon relayed. The message from Gates ordered Somers to arrest Carter and his bunch and try them for mutiny.

Two days later, Governor Gates, fearing the mutiny might spread, wrote a long letter to Admiral Somers requesting he seek out the runaway seamen and do his best to get them to return to duty. Somers, after a few more days, finally persuaded most of the mutineers to return and finish the work on the *Patience* so all could complete the voyage to Jamestown. All returned to camp except Christopher Carter and Robert Waters.

Unknown to the admiral during the time of the mutiny, Robert Waters had killed another seaman named Edward Samuel with a shovel for trying to get the group to give up the mutiny. Bad blood had been building for some time between Waters and Samuel. The mutineers had buried Samuel's body in a shallow grave on a nearby island. Carter was convinced that having rebelled twice, Sir Thomas might have him shot. So both Waters and Carter fled to another island in the chain and refused all pleas to rejoin the camp. They would be left behind when the rest sailed for Jamestown.

Ten days after all mutineers, except Waters and Carter, had returned to Admiral Somers' camp, the final work on the *Patience* was completed, including sails and rigging. The *Deliverance*, under Captain Newport's supervision, was finished five days late on May 5. It was forty feet long with a beam of nineteen feet, and weighed approximately eighty tons.

That afternoon, Sir Thomas called a meeting of all the camp and made the following announcement: "Gentlemen, ladies, sailors, and passengers, I want to thank you all for the excellent work our people have done in building the two pinnaces that will take us the rest of our journey to James City. I especially thank Admiral Somers and Captain Newport, and their teams, for building two fine ships. And I want to announce that we shall set sail for the plantation of Jamestown one week from today."

The governor was interrupted with cheers at the mention of this sailing date.

"This means we must break camp, gather food for at least a fortnight, and give our two pinnaces a short cruise around these islands to make sure they will carry us safely to our colony. It will take the ships a couple of days to circle these islands and do any final repairs or changes. You will receive your ship assignment in a day or two. You will need to pack only the things you absolutely need, since space will be limited. Things you have accumulated while here will have to be left here. This is all I have to say for now."

As soon as the meeting broke up, John looked around for Rachel and waved.

She moved toward him, and they walked to the edge of the encampment.

"Would you like to take a little walk before supper?" he asked, smiling.

"Sure, which way?"

"Oh, down along the inside bay."

"Fine, but let's walk over toward the vale first. It may be our last time to see the final resting place for those poor souls who perished here. Still, I can't think of a more beautiful place to be buried than these islands. Don't you agree, John?"

"I would rather live here than be buried here. I'm anxious to get on to Jamestown. Are you?"

"Oh surely, John. It just saddens me to leave some of these behind. That's why I wanted to see the vale and the crosses once more before we sail."

"I think I understand."

They walked along for a few minutes with only the chirping of birds breaking their thoughts. John reached over and took Rachel's hand. She didn't pull away, but squeezed his hand slightly.

He had never tried to hold her hand before, though he had wanted to. He felt some guilt at first, but soon dismissed it. After all, what did it hurt to show his friendship in this way? When he arrived in Jamestown, he would write Dorothy and tell her about Rachel. Of course, he wouldn't mention anything else.

Soon, they came to the burial vale, northwest of their camp. The dirt mound from Henry Paine's grave still had a fresh look from his burial a week earlier. Five crosses now dotted the sacred plots.

They both stood, silently taking in the little vale, no larger than an acre or two, flanked on three sides by birch-forested hills. The five mounds had been covered with stones to keep wild hogs from disturbing them.

"I'm ready to go now," Rachel whispered to John with sadness in her voice. "May they all rest in peace."

John noticed tears in her eyes as he turned. Without thinking, he gave Rachel a hug. She stiffened, but didn't pull away. With her head on his shoulder, and tears now flowing, she cried.

"I'm sorry, John. I shouldn't have asked you to walk by here. I'm not usually given to this kind of emotion, but I couldn't help thinking about Virginia Rolfe's baby girl and Lady Gates and all the others."

"It's all right, Rachel." Thinking mostly of Henry Paine, he said, "Death is no friend, even to those who deserve it. It is hard for all to bear. It affects us and reminds us of how fragile our lives are."

"Thanks for being here with me, John," she said, composing herself. "I needed that hug. You made me feel better. Let's walk down to the bay."

They turned and walked slowly down the path that led to the inner bay near the camp. They passed several others who were sitting on large boulders or strolling along, waiting for the supper bell to sound.

"Are you anxious to get to Jamestown, Rachel?"

"I have been ready for months. I wonder what it will be like. Are you anxious to get there, too?"

"Yes. I want to get on with my life, and repay the indenture. I think I will be in debt for at least the next five to seven years. Then, I hope I will know what I need to do to make this venture pay. Do you plan to stay more than one year, Rachel?"

"I'm not sure yet. That depends on lots of things. I will just have to wait and see what my future holds."

"I hope we get assigned to the same ship for this last voyage."

"Me too, John. Doesn't that depend on your sponsor, Sergeant Sharpe?"

"Yes, it probably does. However, if we shouldn't get assigned together, I want to stay in touch with you after we get there. Have you decided who you might want to work for?"

"Mistress Horton asked me a few weeks ago if I would like to stay with her in Jamestown. She misses Elizabeth since her wedding to Thomas Powell. Does Sergeant Sharpe know what he is going to do once we arrive?"

"No, except he said he wants to build a plantation after he has explored some other options. Since I belong to him for the next few years, my location will have to be where he decides."

"It sounds like we both have quite uncertain futures."

"Yes, but I am hopeful we can stay in touch."

"Me too."

They had just walked past the main path from the bay leading up to the camp when the supper bell sounded. Turning, they joined others making their way back to the encampment.

The final week dragged by for everyone. All the camp kept busy gathering extra food supplies. Hogs, turtles, fish, and edible berries were gathered, processed for the journey, and stowed aboard the two pinnaces.

The *Deliverance* had a manifest of ninety passengers and ten crewmen. Captain Newport was skipper. The *Patience* had thirty-eight, plus five crewmen, with Admiral Somers at the helm.

At daybreak on May 12, all tents were taken down. Supplies, personal belongings, and passengers were ferried out to both vessels safely anchored a couple hundred yards offshore. John waved to Rachel as she was ferried out to the *Deliverance*. His skiff took him to the *Patience*.

Standing at the rail, he watched as Governor Gates and his staff boarded the *Deliverance*. A small cannon, salvaged from the *Sea Venture* and mounted on the bow of the *Deliverance*, fired a final farewell salvo followed by cheers from both ships.

The crews immediately hoisted the anchors and, with the *Deliverance* leading, set sail for Jamestown, north by northwest, about ten days' journey.

PART THREE

CHAPTER 26

JAMES CITY

THE TEN-DAY VOYAGE to Jamestown was uneventful. The passengers were cramped and space was very limited, with many sleeping on deck. However, John heard very few complaints, because most were happy to leave their "island prison" of the past ten months.

On the afternoon of the ninth day, John began to see signs of landfall. Flocks of ducks and other shorebirds began to dot the skies to the west. An occasional sea eagle with its white head and tail would swoop low and snatch a flying fish gliding over the waves.

The next morning, May 22, the *Deliverance* reached the mouth of a large river and anchored off a small fortification the travelers later learned was Fort Henry. The crew of the *Patience* threw out her anchor near their fellow ship.

John tried to spot Rachel on the deck of the *Deliverance*. He wanted to wave to her, but she was not visible. He wondered if Jamestown was similar to this small fortification. Sergeant Sharpe, standing next to John, said it should be larger.

Admiral Somers, Governor Gates, and Captain Newport were ferried to the fort to confer with its commander. An hour later, they returned, and the two vessels began their voyage up the broad river known as the James. John mused it must have been named after King James, just as the town they would soon reach.

He located Sergeant Sharpe near the bow of the ship.

"Sergeant, how far is James City?"

"I believe it is about a long day of sailing."

"I will be glad to leave these cramped spaces aboard the *Patience* and just stretch my legs again on solid ground. How about you?"

"Yes, I am with you."

Even though the voyage from Devil's Islands had gone fairly smoothly, John had had enough sailing to last a lifetime. He would make his living on land.

After leaving Point Comfort and Fort Henry, the two vessels sailed slowly up the wide, meandering river. Both vessels stayed near its middle. John scanned the shores for signs of human life. He saw only animals; mostly, it was the occasional deer with its neck stretched downward and front legs apart, drinking from the river's edge. Gray pelicans, loons, ducks, and other seabirds fished the coves and riverbanks.

As the day wore on, John found a little shade beneath the sails on the starboard side and dozed to the hoots, quacks, and cries of the waterfowl. He napped for several hours, oblivious to the heat and buzzing of flies and insects. It was the middle of the afternoon when he awoke. He took some dried fish and stale sea biscuits from his backpack as well as a small flask of warm water to wash them down. After satisfying his hunger, he located Wooley sleeping on the port side of the ship. He sat down beside his sleeping friend and coughed a couple of times. This was enough to awaken him.

Opening one eye to John, he said, "Are we getting close to James City?"

"I think we still have another half day of sailing. We may not get there until after dark."

"Any signs of life along the river?"

"No," said John.

"Does Sergeant Sharpe know the size of James City?"

"I have not asked him, William. I think it is just a fort, not a city."

"I will be very glad to reach it and just walk around for an hour or two."

"Me too," said John, sighing.

Using their knapsacks for pillows, they stretched out and were both soon snoring once again. Shouts and the roar of a musket abruptly jarred them out of their sleep. They discovered it was twilight, and the ships had anchored in a little bay near a small island.

Was this Jamestown? They could see huts and a stockade with a small fire near the main gate. The place looked deserted. Two boats, larger than the *Patience*, were tied up at a log landing. They, too, looked deserted. When no one appeared after several minutes, Captain Newport fired off another shot from his musket.

This time, two men ambled down to the dock and waved. They looked like scarecrows. They were scrawny, their clothes in tatters.

Lowering a small skiff, Sir Thomas, plus his aide and two sailors, left the *Deliverance* and headed for the log landing. By the time they reached the dock, several other men had left the fort and were walking down to join the first two.

John noted that Jamestown was not a village. It was indeed a fortification situated on one end of an island of land nestled along the riverbank. The island was perhaps several hundred acres in size. A narrow strip of land connected it to the mainland.

He noticed there were no other signs of life except the few men who were now greeting Sir Thomas and his aides. John wondered where all the others were in the *Third Supply* fleet, who had left England with the *Sea Venture*. Had they made it to Jamestown?

Captain Newport and Admiral Somers soon joined those on the dock. After a short meeting, Sir Thomas and the others returned to the ships. Their message was that all would remain onboard until the next morning. Space would be made at the dock for their two vessels.

John sighed; one more night aboard their cramped boat. However, the sheer joy of finally reaching their destination outweighed the discomfort of a few more hours.

After more dried fish, water, and biscuit, he and Wooley staked out their sleeping places and watched a full moon rise downriver over the rippling waters of the James. It promised to be a long night. The hoot of an owl and the croaking of frogs finally lulled them to sleep.

The next morning, John awakened to the sound of a flying fish flopping on the deck near his head. A red ball of a sun was rising downriver. The day was going to be hot. It was humid already, and the smell of fish was in the air.

He picked up the flopping fish by its fins and flung it back into the river. Some of the crew were up catching fresh fish for breakfast. "They must have succeeded," thought John as he glanced at a large string of fish tied to the gunwale.

He rolled over and raised himself on one elbow. Most of the passengers were awake and putting together their meager bedrolls and clothing. John shook Wooley, then stood and surveyed the deck of the *Deliverance* for signs of Rachel.

She was nowhere in sight. John turned and looked upriver to the dock where two other ships were tied. Signs of life aboard these showed they were getting ready to move to an anchorage around the island. This would make room for the two recently arrived vessels.

The crew of the *Patience* hoisted just enough canvas to propel her to the wooden landing. She would be the first to land. "Good," thought John. "I will be able to get off and finally see this place and greet Rachel when she lands."

He and Wooley were among the first off the ship. Sergeant Sharpe, acting for Admiral Somers, called all the passengers to gather near the landing. He instructed them to remain in place until those aboard the *Deliverance* had assembled with them. Sir Thomas would then give a briefing and further instructions.

John found a stump and sat down, waiting to catch a glimpse of Rachel. He had caught only brief glimpses of her since leaving Devil's Islands. She was among the last off, with some of the other single lassies. She smiled when she caught sight of him and walked over to where he was sitting. He stood and moved as close to her as custom allowed. They smiled and John broke the silence.

"How are you, Rachel?"

"I'm tired and could sleep for a fortnight."

"Was it very uncomfortable aboard the *Deliverance*?"

"Very much so."

John wanted to hold her hand again, as he had that last day they had walked along the beach on Devil's Islands. However, Sir Thomas interrupted the small talk and reunions. He mounted a stump in the middle of the gathering.

"Gentlemen, ladies, and passengers of our two noble vessels, by the grace of God we have now finally arrived at our destination. However, the news is not good. George Percy, one of the original settlers and acting president of the council has told me of the terrible times Jamestown has just come through these past six months. James City has barely survived. Only sixty people are alive."

He paused briefly to let his first remarks sink in. Clearing his throat, he continued. "This past winter, and even now, these settlers are slowly starving to death. Their food supplies are almost gone. We will share some of our food with them, but most of those who came with us on the *Third Supply* are dead. They died of starvation last winter and more recently. Some did return to England with Captain John Smith, who was wounded in an accident last October. A few left later."

He paused again to gauge the reaction on the faces before him. "There is talk now and a strong desire on the part of these settlers to return to England. This might be the best course of action. We will wait a week or two and then decide. Until we do, we will ration all food and begin to help those who are weakest with nourishment, to save as many as possible from death."

Wiping the sweat from his brow, Sir Thomas gave his final orders. "There are a few houses in the stockade that are vacant. We will occupy these and hold this fort until we decide our next move. Work with your assigned leaders to set up housekeeping and help these settlers where possible."

With that, he stepped down and joined George Percy, Admiral Somers, and Captain Newport for a further meeting to decide on a proper length of time before abandoning the fort.

CHAPTER 27 ❧

THE FORTNIGHT

SERGEANT SHARPE WAS placed in charge of the group of men who arrived on the *Patience*. They occupied four of the vacant houses in what was left of the stockade. Several of the houses and parts of the stockade had been torn down and used as firewood during the preceding winter and spring.

Jamestown wasn't much of a fort anymore. They were crowded, with ten men in a single room. However, it was better than sleeping under the stars. They were also in charge of guard duty.

The Indians were in the woods on the shoreline, keeping watch on the dwindling inhabitants of the doomed and dying settlement. Sergeant Sharpe said they would hold the fort for at least a fortnight.

Why the Indians never attacked or tried to wipe out the settlement was a mystery to John. The sergeant said it was most likely due to the leadership of Captain John Smith, who had been taken back to England last fall for medical treatment. Who was this Smith? He sounded like a man John would have liked to have known.

Jamestown was a three-year-old settlement. What had happened during those three years to bring it to such failure and likely abandonment? What would happen to John's plans and those of the others? He wasn't ready to go back home. There had to be something else. Perhaps Sergeant Sharpe had some answers or at least a suggestion or two.

Rachel, too, would be going back. Perhaps she had some news as to her brother Larry who had come over two years ago. They would have a lot to talk about when he was able to arrange time for conversation. However, that would have to wait.

The single lassies and Lady Horton were housed across the open square from John's group, near the middle of the fort. John waved to Rachel as he left with his detail of men to fetch the supplies requested by Sergeant Sharpe. She waved and then went inside her cabin with two other lassies.

John noticed the fort was in terrible shape. Half of the palisade was missing. A few cabins had been partially torn down. What had protected the settlers from being overrun? It must have been only the providence of God, the same God who had brought John and the *Sea Venture* through that terrible tempest.

One of the healthier settlers, a man by the name of Jim Tweed, came along with John's detail to roll back the casks of food for the starving in the fort. John figured Tweed should be able to answer some of his questions, as the man was one of the original settlers of Jamestown.

Later that morning, the detail rolled four casks of food from the hold of the *Deliverance* and placed them in a storehouse next to George Percy's cabin, the acting president of the Jamestown council.

Two of these were quickly broken open and the contents taken to those too ill to leave their beds of straw. Of the sixty survivors of the past winter, only about half were able to move about and care for the others.

The food detail was resting beneath the shade of an oak tree at the side of the storehouse when John began to ask Jim Tweed some of the questions on his mind. Most of the other men lay down in the shade or just sat and listened.

"Mr. Tweed, do you recall how many of our ships made it through the tempest last year that wrecked our flagship, the *Sea Venture*?"

"I believe there were seven ships that finally made it here, with about 350 people aboard. They came in a few at a time, all battered up."

"How many of those people returned to England?"

"About half of those people left us last winter on five of the ships," said Tweed. "Most of the rest died last winter and this spring, during our starving time."

"How did you manage to survive?"

"By sneaking out after dark and before dawn most every day to fish off the other end of the island. I usually didn't catch very much, just enough to keep the two other men in my cabin and myself alive."

"Why didn't the natives capture this fort?" asked Wooley.

"They tried several times, but each time we fought them off and killed several with our muskets. They soon gave up and decided to starve us out by preventing us from hunting game, trading for corn, or digging up roots in the forest."

John stared at Tweed, trying to imagine from his sunken cheeks and hollow eyes the extent of his suffering. This was a depth of suffering that neither John nor any of the other men had ever experienced. Jim Tweed must have lost half his weight during that starving time.

Leaning back on his elbows, John said, "Do all the people here want to go back to England?"

Tweed coughed and took a moment or two to answer. "Most, if not all, are too weak and discouraged to do anything to survive or defend this fort. It would take a lot more new settlers and supplies to save us. We need farmers and the means to grow food and meat to feed ourselves. This has been our main problem from the beginning. Only Captain John Smith saw this. When he was president he tried to get the council and the others to understand this. So when he was wounded and sent back to England, no one had his skill to lead us, and you see what happened. We all just about starved to death."

John and the other men nodded silently. For the first time, John began to realize that they didn't have a choice if they wished to survive. It looked as if the only decision left would be to load everyone aboard and leave. The four ships, the *Deliverance*, the *Patience*, the *Discover*, and the *Virginia* could return to England. Surely this didn't require a fortnight. There must have been another reason for them to delay the journey for two more weeks.

Tweed raised his hand to his mouth and coughed several times, then said, "I've only told you part of the story of our starving time. The worst part was the cannibalism that took place. There were some who were so starved and desperate for food that they dug up remains of those poor souls who had died and cooked their remains. Others lost their fear of the savages and slipped out of the fort at night to seek food from them. We could hear their screams in the night as the red men hacked them to death. The Indians didn't have enough food for themselves, we were told, so they were not going to rescue any of our people. Thus, it was either slowly starve to death here in the fort, or go out and let the savages put you out of your misery. The worst case of cannibalism was when one of our men killed his sick wife, then cooked her body parts. When our council found out, they called a meeting for those of us able to attend and passed the sentence of death by firing squad. He was shot and then buried. I am very fortunate to have lived through all those desperate days."

John and the other men were speechless after Tweed finished his tale of horror.

CHAPTER 28

THE COUNTDOWN

JOHN AND THE rest in his cabin soon heard the reason for the delay in sailing. Without instructions from the Virginia Company, Governor Gates had to show he had waited a reasonable length of time before leaving. If more supply ships arrived, they would stay. Otherwise, they would sail for home June 7. The next two weeks were spent fishing and collecting clams, oysters, and waterfowl for the long voyage home.

Sergeant Sharpe and his forty-man team were divided between the two vessels and put to work. When John asked about their route back to England, Sharpe explained it to him. "We will take a northern route along the coast of Virginia for several hundred leagues, then turn east and follow a shorter, more direct track back to England. Our two vessels will be more crowded, and we will need to catch extra fish as we sail the coastline."

John was kept busy for most of the fortnight sailing up and down the river aboard the *Patience*, fishing and digging on sandbars wherever oysters or clams could be found. Their catch of fish was sizeable. These were cleaned and salted down, placed in casks, and stored in the holds of their two vessels.

He had little time in the evening to visit or even talk with Rachel. She along with Lady Horton and the other lassies were assigned to feed and nurse those who were sick or too weak to care for themselves. It was hoped that all would be strong enough for the voyage home.

All the residents of the fort, as well as the newcomers, were put on a restricted diet. It left John hungry most of the time. However, it was necessary, in light of the long voyage ahead.

The days were long and hot as they prepared to load the four ships and strike sails on the morning of June 7. John and Wooley would sail aboard the *Patience*. The extra sixty survivors of Jamestown were divided among all four vessels, the *Patience* receiving ten more passengers.

Thursday, June 7, dawned bright, but warm, with a light breeze from the south. Chaplain Bucke held an outdoor chapel service in the center of the fort. All were present, including Sir Thomas, Sir George, Captain Newport, and George Percy. The chaplain prayed for a safe journey back to England.

Following this, to the slow beating of a drum, everyone boarded the four ships and began their long journey down the James. Due to light winds, they traveled only fourteen miles and anchored for the night off a small island.

The next morning a small boat from downriver intercepted the *Deliverance* and other vessels. The messengers brought news that Lord Delaware had arrived at Point Comfort at the mouth of the James. He had three ships, heavily supplied, and three hundred new colonists.

Reversing course, Sir Thomas led his procession of four vessels back to Jamestown to prepare for the arrival of Lord Delaware and his supply ships. Some of the survivors of the starving time protested and wanted nothing more than to return to England, but all ships were unloaded and preparations made to welcome the newcomers. Two days later, the supply fleet of three ships arrived.

Lord Delaware remained aboard his ship until all three were unloaded. He then came ashore and was met by Sir Thomas Gates, Sir George Somers, Captain Christopher Newport, and George Percy, council president.

They knew Lord Delaware was aware they had abandoned the fort but had been saved by a warning of his coming. Thus they were able to stand before him now by the mercy of God. Upon approaching them, Lord Delaware dropped to his knees and gave thanks to God. Then, at the new governor's command, the red cross of St. George was hoisted on its pole above the fort. The flag waved in the breeze as a three-gun salute roared from cannons aboard the ships anchored near the shore.

As soon as John could be alone, he found a quiet place and, taking writing materials from his pack, began to write a letter to his parents. It had been over a year since he had left his hometown. He felt sure his parents had heard the news of the loss of his ship.

He wrote quickly, giving a brief summary of all that had happened on Devil's Islands. He mentioned the building of two pinnaces and their safe arrival in Jamestown. Securing a leather packet from one of the survivors of Jamestown, he sealed his letter and planned to send it by the first ship back to Plymouth.

The next few days life in the fort was disorganized while Lord Delaware sought to bring some order out of the chaotic situation. Some wanted to return to England; others were ready for a new attempt to rebuild the plantation. John, Wooley, and the others were ready to fulfill their hopes, dreams, and reasons for signing up. In spite of all they had been through, John felt God must have a future for Jamestown.

CHAPTER 29

A NEW BEGINNING

ON THE DAY Jamestown was abandoned, it was spared from being torched by orders from Sir Thomas Gates. His reason was that other men might come later to inhabit it. Two days later, he was proven right by Lord Delaware's arrival.

The population of Jamestown swelled overnight from two hundred to five hundred. It became a beehive of activity over the next three months. New cabins, watchtowers, and more palisades were added.

Lord Delaware quickly organized the town by selecting a new council and dividing the men into groups of fifty, with a captain over each. John, along with his former small group of ten under Sergeant Sharpe, was placed in one of these groups of fifty. For the rest of June and on into July and August, John's group of fifty men cut down trees for the expansion of housing and fortifications, as well as to clear land for growing crops.

One hot day near the end of July, Sergeant Sharpe told his small squad of ten that Sir Thomas had persuaded Lord Delaware to mount offensives against some of the Indian camps. These tribes of Indians had become more aggressive toward Jamestown during the past year. A show of force might bring more respect and perhaps lead to peace with these savages.

Specifically, Sir Thomas had requested a force of seventy men to attack the Indian village of Kecoughtan. Kecoughtan was located near the mouth of the James River, opposite Point Comfort.

John and his group were asked to be part of this attack force. Several of John's friends had never fired a weapon. The sergeant said he would give them some training, and within just a few days they would be ready. They all agreed to volunteer. Besides, it would relieve them from cutting timber.

In a glen of trees on the other end of the island, Sergeant Sharpe began training his volunteers. For three day, shots could be heard coming from this area. The men became familiar with the musket, how to load and fire it. Most could hit targets within fifty yards.

Sharpe seemed pleased with their progress and said they would leave on their mission in four days. None of Sharpe's men had ever killed anyone or served in a military force. That evening after more training, the conversation around a small campfire turned to the coming battle with the Indians.

Looking at John, Wooley asked, "How are you going to feel when you kill your first Indian?"

"They have been killing our people before we arrived. I believe we need to teach them to respect us. Killing some of them may be the only way to do this."

"But how will you feel?" insisted Wooley.

"I didn't expect this venture to be without risk or pain to my life. But I'm not going to refuse to go fight for our right to live here in peace. Oh, I might have some fear of getting wounded with an arrow, or even killed, but I can handle it. What about you?"

Wooley didn't answer immediately. In the glow of the flames from the dying embers his face paled noticeably. Breathing deeply, he finally said, "Frankly, John, I'm scared. I didn't sign up to come over to Jamestown to kill Indians."

"None of us, except the real soldiers, probably realized we would have to kill anyone when we left England," another spoke up.

"Right," said John. "But are we going to wait until more of us are killed before we teach these savages to leave us alone or respect us? Furthermore," he continued, "there are not enough soldiers to protect all of us. We are going to have to help them when necessary."

Wooley, interrupting with a wave of his hand, said, "John, I'm not sure it is just fear I have. I just believe it is wrong to kill another human being. Doesn't our religion say, 'Thou shall not kill'?"

"Yes, indeed it does say that. But Chaplain Bucke says that applies to murder, not to defense of your home, person, or country."

"Well, that certainly is another way to look at it," said Wooley.

Most of the others around the fire said they could kill if it would make the colony safer. The conversation dwindled as the campfire slowly died and men sought their bedrolls.

John's cabin was across the town square from Rachel and some of the other lassies. For the past month he had little time for socializing with her. Rachel was kept busy, along with other ladies, trying to nurse back to health some of those who barely survived the starving time.

As John made his way to his cabin from the extinguished campfire, he saw Rachel sitting on a log in the moonlight beside her cabin. The full moon made recognition easy even in the shadow of a tree. He walked the few yards that separated them. He was aware of the curfew and lateness of the hour, but he whispered softly, "Rachel." He seated himself next to her. "I have wanted to talk to you, but there never seemed to be a good time with us both so busy. I have volunteered to go with Sir Thomas on the mission to punish the Kecoughtans."

"When will you be leaving?"

"We have three more days of training by Sergeant Sharpe, and then we should be ready to go."

"How many of you are going?"

"Seventy."

"Are you afraid you might get killed?"

"Yes, I am afraid, but I believe God will protect us and we will be successful. Will you keep me in your prayers?"

"Of course, John. But God has told us in His Holy Book to love our enemies. I have trouble praying both to destroy them and to love them. Don't you?"

"Yes, what you have said troubles me. But I also believe that when your enemy has killed your fellow countrymen and will no doubt try to kill you or me if they have a chance, I have a right in God's book to defend us. This action may help bring about peace between us and them."

"I will pray for you, John. I care deeply for you and would not want anything to happen to you or the other men."

"Thanks, Rachel. Just knowing that will help me more than you know."

They spied a sentry walking toward them from the other end of the town square. One of the town's rules was no socializing after curfew outside the cabins. This prevented one from being mistaken for someone up to no good, or an enemy. The sentries were charged with enforcement.

Rising quickly, John squeezed Rachel's hand and promised to talk again before he left on his mission. Both made for their cabin doors before the sentry reached their end of the town square.

One week before the attack on Kecoughtan, Virginia Rolfe came down with a raging fever and died three days later. The loss of her only child on Devil's Islands had taken its toll. Virginia's battle against depression, a poor diet, and the unhealthy climate of Jamestown had been too much for her frail body.

Chaplain Bucke led his friend John Rolfe and a procession of mourners to the now overcrowded graveyard on the south end of Jamestown's peninsula. John Thomas and Rachel were among those who witnessed the burial. This sad event closed the last days of August.

Three days later, shortly before sundown, Sir Thomas assembled his seventy armed men near the river's edge close to the anchored ships. They were in a military formation of three ranks. Behind them stood a crowd of well-wishers, including several ladies, lassies, and Rachel.

"Men," he began, "we will be sailing at dawn. It will take us two days to reach our destination near Point Comfort. Your group leaders will give you more detailed plans of our attack. Get a good night's rest, and be ready to sail tomorrow."

As soon as the men were dismissed, John made his way to Rachel's side, and the two walked slowly toward their cabins.

Four cooking and serving tents had been placed at each end of the town square where food was prepared for distribution. Settlers could take their food to their cabins, or eat in one of the serving tents.

John and Rachel rarely had dinner together, choosing rather to eat with those in their respective cabins. This evening they decided to eat together then go for a walk along the river. It was cool, and mosquitoes buzzed around them. They found a log, and John built a small fire whose smoke drove most of the insects away. The sounds of the river lapping at their feet and croaking bullfrogs added to the peacefulness in the fading twilight.

Rachel broke the silence first. "Do you feel prepared to go against that Indian village?"

"I didn't a week ago, but since our training I feel I can hold my own in a battle."

"But you are not a soldier, John. I can't imagine you killing someone, even an Indian. You are a kind-hearted man, gentle and sweet. I think it takes a certain kind of person to be a soldier, one who is gruff and tough. Am I mistaken? Do you have some of those qualities that you have kept hidden from me?"

"No, what you see is what I am. I think courage, strength, perseverance, and a strong belief in right and wrong are not always apparent like one's physical stature. They are only obvious when one is tested or challenged by evil, danger, or risk to one's life, or the lives of others."

Rachel was silent for a moment. "I guess I have never thought about it in quite that way. I think you have many of those qualities you said are vital for this task. I think you will be successful in this coming battle. I realize you are going in order to make this town and our lives safer. You know where my heart is, don't you?"

"Yes, and your words and prayers will give me a lot of strength and hope. I'll be thinking of you and how much you mean to me while I am away. Have your heard anything about your brother, Larry?"

"Nothing," said Rachel. "None of the people who were here when we arrived ever heard his name. He may not have survived, or he may have returned home."

They stared into the dying fire, lost in their thoughts. It had grown dark by this time. John put his arm about Rachel's waist and held her close. The fire slowly turned into red embers. Rachel turned and felt John's lips gently brush her cheek as the curfew bell shattered their blissful moment.

John wanted to linger for a few more minutes, but both knew this would not be wise given the strictness of the curfew. Rising first, Rachel led the way back to the center of the fort where they said their goodnights, then made their way to their respective cabins.

CHAPTER 30

THE BATTLE

AT DAWN, SIR Thomas transported his seventy men, a mix of soldiers and volunteers in two of the smaller ships, downriver toward the village of Kecoughtan. Two days later, they anchored a safe distance below the village. Disembarking, the raiding party split into two platoons of thirty-five each. Sir Thomas led the first platoon, and Lieutenant Earely led the other. Sergeant Sharpe, with John's comrades, was in Earely's platoon.

John's platoon was sent behind the village to prevent those fleeing from escaping. No sooner were they in place when they heard sounds of a drum coming from the other side of the village. This was meant to draw out the Indians from their thatched huts. It was also the signal to alert Earely's platoon.

John and the others in his platoon took up positions behind trees thirty yards from the nearest hut. Soon, they heard musket fire and saw Indians running toward them.

The Indians were offering very little resistance. One arrow narrowly missed John. Some of those approaching appeared to be wounded. John took careful aim at one Indian warrior and fired his musket. The shot hit the man in his shoulder, and he fell close enough for John to see the terror in his face. Quickly reloading, John and his fellow citizen soldiers continued to shoot.

Those not killed or wounded by fire from Earely's platoon ran back among their huts or escaped into the forest. The firing gradually ceased, and soon the battle was over. At least a dozen Indians had been killed and several more wounded. Sir Thomas ordered the village burned and the Indians' crops destroyed.

A couple of men in John's platoon, and several in the other platoon, had been hit with arrows. All were treated, and by that evening, all seventy men were able to return to their ships and sail to the mouth of the James River.

Anchoring overnight, they arrived back in Jamestown two days later. Rachel was among those who ran down to the river as the two ships tied up to the trees along the shore. She waved her bonnet and smiled as John walked down the gangplank.

The crowd cheered the men, and Lord Delaware warmly greeted Sir Thomas and his lieutenant. The men were instructed to go directly to one of the food tents, where hot victuals awaited them. Rachel walked along with John, Wooley, and their friends, smiling and saying how happy she was to see them safely back. John promised to tell her of the battle the next day.

The next morning, several of the men in the raiding party told John over breakfast that they were originally selected over a month ago to go to Devil's Islands with Sir George Somers and Captain Argall. They understood the mission was to bring hogs and other food from the island paradise that had been the home of the *Sea Venture*'s passengers and crew for ten months. John simply nodded.

After breakfast, John looked for Rachel and found her near one of the wells, washing some clothes. They walked over to a nearby tree and sat for a spell on a bench hewn from a large log.

"Sir George Somers should be back by now from Devil's Islands to bring hogs and other foodstuffs," began John. "Several of the men in our raiding party told me they had wanted to go with him. Have you heard any news about when he should be back?"

"Yes, Lady Horton said Lord Delaware informed her he should be back any day now. He said we needed the hogs to help us make it through the winter months."

"I'm glad I didn't go. I've had enough excitement the last two weeks to last me for awhile."

"Do you think they will send you on another raiding party against the Indians?"

"No, I don't believe so. Sergeant Sharpe said George Percy is planning to lead a different group of seventy men upriver against two other Indian tribes. He told me which tribes, but I can't pronounce their names. He said Lord Delaware wants to put some fear into the surrounding tribes, so we will be safer before more colonists arrive, and during the winter months."

Their conversation was interrupted when Sergeant Sharpe walked up. He said he needed to talk to John about some plans he had for their future work. John had temporarily forgotten that he had a debt to pay to his sponsor.

John had signed an agreement of indenture for at least the next five years. Or was it seven? He couldn't remember. He needed to know exactly, so he could start making plans for his future. He arose, telling Rachel he would see her later.

Two weeks after his arrival in June, Governor Delaware had sent Sir George Somers and Captain Argall back to Devil's Islands. Late in August, word spread that Captain Argall and the *Patience* were approaching Jamestown. Sir George Somers' ship, the *Deliverance*, was not with him.

Many of those who had been on the *Sea Venture* and spent time with Sir George rushed down for some news about him. John and Rachel were among them. Captain Argall, standing in the bow of the *Patience*, waved to the motley crowd who welcomed him. With flags waving in the breeze from its masthead, the ship glided to the landing. Hands quickly secured it to the dock.

Lord Delaware welcomed him. Word quickly spread that Sir George had died shortly after reaching the islands. His body was buried there, but his heart was removed and taken back to England aboard the *Deliverance* for burial.

It appeared that Matthew Somers, nephew of Sir George, had found a block of ambergris in the islands and took it to England for the Virginia Company. The company could sell it for 120,000 pounds, a colossal sum. Ambergris, a waxy substance found floating in tropical seas, is a secretion from the sperm whale and was valued in the manufacture of perfume. Captain Argall believed this valuable find by Matthew Somers was his primary motivation for going back to England.

Early in September, after the battle and razing of Kecoughtan, Sir Thomas Gates and his secretary, William Starchy, left for England. Lord Delaware ordered Captain Howldcrofte to build a fort near the destroyed Indian village. It would be named Fort Charles, in honor of Prince Charles.

Sergeant Sharpe and his small squad of men, including John, were part of a company of men sent to help in the construction of this new fortification. However, before they left on this mission, they were part of a farewell for Sir Thomas Gates.

Sir Thomas was returning to England to generate more support and arrange for relief shipments to the colony. William

Starchy would publish his journal covering the great tempest of 1609, events in the colony, and its future potential.

The new governor, very quickly after his arrival, instituted strict rules for all those in Jamestown. Every able-bodied person was expected to help plant and harvest crops, as well as conserve food and supplies. Suitable punishment was promised if these rules were not enforced and obeyed.

In addition to these laws, Lord Delaware set about building one fort up the James River and another one across from Jamestown. Hostile Indians were his main concern, but raids by the Spanish were a concern as well. However, as winter came on and his health began to suffer, plans were made for his return to England in the spring.

John and the rest of Sergeant Sharpe's crew were kept busy for the next two months building the new fort downriver near Point Comfort. During the first week in November, Fort Charles was completed, and a small garrison was stationed there. John was glad he was not asked to be part of it. Actually, John's agreement of indenture with Sergeant Sharpe meant that wherever the sergeant was assigned, or needed, John was fairly certain he would go as well.

The sergeant was interested in putting down some roots somewhere near Jamestown and building a small plantation of his own. He had been married at one time, but his wife had died during one of his many sea and land missions for the Crown. Some of Sergeant Sharpe's assignments had been with Sir George Somers in the Caribbean. Now in his late forties, William Sharpe was not looking for another wife, but rather for a place of his own that he could cultivate and live partly off the land. Money saved over the years, an inheritance from his father, and his stipend from the Virginia Company gave him a comfortable income. His present mission was to help the Virginia Company make Jamestown a profitable venture and plantation for those who had invested in its future.

Now the sergeant had ten men who were indebted to him for the next five years to help make his dream come true. If they all turned out like John Thomas, the sergeant would be very pleased. All his men had performed better than expected in the military action against the Indian village. None had asked to be excused or given a less dangerous task. They had trusted his leadership and could be counted upon as a squad of volunteers if called to engage in some future action against the Indians.

Though a professional soldier, Sharpe would be happier to lead his indentured ten on building missions, rather than military ones.

CHAPTER 31 ∾

DOCTOR LAWRENCE BOHUNE

DURING THE SECOND week in November, the first doctor arrived in Jamestown. Doctor Lawrence Bohune, a professional physician, was a welcome sight in the colony. His arrival brought comfort to the colonists, but his battles against rampant disease and malnutrition seemed an insurmountable challenge.

The previous winter of 1609 was known as the "Starving Time." When John's two ships arrived the following May, the population of Jamestown had shrunk to just sixty starving persons. Although malnutrition was a major cause of death, more had probably died from other illnesses since the founding of the colony in 1607.

John's health had been good since leaving Wales, and in the first months at Jamestown he had suffered no serious illness. However, shortly after the arrival of Doctor Bohune, John came down with a high fever, chills, and a hacking cough.

Sergeant Sharpe summoned Dr. Bohune to treat his indentured young man. John had earned the respect of William Sharpe, and his friendship as well. Thus, when John fell ill, Sergeant Sharpe reacted as if John were the son he never had.

Doctor Bohune arrived and found John lying on his bunk about a foot off the floor. Lawrence Bohune, while highly trained in the latest treatments, expressed his private reservations to Sergeant Sharpe regarding John's recovery. Nevertheless, he prescribed that John be kept as cool as possible, in spite of his chills, believing that his high fever might be more damaging than the discomfort of his bodily chills. He also recommended John's upper body be bathed every hour to lower his fever. If John's condition had not improved after a day or two, he would bleed John to see if some of the poisons in his system could be eliminated.

Shortly after the doctor left, John sent Wooley to tell Rachel he was ill. Sergeant Sharpe had assigned Wooley to take care of John's treatment, and he was in the middle of applying cold water compresses to John's upper body when Rachel knocked on their cabin door.

Wooley yelled, "Come in!"

Entering, Rachel saw John with his eyes closed, his face flushed with a burning fever. "Greetings, John!"

Opening his bloodshot eyes, John whispered weakly, "Greetings, Rachel. I'm not feeling very well. William is trying to help me."

"Is his treatment helping?"

"Yes, it cools my burning briefly, and that helps."

"How long have you been sick?"

"Since day before yesterday. Doctor Bohune just left a while ago. He may bleed me tomorrow if my fever hasn't gone down some."

"I would have come to see you sooner, John, if I had known you were ill."

"I know. I didn't want to worry you. I thought I would improve, but I got worse each day. I believe if my fever were to break I would get better faster. Have you met our new doctor?"

"Yes, he came to call on Lady Horton soon after arriving last week. I believe they had mutual friends back in London."

"Does he have a wife?"

"I don't think so."

"Lady Horton doesn't have a husband, either, does she?"

"Not to my knowledge, and she has told me a lot about herself," said Rachel.

Noticing that John had drifted off, Rachel said to Wooley, "He is resting. I will come back later today, or in the morning. If he should get worse, come and get me, will you?"

"Of course. Keep him in your prayers."

"I will. It hurts me to see him suffer like this. When he awakens, tell him I shall return."

Shortly after Rachel left John's cabin, Chaplain Bucke paid a pastoral call. John was still sleeping, but turned over and opened one eye to see Wooley greeting their chaplain. John had warm regards for the chaplain, who was providing much comfort for Jamestown as he had for the *Sea Venture*'s passengers coming over.

"Hello, John! I am sorry to see you come down with this flux and fever. I came by to pray for you."

"Thanks, Chaplain Bucke. I hope I will soon be better."

"Has Dr. Bohune been to see you?"

"Yes, sir. He was here earlier and said he would be back tomorrow."

"Well, I don't have anything to give you but prayer and encouragement."

"That would be fine, Chaplain. I've read in my Bible where Jesus healed the sick, and I believe God can heal me."

"His power and grace brought us through that terrible tempest and preserved our lives on Devils' Islands, did He not, John?"

"Yes, Chaplain. That was sure some miracle. I hope I never have to go through something like that again."

"If God had a hand in that, I'm certain He can help you now. Let us pray. Heavenly Father, look down upon John and his sickness and, as You have shown Your power and grace before, may Your Spirit touch John now and heal his affliction. We ask for this in Jesus' name. Amen."

"Thanks, Chaplain Bucke. I feel better than I did before."

"Good. I hope to see you up and about real soon."

With that, the chaplain turned and left the cabin. John could not explain the sensation he felt as Chaplain Bucke had laid his hand on his forehead and prayed for him. It was as if some new strength and energy swept over his body.

"William, touch my forehead and see if you think my head is as hot as it was earlier."

"I believe your head is cooler. It seems as if your fever has broken."

"I felt something in my body as the chaplain prayed for me. I believe it was God's power."

"This is great, John. I was getting tired of putting these wet towels on you. I believe I will stop for a while."

"I agree. Thanks for helping me."

"You would do the same for me."

"Yes, I would, but I hope I don't have to."

"Me either."

The next morning, John's fever had definitely broken, and he felt well enough to sit up and take some broth Rachel had brought him. By the end of the day, after the doctor had come and gone, John's cough was also better. He almost felt like a new man. Doctor Bohune was amazed at how quickly John had recovered. John didn't tell him that it all began to happen after the chaplain prayed for him.

Rachel came by to see him again shortly after sunset. John was sitting on a log under a tree near his cabin when she walked up.

"I am amazed to see you are up so soon. I just came by to see you and to know how you liked the broth."

"I feel much better. After the chaplain prayed for me yesterday, I suddenly felt better. I can't explain it except to say that God healed me."

"That is just wonderful. I'm so happy you are better."

"Me too. And, yes, Rachel, your broth was very tasty. Did you make it?"

"Yes, I cook some for Lady Horton. That is, when she is not dining with Lord Delaware and some of the town council."

"Does the good doctor also eat with that group?"

"Yes, and that reminds me of something I wanted to tell you. It looks like the good Doctor is starting to court Lady Horton. He walks her to our cabin after meals. Also, they take daily walks together down by the river before coming back to the cabin for the evening."

"Do you think they are serious about each other?"

"Yes, I do. She doesn't talk to me about him, but she takes more time with her appearance and dress. Also, her face is more flushed after he returns with her to the cabin."

"Do you think a wedding might be in the offing?"

"I would not be surprised if something like that happened."

It was beginning to get dark. "I must leave now," Rachel said.

"Yes, thanks for coming. I should be strong enough by tomorrow to take a little walk with you."

"I would like that." Smiling, she arose and left the cabin.

No sooner had she left than Wooley entered and said, "I think that lassie likes you more than you realize. What about that lassie you left behind in our village, John?"

"Well, I am in no position to do anything regarding either. I can't return to Wales for at least four more years. And I can't make any lasting promise to Rachel. But the least I can do is be her friend."

"Has the sergeant made a decision where he wants to build his own plantation? He seems to tell you more about his plans than any of us."

"Yes, I suppose you are right. He has not told me anything thus far. I believe he has an agreement with the governor and the Virginia Company to get Jamestown firmly established. Then he will request his land patent."

"How much land have they promised him?"

"I believe he told me he would receive one hundred acres for himself and fifty acres for each indentured servant he has sponsored."

Wooley paused a moment to do the math. "That would give him about five hundred or more, would it not?"

"Yes, your ciphering is correct."

"Are you going to request your land patent when you have finished paying your debt to the sergeant?"

"I have not decided if I will want to stay or not."

"What have we got to go back home to? Your Dorothy will probably get tired of waiting for you to come back and marry her."

"Yes, I suppose you are right," John sighed. You see, I'm in no position to take on a lassie or start a family until I find a way to earn a living for myself. I may decide to work on with the sergeant after I have paid off my indenture and earn enough to start a plantation of my own."

"That also sounds good to me. I may decide to try that."

The two of them continued to talk until Wooley excused himself for his turn of guard duty at watchtower C. Scouts from neighboring tribes of Indians were constantly roaming the woods on three sides of the fort, testing the defenses of those inside the palisades. They barely stayed outside the range of fire. Occasionally, in the stillness of the night, a nervous sentry would fire his musket at the shadowy figure of an Indian testing the defenses of the fort. Sometimes this was followed by a scream as the musket ball found its mark. Such sounds would awaken John, who was a light sleeper, reminding him he was living in a dangerous country. Tonight was one of those nights.

Instead of going back to sleep, John arose, lit a candle, and decided to write his folks. His mother had been good about writing him, but for some reason, she had failed to answer his last letter, written after his return from the battle with the Indians.

It usually took, at the very least, four or five months to get an answer to a letter even when its timing coincided with the sailing of ships to England from the plantation.

He wrote the usual, three or four paragraphs telling what he was currently doing and that he was feeling well, then inquiring about their health. He had secured several leather address packets. These protected the contents written on parchment and sealed them inside from the weather. Placing his letter on the small bench beside his bed, he turned over and was soon fast asleep.

The next morning, John took his letter packet to the headquarters, where mail was routinely collected to be placed on the next vessel sailing for Plymouth and London. Sometimes letters would collect for a month or longer before leaving Jamestown.

CHAPTER 32

THE FOURTH WINTER

BY THE THIRD week of November, most of the gold and brown leaves had fallen from the trees surrounding the palisades. Signs of an early winter were everywhere. Squirrels scampered up and down, hoarding their finds high up in oak and walnut trees.

Lord Delaware had instituted a rationing program soon after his arrival in June for every person in Jamestown. His purpose was to guarantee that food supplies would last until crops could be harvested later in the fall. He had asked for more relief supplies from London.

Extra land had been cleared and planted during the summer months. In addition to this harvest, the council had sent out several vessels and crews to barter for corn with the Indians. Hunting parties stalked deer that came to feed off the cornfields close to the fort.

Even so, a strict control was set over the town storehouses. The quartermasters were accountable to the town council and governor for any thefts or shortfalls. Every measure was taken to avoid a repeat of the previous winter's starving time. John was thankful he had escaped the famine that took most of the lives of those in the *Third Supply* convoy who chose to stay in Jamestown.

Winters in John's native Wales were not as mild as his last in Devil's Islands. He didn't know what the weather might be like here in the colony. There were few original colonists left who had spent the previous three winters here. Of those who had, all said the shortage of food was their greatest danger.

John was a light eater. He usually ate just enough to curb his appetite. On the other hand, Wooley was always hungry. He outweighed John by at least twenty pounds. If rations became scarce during the coming winter, no doubt Wooley would feel it the most.

The first heavy snow fell in early December. It snowed all of one night and late into the following day. By that time, the white stuff was over a foot deep. It brought memories of home to John.

There were moments on Devil's Islands when he was nostalgic about home, his parents, and Dorothy, but that was nothing compared to what he felt now. The first snow and cold winter winds brought memories of his family and gave him a bad case of homesickness.

Rachel noticed John's somber features when they met near the chapel for evening prayers. The lassies and married women sat in a section of the chapel apart from the men, across the center aisle. John sat across the aisle from Rachel. Chaplain Bucke, in his sonorous voice, read Psalm 23 from his evening prayer book. The pews were benches made of logs split lengthwise and were far from comfortable. At least they kept one awake. John looked up at some of the bare rafters his crew had cut and installed to expand the chapel to accommodate more worshippers. Twilight from the gray, somber sky filtered in through spaces between logs where chinks of moss and mud had fallen away.

The cold wind whistled through these cracks and chilled everyone; especially those who were sitting. As John grew more uncomfortable, he remembered the warm sanctuary of his home church and the soft, melodious voice of his old sexton. He tried to focus on what Chaplain Bucke was saying. He wanted to believe that God was truly like a shepherd who attended to his wants. But now, he would trade what he had in Jamestown for a one-way journey back home.

Would it ever get better? Would this heavy depression he was feeling ever lift? Why was this sadness hitting him again? After the evening prayers were over, he would share his feelings with Rachel. Talking with her always lifted his spirits.

In the meantime, he would listen to the chaplain's meditation and try to believe God would help him throw off these painful feelings of loneliness. Could faith melt them away like snow under a warm sun?

On the way to supper, where a hot meal awaited them, John said to Rachel, "Do you ever get homesick?"

"Oh yes. Not very often, but sometimes during the night when I awaken, I wonder why I ever left the comforts of home for this venture."

"Do you think God really cares how we feel?"

"Yes, I believe like Chaplain Bucke said; God is like a shepherd. He has all knowledge, or else He wouldn't be God."

"Sometimes I feel as if there is a wall between me and God, and I can't get over it with my prayers. It's like shouting down a well, and all I hear is the echo of my own voice. If God hears me, I would like to have Him lift this sad feeling. It began yesterday when it started snowing."

"I will pray for you tonight, John, when I go to bed."

"Thanks, I usually feel better after I share my feelings with you."

"I'm glad it helps you. We have grown pretty close over the past year and a half, have we not?"

"Right you are. I thought you might be leaving for England after we finally arrived here in Jamestown. I was very happy when I heard you had decided to stay another year."

"You know, I signed up to come to Jamestown for at least a year. So I decided to fulfill that agreement, even though we were delayed about a year on Devil's Islands."

"Do you plan to leave next summer?

"I don't know what I might do by then. My other brother, James, has written me that he might come over for a visit to see what future this colony could hold for him. He didn't mention Larry, however. I am worried that Larry might be dead."

"I hope not. I would like to meet both your brothers."

"You will if James decides to come. I will keep asking about Larry."

He smiled at her as they entered the dining hall and separated to find their respective tables. Rachel ate with the lassies, and John with his friends. The smell of hot food gave John an added boost to his morale as he seated himself.

This building for common dining was erected in early September next to the marketplace at the center of the fort. Since most in the fort were single, this hall provided a more comfortable place than the original food tents for those who chose to eat together.

The celebration of Christmas on Devil's Islands the previous year could barely have been called a celebration. Most of the men had been busy building the two pinnaces that would bring them to Jamestown. John recalled Chaplain Bucke had conducted a special worship service on the evening of Christmas Day, which fell on a Monday. It was mostly a service of thankfulness. God's providential care had brought them all safely through the great tempest and provided so bountifully that island paradise.

On Tuesday, December 25, 1610, Lord Delaware proclaimed Christmas Day an additional day of rest for feasting and celebration. Chaplain Bucke held two morning worship services to accommodate all. Attendance was mandatory.

Extra food rations were made available for everyone. All were assured they would not leave the Christmas table hungry. Even Wooley, who was always complaining about being hungry, was satisfied when he saw the heavily laden tables that were decorated with boughs of holly and candles. A large evergreen tree graced the dining hall. It was decorated with strings of brightly colored beads usually reserved for trading with the Indians.

Several casks of ale were rationed out to the celebrants. It was a welcome addition to the meal, replacing the usual poor quality drinking water. Drunkenness was not tolerated in the fort, so nearly everyone drank in moderation. Yet, enough was consumed to lift the spirits of most.

Lord Delaware made his entrance near the end of the meal and gave a short speech. He, the town council, and other officers usually dined privately in a separate smaller dining hall. Dressed in his finery, he began his talk.

"Men, ladies, and lassies, I want to congratulate you on this special day of our Lord's birth for your hard work, frugal living, and willingness to pull together to make our Jamestown livable. I believe we have shown the Indians we will not tolerate their attacks on our presence here. We choose to be peace-loving neighbors to them, but if they refuse to accept us on these terms, then we must defend ourselves against them, or the Spanish if they should arrive in these parts. I hope you have enjoyed Christmas Day, and your dinner, and will use your time to express good cheer to your fellow residents of our fair town. God bless you and may God save the king."

On Christmas night it began to snow and soon turned into a howling blizzard that lasted the next several days. In fact, the rest of December was a mixture of snow and ice storms that kept the town's residents cabin-bound.

By the time a break in the weather came, the fort's supply of firewood was almost exhausted. Teams of woodcutters were dispatched to the east end of the peninsula to replenish it before more blizzards moved in.

CHAPTER 33 ❧

JOHN ROLFE

JOHN ROLFE, DEEP in thought, continued to stare into the red coals of his fireplace long after supper. He was alone with his memories in his two-room log cabin in Jamestown. The winter nights were cold, so he had built a fire after coming in from dining with Samuel Argall and Chaplain Bucke.

It was six months ago that Virginia had died, shortly after they had completed construction of their new cabin in Jamestown. First, they lost their baby girl in Devil's Islands, and now, Virginia. Losing both in less than a year was almost more than he could bear.

If it hadn't been for his friend and pastor, Chaplain Bucke, Rolfe would have given up and left on the first ship back to London. But the prayers, faith, and comfort of Chaplain Bucke, in addition to something else, made him want to stay a while longer.

The additional incentive was a bottle of tobacco seeds he kept safely tucked away in a wooden box under his bed. He had jealously guarded them on the *Sea Venture*, even during that terrible tempest when it seemed all would be lost. Later, on Devil's Islands, he had started to plant some, but decided to wait until he reached Jamestown.

These were not tobacco seeds of a common variety. They were a superior strain from the seeds of Trinidad and Orinoco tobacco. He obtained them indirectly from a Spanish trader with whom Captain Newport had bartered. These quality seeds were one of Rolfe's reasons for wanting to come on this new venture of the Virginia Company. He wanted to see if these seeds could grow and produce the quality and abundance of tobacco the Spanish trader had promised.

It was these thoughts that gradually pushed the painful loss of his wife and infant daughter from his mind. The red embers and the warmth of the dying fire soon lulled him to sleep. He dreamed he located a small plot of ground near the edge of the graveyard and planted a small portion of his precious seed to see if it would thrive in this spot. The town's cornfield, all of four acres, was located at the opposite end of their peninsula.

The room was dark and cold when Rolfe awoke, and he couldn't remember if his dream had shown any results from his planting. Anyway, it was too early in the year to plant. He would find a better place to begin his experiment in the spring. Then, he would know for sure if his dream would come true.

The next morning, Rolfe thought again of his dream. Maybe he should take a closer look at the place in his dream near the graveyard. After breakfast, he headed west of the fort and quickly reached Jamestown's places of burial.

He paused briefly at Virginia's grave. The small cross bore her name and dates of birth and death. Since her death, Rolfe had come to this spot to pray and grieve his loss. This time, he spoke her name and said, "Virginia, I've had a dream of where to plant those seeds I guarded so carefully on our journey over. I believe it will give me a reason for staying here a little longer. I miss you so much."

Wiping away the tears, he walked through a row of trees left standing by Sergeant Sharpe and his work crew during the rebuilding and enlargement of the fort. On the other side of this tree line, he found an acre of land filled with brush but no large trees. It was no more than a stone's throw from the river as it flowed around the west side of the fort. Jamestown was mostly an island, surrounded by water on all sides but one and separated from the mainland by a narrow neck of land.

Rolfe looked at the plot of land and decided to ask permission to use it as a testing ground for his precious seed. Between now and next planting season, he would have time to clear enough brush to give it a good test.

As he turned to leave, two Indians walking toward him caught his eye. Just beyond them, their canoe waited on the bank of the river. One was a young girl in her teens, the other a tall male a few years older.

Making the peace sign, they cautiously approached him. He didn't know whether to sound the alarm with his weapon, or to wait and see. They didn't seem threatening, so he let them come within ten paces of him.

The girl was the first to speak in broken English. Pointing to her chest, she said, "Pocahontas."

Rolfe had heard that name before. This must be the girl who saved Captain John Smith's life and had returned to Jamestown once or twice after Smith was taken back to England for medical treatment.

Pointing to his chest, he said, "John Rolfe."

Pocahontas, touching her companion's chest, said, "Brother."

Rolfe nodded and held up his open palm in the universal sign of peace and welcome. He had heard the story of how Pocahontas had saved John Smith's life and probably the whole colony. Jamestown, like Roanoke's Island, would probably not have survived the second winter had not this young lady's love for Captain Smith provided corn and friendly relations with the Indians.

After Smith was hurt in an explosion of gunpowder and left for England, it was reported Pocahontas came back several times looking for her hero. Smith must have made quite an impression on this young daughter of the chief of the Powhatan Confederacy.

Rolfe looked at her more closely as he began to understand what might have drawn her back again to Jamestown. This young lady, already showing signs of her feminine attractiveness, probably wanted some news of Smith.

Pocahontas walked up to Rolfe and touched his palm with her palm. The touch sent shivers up John's spine. It brought memories of his Virginia, and how much he missed her gentle touches. He wanted to reach out and embrace this lovely young lady, but he knew that would not be received the proper way. He sensed that her brother had come with her to protect her and see how she would be treated.

Rolfe turned to her brother and smiled as he moved a step closer to him. Her brother acknowledged his smile, but remained stoically in his tracks.

Pocahontas took a step backwards and asked, "Know John Smith?"

Nodding, he made the sign of a small amount with his thumb and forefinger and then added, "Yes."

"See him?" she asked, pointing to her eyes.

"No," Rolfe shook his head.

He could see the disappointment in her eyes as she turned and looked at her brother, as if to say, "I'm ready to leave."

"You speak much English?" Rolfe asked her.

Using Rolfe's sign for small, she held up her thumb and forefinger with a small space between.

To show appreciation for her skills, Rolfe pointed to her hand, then himself, widening the space between her thumb and forefinger with his two hands, saying, "Much English."

She smiled her understanding then looked at her brother for approval. He smiled and nodded his head. With another smile and a slight wave, Pocahontas turned and headed toward the canoe, followed by her brother.

Rolfe walked a short distance behind them, then waved as they pushed out against the current and headed upriver, keeping close to the shoreline. Just before they were out of sight, Pocahontas turned and waved with a motion that indicated she would be back.

Walking back to the fort, Rolfe felt the load lift from his heart for the first time since Virginia's death. He couldn't understand how meeting two heathen Indians could have helped do that. Perhaps it was the touch of Pocahontas's hand that proved to be the healing balm. Time would tell.

That evening at supper, he mentioned his plan for the plot of land beyond the graveyard to Lord Delaware and Chaplain Bucke. The governor quickly gave his permission to proceed come spring.

Rolfe thought it best to keep quiet for now about the visit of Pocahontas and her brother. Only if she returned would Rolfe speak about teaching more English, plus something about Christianity.

In March, Rolfe cleared a small plot in the middle of his acre of brush and small trees to test his precious seed. If it produced, as his Spanish trader friend had promised, then John would have even more seed, perhaps enough to plant the whole acre. This would give him another year to clear the land. Next, he would prove to the colony that his tobacco venture might be something the Virginia Company would want to exploit.

Rolfe believed he had a product that would do well in this climate, though it was much colder than plantations in the tropical climate where Spain raised its crops. Most of Europe, England included, was consuming vast amounts of tobacco. If Jamestown could get even a small share of this market, it would give the London Virginia Company some much-needed returns for its stockholders. In addition, this could give the colony and its planters a means of livelihood that had escaped their attention thus far.

CHAPTER 34 ❧

SPRING

LORD DELAWARE, DUE to ill health, made plans to leave for London shortly after the arrival of spring. On Tuesday, March 28, the governor boarded his ship, the *De La War*, and sailed down the James River on the first leg of his journey home. He had suffered from dysentery and scurvy, due in large part to the inadequate and unhealthy diet of the colony. He left George Percy, his second in command, and the town council to govern the colony until his replacement, Sir Thomas Gates, would arrive in May.

Early in May, Sir Thomas Dale, the temporary acting governor, arrived at Jamestown with supplies, cattle, and three hundred passengers. The roar of a cannon alerted all in the fort that three ships were about to land. Word spread quickly that Lord Delaware's replacement would not arrive until later in May.

John and some of his friends rushed down to the pier to see the newest arrivals. Acting governor George Percy, the town council, and a respectable crowd were on hand to welcome Sir Thomas Dale, Admiral Newport, and William Starchy.

Percy saluted his replacement, then Starchy, in a loud voice, read the commission from the Virginia Company installing Sir Thomas Dale as the new acting governor until the arrival of Sir Thomas Gates.

Soon, all three ships were unloaded. John, along with other men, helped carry the supplies to the storehouses inside the fort.

Though the past winter had been less severe than the previous one, there had been some threats of lawlessness, especially as food supplies dwindled. The new acting governor, major general, was made aware of these threats. To counter this spirit of desperation on the part of some, Sir Thomas Dale immediately instituted the "Dale Code." Essentially, this was a declaration of martial law to guarantee the survival of the colony and turn it into a profitable commercial venture. Severe punishment was promised to those who broke the code. In addition, all able-bodied persons, regardless of rank, who did not have assigned tasks, were expected to help cultivate crops and food for the colony.

To provide more security and protection for Jamestown and the downriver forts, Sir Thomas Dale began construction of two stockades and a new settlement up river. The new settlement, named Henrico, would be similar to Jamestown.

Sergeant Sharpe and his squad of indentured men were to be part of the company of men going to build the stockades and the new settlement. John was glad for this change in his job.

His sergeant had given him a break after his serious illness so he could regain his health, loaning him to those in charge of the storehouses of food and other supplies. This job had kept him indoors, out of the cold winter storms that swept down from the north.

Also, this had allowed him more opportunities to see Rachel when she came for rations and miscellaneous supplies for Mistress Horton and herself. Sometimes Rachel would linger for small talk, especially when no other residents were requiring John's services.

One day, shortly before John was to leave with the building party, Rachel came into the storehouse next to the marketplace for a bolt of cloth.

"John," she began, after he had brought her the cloth, "do you know when you will be leaving to build that fort?"

"No, not exactly. I think we will be leaving later this week."

"Did you realize that we have been here in Jamestown a little more than a year?"

"No, I hadn't thought about that, but you are right. It has been almost thirteen months, hasn't it?"

"Remember when I said I had planned to stay here for another year?"

"Yes."

"Well, that year is up, and I believe I will stay longer, at least until my brother James arrives. I received a letter from him when Sir Thomas Dale arrived. He said he would be coming over in the next supply fleet."

"Do you know when that will happen?"

"No, but I think it will be before summer. Lady Horton wants me to stay. She and the doctor are getting very serious and may be married. If so, she has said I could stay and work for her as long as I cared."

"That is just fine. I think it will take us until the end of summer, or early fall, to finish building the forts. Then I believe we will be coming back for a while."

"Will you write me?"

"Yes, I will let you know our progress."

"Thanks. That will make the next few months easier for me if I can hear from you."

"You will, then. I care for you and want to be near you as much as possible."

"I feel the same about you, John. You are my dearest friend."

"And you are mine."

"Does your Dorothy back in Wales know about our friendship?"

"Yes, and I have told her that if she meets some lad to be friends with, it is all right with me."

"What did she say about that?"

"She said she understood. I also told her it would not be fair for me to hold her to a promise to wait for me for an indefinite number of years. I said I didn't know for sure that I would return before I had secured land and could support myself or a family."

"Could you take on the responsibility of a wife or a family before you finished your indentured service?"

"I am not sure. I would have to have permission from Sergeant Sharpe. It might be possible. That is a question I will pursue with the sergeant."

Rachel smiled as John walked her to the door and handed her the cloth.

"Will we see each other before you leave?"

"Of course. I couldn't leave without holding your hand and telling you how much I will miss you. I will be counting the days until we can see each other again."

"You say the sweetest things that make me feel so special to you."

"You are special to me, Rachel, and don't ever forget it."

John squeezed Rachel's arm, then stood in the doorway and watched her walk slowly down the main street of the fort. As she turned into the street leading to her cabin, she looked back, waved, and was gone.

Early in June, Sir Thomas Gates arrived, replacing Lord Delaware as governor. Sir Thomas Dale was named marshall of the colony and was given a free hand to enforce his "Dale

Code." His other mission was to build a new settlement upriver by the end of the year.

PART FOUR

CHAPTER 35 ❧

THE SETTLEMENT

FORTY MILES UPRIVER from Jamestown, a new settlement was built. Lord Delaware had built a stockade yet farther up the James River at a place called "The Falls." He spent most of the winter of 1610 there before returning to England the following spring. The Falls was as far upriver as sailing vessels could go. This latest settlement Sir Thomas Dale would build would be about fifteen miles below The Falls.

John and his other indentured friends in Sergeant Sharpe's crew, with about twenty other men, left Jamestown near the end of May with enough supplies for three months. They sailed in one of the smaller vessels up the James and selected a peninsular site. It was on the north bank of the river, close to a tributary.

Timber was plentiful. The men set to work almost immediately once the site for this settlement was determined. For several weeks the men slept on the ship. They were always on guard for the Indians, who were not long in coming to survey the construction.

This settlement, Henrico, was approximately twelve miles from the Indian village of Powhatan. Chief Powhatan, of the

Algonquians, was over a confederacy of Indian tribes known as the River Tribes. A few battles and skirmishes between the colonists and the Indians had occurred to date, but there had been no all-out war to drive out the English.

Guards were posted at strategic points on the peninsula, ready to fire warning shots when an Indian warrior got too close. Sergeant Sharpe's men took their turns standing guard as others felled trees and gradually enclosed an area of approximately five acres.

This settlement, built on a triangular pattern similar to Jamestown, had three blockhouses and two gates, one facing the east, the other the west. It was laid out with three lanes to be lined with small one-room huts. In the center of the town, Sir Thomas Dale ordered a church and storehouse built first.

The work was slow and the weather humid. The small tributary that emptied into the James on the west side of the fort afforded the men no small comfort for bathing and cooling off at the end of the workday.

All of summer, October, and most of November were spent in building this settlement. Henrico was Dale's new town. Additionally, two small stockades—each with one blockhouse, a gate, and five small huts within—were built across the James River from Jamestown and Dale's new settlement. These stockades were meant as temporary shelters for small patrols exploring the surrounding territories and protection for future small plantations.

John had written Rachel describing the work and when he hoped they would be finished. The sailing vessel that had transported the crew upriver had made several trips back and forth to James City. Each time it left, John dispatched a letter for Rachel. And each time it returned, John met the skipper to see if he had a letter. Most of the time, he did.

In June, Rachel had written that with Sir Thomas Gates' arrival as governor, her brother James had finally arrived, and she was very happy to see him. She was anxious for John to meet him. In her next letter, she stated that Lady Horton and the good doctor were definitely making plans for marriage. They were also talking of locating their new home at the new settlement when another doctor arrived to serve Jamestown. She stated further that if they married, Lady Horton wanted her to move so she could continue to work for her. She concluded with how this might affect her relationship with John and where his duties would take him.

John questioned Sergeant Sharpe, who told him he was not aware of where his next work would take them after Henrico. In his next letter to Rachel, he said he hoped he would not be part of a project that would separate them or make it harder to see and be with her. However, he said he would have to go where his sergeant went. He expected to see her shortly, since their work was practically completed.

By the end of November, Sir Thomas Gates sent parties to occupy the stockades and the new settlement and ordered John's work party back to Jamestown. John was anxious to see Rachel and meet her brother James.

As soon as their vessel tied up, John took his belongings to his cabin then went to find Rachel. Not seeing her for over five months had made his heart grow, if not with love, then something very close to it.

As he walked up the path to her cabin, he wondered how long he could keep these deeper feelings from becoming obvious.

No one responded to John's rapping on Rachel's cabin. A lassie next door said she thought Rachel and her brother James were down near the river. Indeed, he found them sitting on one of the several logs near the river's edge.

As John approached, Rachel let out a little squeal of pleasure, jumped to her feet, and ran to greet him. After clasping both of his hands in hers, she turned and led him to her brother, who was standing awaiting their approach.

"John, this is my brother James."

"I'm pleased to meet you, James," John said, reaching out his hand. "Rachel told me of your arrival and how happy she was that you were here."

"Yes, I am happy to be here with Rachel. We were both hoping to find my brother, Larry, but the government thinks he was one of those who perished in the Starving Time two years ago."

"I'm sorry to hear that. Were it not for the grace of God, Rachel and I and our party aboard the *Sea Venture* might have perished during the great tempest."

"Yes, Rachel has been telling me about you all, and how Devil's Islands seemed to appear out of nowhere in the nick of time to save you."

"Indeed, we were very fortunate. What do they have you doing, James?"

"I'm a glass blower, so I will be working with those who are busy with that guild. I have been taking a few days before I begin to get settled to spend some time with Rachel. She tells me you and she are very close friends."

"Yes, indeed. I care deeply for your sister. She has been a dear friend to me and helped nurse me through my sickness with the flux last winter."

"She tells me you are indentured to a Sergeant Sharpe, along with about nine other men from your village in Wales."

"Yes, that is so. I have about four more years of servitude and then I can get a land patent of fifty acres if I decide to stay here."

"You are a brave lad to have left family and all to come here."

"I suppose so. But I would not exchange what I have experienced since coming. And if I hadn't come, I wouldn't have met Rachel," he said, smiling at her. "Did you leave a family in London, James?"

"My wife died two years ago. We had one son, who is now four years old. My mother is caring for him. If I decide to stay, I will try to send for him when he is a little older."

While John and James were getting acquainted, Rachel stood silently by, holding John's hand. Occasionally, James would glance down at their hands and smile knowingly at Rachel, as if to say, "I think you are more than just friends with this young man." Rachel, mindful of her brother's thoughts, smiled back at him and then at John, unashamed of her open display of affection for him.

Just witnessing his sister's love for John in this hostile land brought memories of love James had lost in the death of his wife. Yet he wondered how a couple who so obviously cared for each other could wait four more years to announce to the world their real desires.

Hearing the supper bell, they ambled toward the dining hall and joined others streaming in from different parts of the town. The three had their dinner meal in the main dining hall. Over their meal, John asked James more questions about his glass-blowing trade.

"So, do you believe you can make a living here in this colony with your trade?"

"Yes. However, it will require a year or two before the forts and small plantations begin to see the value of the products our guild can supply."

"I wish you much success, James. I hope to be one of those plantation owners one day who will be one of your customers."

CHAPTER 36 ✍

HENRICO

AFTER THE INITIAL phase of building Henrico, John and the rest of Sergeant Sharpe's men spent the remainder of their second winter in Jamestown. There would be more expansion to Henrico come summer. They were kept busy doing minor repairs on the fort. This included clearing the acre plot of land for John Rolfe and his tobacco experiment.

During the winter, John and Rachel got to see more of each other, and John became better acquainted with Rachel's brother. James began work at his trade of glass blowing. With the growth in the colony, and now Henrico, he found a ready market for his products.

One evening after supper in March, John and Rachel were sitting on their favorite log close to the river. The subject of Pocahontas, Chief Powhatan's daughter, came up. John had heard the name but knew little about her.

"John, have you heard the story about Pocahontas and Captain John Smith?" Rachel sighed.

"No," he said. "What about her?"

"Well, Captain Smith was one of the first group of settlers to come to Jamestown. He was the president of the council that governed here before Sir Thomas Gates and Lord Delaware were sent over. He was captured by the Indians and was about to be killed when Pocahontas saved his life. She fell in love with him. However, due to her youth and being the chief's daughter, Captain Smith was very careful with her. He was wounded and had to return to England for treatment. She kept coming to the fort every month or so asking about Captain Smith. I noticed her shortly after we arrived almost two years ago. Then some lady told me the story."

"That's all very interesting," said John.

"But there is more to the story. Last fall, she and her brother began visiting with John Rolfe. I heard he is teaching her and her brother the English language. Lady Horton said it seems that since John's wife died, he has become somewhat taken up with this relationship with Pocahontas and her brother. Mistress Horton also said Mr. Rolfe thinks his relationship with Pocahontas and her brother will be helpful to the colony in dealing with Chief Powhatan. So, our dear governor has given his blessing to Rolfe to cultivate this friendship with this young maiden and her brother."

"Speaking of cultivation, have you heard about Rolfe's tobacco farm?"

"No," said Rachel, lowering her voice.

"Well," said John, clearing his throat, "Sergeant Sharpe and our team have been clearing an acre or so of land beyond the graveyard for his experiment. Since it is getting late, I believe we have time to walk over and see it on our way back inside the stockade."

"Fine," said Rachel as she got to her feet. "I need a short walk before we go to our quarters."

John led Rachel along a path near the edge of the river, then skirted the graveyard and entered the cleared land. Rolfe had already started his planting. Neat rows of freshly turned soil were still visible in the fading twilight.

"Rolfe thinks there will be quite a market for his product, if it grows as he hopes," said John, breaking into the chorus of frogs, crickets, and other evening sounds.

"Ugh," said Rachel. "Tobacco smoke makes me choke."

"Me too."

And with that, he took her hand in his and led her through the graveyard to the open gates of the fort. They quickly came to the street where Rachel lived with Mistress Horton.

Saying goodnight, John made his way to the quarters he shared with Wooley and two of the other men in Sergeant Sharpe's squad.

By the end of May, the acre of tobacco showed signs of becoming a bumper crop, even beyond Rolfe's wildest dreams.

He now realized he had the makings of a new commercial business that would find a ready market in England, and perhaps even in all of Europe. Getting it cured and ready for market would be his next project.

CHAPTER 37

SERGEANT SHARPE'S PLANTATION

ONE OF SERGEANT William Sharpe's dreams was to own some land and become a gentleman farmer. His rank would not allow him to ever become one of the landed gentry in England. However, his twenty-five years of service to the Crown and his rank of staff sergeant had opened some doors for him with the Virginia Company.

Sergeant Sharpe was part of a number of men with military backgrounds who had signed on with the London Virginia Company and its leadership. These included officers and non-commissioned officers.

The sergeant was also permitted by the Virginia Company to indenture up to ten men to help him establish his own plantation after several years of service to the company. He was part of the *Third Supply* that sailed in 1609, so his service would be up in 1614, two years hence.

He had surveyed several sites upriver across from Henrico, in addition to sites across from Jamestown. He preferred a site directly across the James.

He would be granted one hundred acres for his plantation. Those he had sponsored would receive fifty acres each. If he could persuade his team of men to acquire land next to his, they could help each other clear the property and begin to harvest some of this tobacco Rolfe had discovered.

Some of his team had already said they were returning to Wales. Perhaps he could persuade them to sell him their head rights of fifty acres. He would have to work on that, he told himself.

If John Rolfe's tobacco experiment proved successful, it would provide seed for the sergeant's plantation, as well as crops at Henrico and elsewhere. His relationship with Rolfe and Sir Thomas Dale would help when his time came to secure land for his plantation.

At first, Sergeant Sharpe had found it difficult to work with Sir Thomas Dale, the new marshal of the colony. Gradually, as he carried out Dale's strict orders, he had won the marshal's respect.

Sir Thomas Dale's arrival the previous year had brought some changes to the easy-going life in Jamestown. The colony had needed something like the Dale Code. It brought order out of the chaos that had been characteristic of the governing of Jamestown by previous administrations. A lack of strong leadership had led to many deaths that almost destroyed the colony.

Sergeant Sharpe remembered that only sixty of the many hundreds of colonists were still alive when he arrived two years ago in May. Starvation, disease, and Indian attacks had taken their toll, but so had a lack of strong and able leadership.

Dale laid out very strict rules that would strengthen the colony. Those who failed to obey were immediately punished. A few lost their lives, and others were punished very severely. This harsh, and some would even say cruel, treatment made the colonists realize those in authority meant business and intended for the Jamestown plantation to succeed.

Sergeant Sharpe and his ten men had no trouble obeying the Dale Code. They were now a team that worked closely with their leader and wanted nothing more than to survive and gain their freedom from the contract they had signed with Rolfe, Sharpe, and the Virginia Company.

By early August 1612, all of Jamestown and those in other forts had seen or heard about Rolfe's success with his small tobacco farm. The governor and Sir Thomas Dale were especially pleased.

Although none of the tobacco leaves had been harvested and cured, dreams of producing a commodity that would sell and even be exported to the homeland, and perhaps all of Europe, became topics of conversation.

In addition to a bountiful harvest, Rolfe's field produced enough seed to plant many acres of tobacco. Soon, other plots of ground were vacated of their brush and growth to make room for more plantings the following spring.

Early in 1613, Governor Gates, Thomas Argyle, and Sir Thomas Dale hatched a bold plan for dealing with the Indians who had become more and more hostile toward the plantation. Pocahontas and her brother had not been seen at the fort in over a year, or met with Rolfe. The Indians under Powhatan's control had killed and captured several settlers and stolen much equipment.

Thus, they decided to take a bold approach with the Indians. This meant capturing Powhatan's daughter, Pocahontas. They hoped this would force the old chief to make peace and bargain in good faith with the colonists.

In April, Sir Thomas Argyle led a force of men on his ship, including John Rolfe, to capture the Indian princess. She was tricked into coming aboard Argyle's ship, along with another friendly chief's wife. The plan worked, and Pocahontas was taken back to Jamestown, where she was kept for a while. Her father was informed, but he was not too concerned. He may have thought, "My daughter's loyalty has slowly been eroded by her previous relationship with Captain Smith and now, perhaps, with John Rolfe or someone else."

Two months later, Pocahontas was taken to Henrico and converted to Christianity by Reverend Whitaker, the first Presbyterian minister to arrive in the colony and establish his church. He christened her "Rebecca."

John Rolfe continued to visit Pocahontas and teach her English. Their relationship began to blossom, due in part to John being a lonely widower and the Indian maiden a lovely young lady.

In April 1614, the year following her capture, Rolfe obtained permission from the governor to marry Pocahontas. By now she felt betrayed by her father, but loved and accepted by Rolfe and the colony.

Chaplain Bucke, Rolfe's personal friend, married the two in Jamestown later that month. Powhatan sent one of his sons to attend the wedding and announce his blessing. Thus, a new era of peace between the Indians and the colony was ushered in by this unusual covenant.

CHAPTER 38 ❧

VIRGINIA GOLD

TWO WEEKS AFTER Rolfe's wedding to Pocahontas, Sergeant William Sharpe requested a land patent for one hundred acres from Sir Thomas Gates. This was a deed, with conditions, from the Virginia Company.

Rolfe's planting of his superior strain of tobacco was already furnishing seed for plantings at Henrico and Bermuda Hundred, a plantation downriver from Jamestown. Rolfe had urged the sergeant to request his land patent and begin planting the lucrative crop.

Three weeks after his wedding, Rolfe met Sharpe at the acre of his first planting on Jamestown Island. "William, I am moving to Henrico with my bride and I need someone to tend and harvest this crop for me. I promised you seed two years ago when you and your men cleared this land for me."

"That you did."

"So here is my offer. You can have all the seed you need for your plantation, plus, if you will tend this field for me, I will give you sixty percent of the sale of this crop. It will give you some experience with growing and harvesting that you will need as you move ahead with your own plans. Is this a fair offer?"

"Indeed it is. I accept your terms and appreciate your generous offer."

"Also," said Rolfe, "you can count on my help in marketing and shipping your crops over the next few years as you get your plantation going. I believe tobacco is the gold, the Virginia gold, the company was searching for and must have in order to become profitable."

"I think you may be right. I've always wanted to own some land and be a gentleman farmer. When I was fighting for the Crown in the Netherlands and Ireland, I dreamed someday of beating my sword into a plowshare and not studying war anymore. I knew it would never happen in merry old England."

"Well, if anyone deserves a plantation, it is you and your men. In the next few years, I feel we are going to see many more of our fellow countrymen coming here. They will get land to make a good living for themselves and their families. What about your family, Sergeant?"

"I was married once and had one son, but he died in a fire. My wife couldn't bear his loss and my being away for long periods. She left me, and I have lost track of her. For all I know, she may be dead."

"We both have suffered losses: my baby in Devil's Islands, and then my first wife here in Jamestown. Do you ever get lonely for a wife?"

"Yes, sometimes. But then I think of my wife and how lonely she must have felt losing our boy, and with me gone, not knowing if I would ever come home alive."

"War creates so much misery and suffering. I've never served in the military, but I honor and thank you that you have served the Crown."

"Yes, it is a hard life, but someone has to do it, and now after twenty-five years of service, I am glad it is over."

"When will you get your land patent?"

"I applied a week ago, so I should receive it from the governor any day now."

"Have you chosen a location?"

"I like several places. However, I have selected a site across the river from our fort. I like being fairly close to our headquarters. When will you and your bride be moving to Henrico?"

"We are in the process of loading our things and moving within a week. One of the last things delaying us was this field and crop. I needed someone to manage it. I'm delighted you are that friend."

Shaking hands to finalize the contract, the two walked together to the fort and parted company; Rolfe to his cabin and bride, Sharpe to check on his land patent.

CHAPTER 39

THE LAND PATENT

GOVERNOR GATES AND the Jamestown council granted Sergeant Sharpe's request for his one-hundred-acre plantation across the river from Jamestown. He could start it immediately, subject to the London council's final approval. His grant deed would come from them. Also, he could request up to four hundred acres more anytime.

His acreage total was based upon two things. First, there was a desire for more tobacco to be planted. This promised the quickest means for the money-strapped company to begin showing a profit for its stockholders. Second, the sergeant had financed ten men who had worked for the company and the sergeant for five years. The ten months in Devil's Islands were considered service time. Thus, the sergeant had more than earned the acreage for his plantation.

John Thomas and the others would also receive their promised fifty acres of land as an inducement to stay and farm the rich soil. Food for the colony and tobacco exported by the company were almost equally valued, though tobacco harvesting was more desired.

The company desired mostly to trade with the Indians for needed corn and other food, rather than for the colony to produce it. However, it was getting harder to trade for enough corn and other foods to feed the growing numbers of settlers.

Farmers were greatly valued and being recruited by the company. Some farmers chose not to wait for land patents, but grabbed fertile acres on tributaries of the James River to grow corn as well as tobacco.

When the Jamestown council discovered this practice, Sir Thomas Dale quickly hauled them before the governor. However, since produce of both kinds was in short supply, the council didn't punish these men very speedily. At times, they appeared to look the other way.

Two days after the sergeant had secured his first land patent, John Rolfe met with him in the fort's dining hall over breakfast. He and Pocahontas were preparing to leave for Henrico and their new house.

"Pocahontas and I are moving today back upriver and I would like to secure some of your men to assist me with planting another field of tobacco. I heard you received your land patent, and I am sure you will also want to clear your land as quickly as possible."

"I could spare five men for a week or two, if that would be long enough."

"That would be much appreciated, and I will pay for their help in my first shipment of tobacco to London."

"I trust you, John. I'm sorry I can't say that of some of our people over here, but I want to help you and your missus get a good start in your new town. And I'm sure I will need advice and help from you as I get my plantation into production."

"Indeed, you will, and you can count on me to help you."

The next morning Sergeant Sharpe asked John Thomas to pick four of his friends and accompany Mr. Rolfe and his wife on their boat upriver to Henrico. They would work with Rolfe and his other men, planting a fifty-acre field of tobacco. They would leave by noon.

"Thanks, Sergeant. I was hoping you would select me to go because of a certain young lassie I know who is living there with her mistress and doctor husband. It has been almost one month since I saw her last."

"Yes, John, I am very aware of your feelings for Rachel. That did enter into my decision. But I also know you will be responsible and do a good job for Rolfe. Ever since you volunteered on the *Sea Venture* for that lookout assignment, I knew you were a man I could depend on. I am going to place you in charge of the others, even if some are a bit older than you. I will instruct them that if you have any trouble with them doing what is expected, they will also answer to me."

"Thanks, Sergeant, for your confidence in me. I will do my best, and my friends respect me as I do them."

Wooley was not selected to go. John didn't want his friendship with him to interfere with his duties. After loading their personal items and additional tools, John and his crew boarded the boat with Rolfe and his beautiful wife. Several other passengers and the crew came aboard for the day-and-a-half journey.

They reached Henrico late the following day. John, after tending to some duties with Rolfe, took his crew to its quarters. He waited until the next morning to visit Rachel at the home of Doctor Bohune and his wife.

Their home also served as a clinic. The house was extra large to accommodate the medical facility. Until a second medical doctor arrived, Doctor Bohune's practice included the Jamestown settlement.

When John arrived, the doctor was in his clinic. Rachel invited John into the living room, where Mrs. Bohune was very cordial and greeted him warmly. She offered him a cup of tea and a biscuit. "How was your trip?" she asked.

"Uneventful. We didn't see much traffic on the James. How do you like living here versus Jamestown?" John asked.

"We are getting used to it, aren't we, Rachel?"

"Oh yes," answered Rachel.

"Well, I think I will leave you two and let you catch up on things. Nice to have you up for awhile, John."

"Yes, my men and I are here until we finish planting Mr. Rolfe's tobacco field. It may take us ten days or two weeks."

Mrs. Bohune excused herself and left Rachel and John alone. John moved closer to Rachel and took her hand.

"I have missed seeing you," he said.

"I have missed you, too. I take short walks when I get really lonely for you and imagine you are here beside me. When no one can hear me, I even talk out loud to you and ask God to carry my thoughts of love to you."

"Sometimes, I almost feel you beside me, Rachel. Maybe God is transmitting your thoughts to me and from me to you."

"So, now that we are together, I won't daydream, but use all our precious moments to the fullest. How does that sound?"

"Just what I was thinking, too."

Rachel turned and gave John a brief embrace with a big smile as he returned her show of affection. They held each other briefly, then stood as Rachel suggested a little walk around the outskirts of the town.

Rachel told Mrs. Bohune she would be out for a walk with John but would return to prepare the evening meal for them. Mrs. Bohune had already invited John to dinner, and he had quickly accepted.

Leaving the house, they ambled through the main street of Henrico with its twenty-some houses, a few shops, and a brick structure that Rachel said would be Reverend Whitaker's new Presbyterian church. A tailor shop, with its quaint little sign in a small glass window, beckoned to them.

"I need to stop there tomorrow. I'm almost out of shirts."

"Mr. Brown, the tailor, does really good work," said Rachel.

They passed a barber shop with a candle burning in the window. John's hair was in need of a trim, and he made note to stop there before returning to Jamestown. They passed a bakery and the town dining hall where the single men ate.

The smell of the bakery drew them inside. Rachel picked out two cinnamon rolls and placed them in her small basket. John let her pay the one-half shilling for the rolls. Though he received a small stipend once a month for incidentals, he had very little money beyond that. On the other hand, Rachel received a generous amount from her mistress each month, and she had brought an extra amount of money from London, of which she had spent very little so far. She knew that John had brought very little money with him. He would not earn money until he was free from his debt to the sergeant.

They spent the next hour circling the town and ended up near the landing dock, sitting on a log, watching the small amount of traffic on the James, and eating their rolls.

"How's your brother doing with his glass work?"

"Pretty well. He made the glass for most of the windows in the houses and shops here in Henrico. Some of the other settlements and plantations are beginning to give him more business. I believe his work will grow as the colony grows."

"Have you any more news of your other brother?"

"No. We believe he may have returned to London. The list of those who have died in the colony since it began seven years ago does not list his name. Doctor Bohune secured that information for me and James. He may have gone to some other country, or hired on as a crewman aboard some ship. I think we will hear something one of these days."

They talked on for another hour until Rachel remembered her promise to fix dinner for themselves and the Bohunes.

After dinner, John excused himself to check with his crew and Rolfe about beginning the planting of Rolfe's field. He told Rachel he would see her later that evening.

John and his crew spent the next two weeks planting Rolfe's tobacco field, then an extra two weeks clearing another twenty-five acres for more tobacco crops.

Rolfe obtained the extra time and help from the sergeant with the promise of additional payment in the harvested money crop that was increasingly becoming the new medium of exchange along the James. The cured leaves, packed into casks for shipment to London and final processing for pipe, snuff, or chewing, was in great demand. The supply could not keep up with the demand.

During his month in Henrico, John spent all his free time visiting with Rachel. Mrs. Bohune invited him to dinner several times each week. Rachel, without John's knowledge, had arranged with her mistress for John's food out of her allowance.

By the middle of May, John and his crew were ready to leave Henrico. John told Rachel goodbye and said he would come back as soon as possible. Then, he and his crew headed downriver to clear more acreage for Sergeant Sharpe's tobacco crops. The sergeant and his men were able to clear enough land for an initial planting before the planting season was over. It would be harvested later than usual, but still in time for a fall shipment to London and its expanding markets.

CHAPTER 40 ᔑ

THE FUTURE

JOHN HAD BEEN thinking about his future for some time. He had several options once he satisfied his indebtedness to the sergeant. He could stay on as a hired hand and work as he had for the past five years. This would earn him some much needed money. The sergeant had offered to make him foreman for his plantation. He liked John, and treated him more like a son. Sharpe had not been able to raise his only son during his active military career for the crown and had lost him to a fire.

John appreciated his special friendship with Sergeant Sharpe. Sometimes the rest of the crew teased him about this. John never used this as a means to receive special favors or treatment. He always did his fair share of work and was respected by the other men.

All the others were facing an uncertain future, now that their indentured service was drawing to a close. At times they shared with each other their concerns and plans. Some were tired of the rough living, plus dangers from the natives and the elements. They just wanted to earn enough to pay their passage and take the first ship back to Plymouth or London.

Not John. He had heard about the poverty, low wages, and lack of opportunity in his homeland. His future, whatever that might hold, was here. After he had written to Dorothy, releasing her from her promise to wait for him, she had responded with a note of sadness that they and their dreams were over. She said she had found no one she loved as she did him. But, she understood the impossible circumstances of their relationship, at least for the foreseeable future. She had closed her long letter by saying that if John wanted to renew their covenant, she would welcome it. John never told her of his feelings for Rachel. He had wanted to spare her that.

Yet, his future with Rachel, in some ways, was almost as tenuous as with Dorothy. He had to have a means to support a wife. It would not be fair to either party to promise something he could not fulfill. His immediate concern had to be finding the means to support himself in order to ask Rachel to become his bride. He became a bit frightened at the mere thought.

How did his parents ever find the guts to make the choice? At times it almost seemed like jumping off a cliff and not knowing just where one would land. "I suppose this is why they say marriage is for the young who have faith enough to take the leap," John thought.

John just wanted to know where he would land when he took that leap of faith. This much he knew, his future, for better or for worse, for richer or for poorer, had to be here in this dangerous, beautiful, and challenging new world.

Sergeant Sharpe and his men worked on and off at his plantation opposite Jamestown and upriver at Henrico. They cleared more acreage for both Rolfe and the sergeant. They also built the sergeant's home and two curing barns for the tobacco, plus sleeping quarters for the men.

Rolfe introduced the latest methods of growing, cultivating, and finally harvesting the large leaves of tobacco to his and the sergeant's team. Curing the tobacco leaves for shipment was a time-consuming process.

It was hard work that left John and the men little time for relaxation or other pursuits. Yet, John found time, not only for work, but to see Rachel whenever possible. Occasionally, while he was working at Henrico, she would come to the town dining hall to eat with John in order to see him. But usually they saw each other late in the evenings before dark.

Occasionally, John would nearly fall asleep during Rachel's conversations. At those moments, she would say, "John, dear, you need your rest; I'll see you tomorrow at noon, or in the evening."

And, rubbing the sleep from his eyes, he would say, "I hope I can see the trail to my cabin."

Slowly, summer faded into fall, and work was completed at Rolfe's two plantations. Rolfe had been planting and harvesting tobacco for two years. In October, he prepared his first shipment to London aboard the ship *Elizabeth*.

John and his team of men, with their work finished at Henrico, rode the *Elizabeth* down-river to Jamestown. A barge belonging to Sergeant Sharpe ferried them across to their plantation home.

Soon after arriving, Sharpe called a meeting with his ten men. "Men," he said, "we have some very important matters to decide: in fact, two. First, all you men have satisfied your contract of indentured service. You are now free to do as you please. Second, Sir Thomas Dale has instituted a new policy of ownership of land by the settlers. You can immediately have a fifty-acre plot of land."

He paused a moment to let both facts sink in. "If you choose to return to England, you can claim your land first, then either decide to stay and plant a money crop of tobacco or some other produce. Or, if you choose not to stay, I will buy your land for enough to pay your fare back home, plus a little profit."

The sergeant said their plots could be next to his, and he would purchase plots from any who decided to sell. The men talked among themselves for a few minutes.

"Men, I have one more proposition. I have come to appreciate and respect you for the way in which you have fulfilled your contract with me. You are a fine bunch of men and I would like to see you prosper and gain more from your hard work. Therefore, if any of you would care to continue to work for me, as a hired and free settler, I will pay you a fair wage, and you can also work your own plot of land."

He paused again, then concluded. "You do not need to decide today on these matters. Take your time and decide what is in your best interest, then let me know as soon as you have made up your mind."

CHAPTER 41

DECISIONS, DECISIONS

THE NEXT MORNING, John went to see Sergeant Sharpe in his cabin home. Being an early riser, he was there before the sergeant had finished his breakfast. An older Indian female who prepared meals for Sharpe was working in his kitchen. Dismissing her, Sharpe offered John a seat at the table. "What's on your mind, John?"

"I have been mulling over the good news of yesterday, and I would like to secure the plot of land I have coming and go to work for you as well."

"I'm glad to hear your offer, and I accept. I was planning to ask you to stay on and become my foreman."

"Could I farm my plot of land and still take on the foreman's job?"

"Yes, by all means, you could do both. I would be willing to give you extra time, when needed, to take care of your plot of land."

"When could I begin?"

"Tomorrow, if you like. You need to go over to Jamestown and sign for your plot. Make sure it is next to mine. They will ask you. All the plots must be next to an established plantation."

"I have one more favor to ask, Sergeant."

"Call me William, except in mixed company."

"Certainly, sir. I would like a few days off before I begin. After signing for my land, I want to go up to Henrico and share this news with Rachel. Is that possible?"

"Of course. Just let me know when you will return, and we will get to work on some more adequate housing for men such as yourself, who will choose to stay and work for me."

"I'll leave for Jamestown later this morning, then for Henrico tomorrow. Thanks again for the job. I'll do my best for you."

"I'm pleased to have you. I think you have made a good choice."

The next morning, John headed for Jamestown and the headquarters building located in the center of the fort. The red cross of St. George fluttered in the breeze above this cabin that was larger than the others inside the stockade and housed the governor and his staff.

A young clerk John's age greeted him. He was seated behind a large desk. Rising, he said, "State your name and the nature of your business."

"I am John Thomas, and I have come to sign up for my plot of land Marshal Dale has offered to us settlers."

"When did you arrive in the colony?"

"I signed a contract in 1609, and arrived after a shipwreck in May 1610."

"Where are you living?"

"Sergeant Sharpe's plantation across the James."

"Is that the location for your request?"

"Yes."

"If you will wait for a few minutes, I will have the papers ready for you to sign. Have a seat."

John picked a chair among several scattered about the room and waited. Behind the desk and above the clerk's head were two portraits on the wall. One was of Sir Thomas Gates that John remembered from his *Sea Venture* days. The other, John read, was Sir Thomas Dale, lieutenant governor and marshal. Their names and titles were printed in large letters beneath each portrait. John had had very little contact with either since their arrival in 1611, following Lord Delaware's exit as governor.

Marshal Dale, with the strict enforcement of his code of laws, had made quite an impact upon the colony's inhabitants. John had heard of a few who had even been hanged for breaking his laws. None of the sergeant's team had been affected by the code. Sharpe had kept all informed of these rules. Besides, they had been too busy with work to get into trouble.

"I have this ready now," the clerk said, looking up and handing John the ink quill.

John dipped the quill and signed. He felt a thrill of joy as he finished. He breathed deeply and said to himself, "My first owned land. I'm part of the privileged—not a large part, but at least a part."

The clerk smiled. "You will be issued a grant deed in several months. Stop by in a few months to see if we have it for you. You can build and plant on your plot effective today."

"Thanks," said John.

He turned and left the office. After checking at the wharf to see when the next ship would sail for Henrico, he learned a small pinnace was leaving within the next hour. He stowed his bag aboard and went to find some food to take with him.

While waiting for his boat to leave, John scribbled a quick letter to his parents in Wales. He informed them of his good fortune in becoming a landowner. To him, his fifty-acre plot brought almost as much joy as if it had been one hundred or even five hundred acres. It would take months before his letter reached his parents. Mail service, being by guess and by God plus community effort, amazed him that it functioned as well as it did. Anyway, the good news had to be shared. He offered a prayer of thanksgiving to God as he dispatched his letter.

The next day, John arrived in Henrico and went quickly to Rachel's home. She was thrilled with the news of John's new land. They went to the town's dining hall for dinner. Over their meal, they had a wonderful time discussing John's land and his new job as Sharpe's foreman.

"What do you plan to grow on your land?" Rachel asked.

"I'm not sure. The money crop now is tobacco. However, the colony needs corn very much. The natives cannot be depended upon much longer to supply the amount of corn we need."

"Which is easier to grow?"

"Corn."

They continued to talk for the next hour, until Rachel remembered she had to get back to her duties.

John said, "I, too, need to get back downriver and stake out my new property next to the sergeant's plantation."

"You are coming for supper, right?" Rachel asked.

"Yes. Also, I will be staying overnight on Rolfe's plantation. The next boat run downriver leaves at dawn. So, after tonight it may be some time before I can come back up to see you."

"I'll be here, John, waiting for you."

During the remainder of 1614, John and Rachel tried to see each other once a month. In February of 1615, Pocahontas presented her husband with a new baby boy. This somewhat eased the loss of Rolfe's first child five years earlier in Devil's Islands.

The Rolfes were filled with joy. John and Rachel were present for the child's christening by Reverend Whitaker in Henrico. The event took place at the reverend's new brick Presbyterian church during one of John's monthly visits to see Rachel.

For the rest of the year, John was kept busy clearing his property on a small creek next to Sharpe's land. In addition, he supervised four of the men who decided to obtain their property. They would then work for two more planting and harvesting seasons for the sergeant. Following that, if they decided to leave for their homes, they would sell to the sergeant. Field laborers were in short supply in the colony. Some planters sought to entice native men to work their fields. In most tribes, women did almost all the common labor, while men did the hunting and fishing.

William Wooley decided to return home. He, along with three other men from Wales, left in January of 1616, after the sale of their plots of land. Sergeant Sharpe purchased their two hundred acres and added them to his plantation.

In May, John Rolfe, his wife, and their baby boy, along with Sir Thomas Dale, now governor, left for England. Dale was being recalled as governor. The Rolfes' trip was to help the Virginia Company advertise and attract new settlers.

Pocahontas was excited about the trip for another reason. She hoped to see and visit with her old friend Captain John Smith. In addition, her husband planned for her to have an audience with the king and queen as a representative of her native people. Little did they realize the tragedy that awaited them.

CHAPTER 42 ~

JOHN'S FIRST PLANTATION

DALE'S REPLACEMENT AS governor was George Yeardley. John learned this in July on one of his visits to Jamestown to pick up supplies for the sergeant and his grant deed from the governor's office. The same clerk was behind the desk, and Yeardley's portrait hung on the wall behind him.

"Why isn't he a full governor?" John asked.

"He doesn't have the rank yet for that, and a new governor will be appointed next year."

"Why was Sir Thomas replaced?"

"The rumors have it, because he was too strict and this was affecting the Virginia Company's ability to recruit new settlers."

"We sure need more men to come help raise our crops," replied John.

"You are right," said the clerk. "By the way, my name is Samuel."

"Where are you from, Samuel?"

"I came from London."

"Are we ever going to see more women coming over here?" asked John.

"Yes, I hope so. I would love to see more of our English lassies. I would like to get married one of these years. Where are you from, John?"

"Carmarthen in Wales."

"Where's that?"

"About sixty miles northwest of Plymouth."

With that, John picked up the deed and thanked Samuel for his services. He collected his supplies and posted a new sign on the town's bulletin board for hired help. It read, "Any man looking for a farming job, contact John Thomas at the Sharpe Plantation, across the James."

The week following, three men showed up at the plantation and were hired by Sharpe after John had sized them up regarding their experience in farming.

Over the balance of the year, John was so busy with his two jobs that he was only able to visit Rachel when he needed to see Rolfe's foreman, who supplied information to John in the cultivation and curing of tobacco. In between visits, he and Rachel exchanged letters to keep their relationship current.

On his last visit, at the end of December, following Christmas, John had supper with Rachel at the Bohunes' home. After the meal, the Bohunes excused themselves. Before a cozy log fire, the subject of marriage came up. For some time John had purposely avoided this with Rachel. But it was Rachel who brought it up.

"John, have you given any more thought as to when you might like to get married?"

"Perhaps in about two more years. I should have at least two or more harvests of tobacco sold and a nice log house constructed on my land. I should be able to support someone and myself by then."

"And who might that someone be?"

"You will be the first to know, Rachel," he said, with a twinkle in his eye.

"I was just curious. A few single lassies have been arriving here in our town, and they are getting married shortly after they arrive. Has Jamestown been receiving more lassies?"

"I haven't noticed."

"Now, John. I know you well enough to know you would be quick to notice a pretty lassie. It didn't take you very long to get acquainted with me, right?"

Blushing a little, John retorted, "That was different. We were pretty well confined to the ship with a lot of time on our hands. Now I am so busy, I try not to think too much about women, or pretty lassies, except you."

"That's sweet. I don't worry about you noticing other lassies. I feel the same way about you, with other men. Every time I go into the town, and men are around, I am aware of their hungry looks. Living in this colony is not easy for the single woman, or man, is it?

"You're right, but the more I think about you and how much I long to have you for myself, I get miserable, so I get busier, so I won't dwell on it."

"Me too, but how long do you plan to wait?"

"Not any longer than I have to. But it would be selfish of me to ask you to marry me and not have a comfortable place for us to live or the means to support us. Don't you agree?"

"Yes, but there are days when I see how happy my mistress and her man are, and I can barely wait another day. There is also something else. I haven't told anyone else about this."

"What is it, Rachel?"

"I may have to seek other employment."

"Why?"

"Well," said Rachel, lowering her voice, "I'm not too comfortable at times around Doctor Bohune. Especially when my mistress is out of the house."

"Has the doctor done anything to make you feel this way?"

"Not really. But I can feel his eyes on me in ways that make me wonder about him. A lassie can tell when a man is not being a gentleman around her. If my mistress had to be out of the house for an extended period, I would be afraid the doctor might make untoward advances. That scares me."

"Do you have any other possibilities for employment?"

"Not at this moment."

"I hear what you are saying and feeling. I have an idea. I will talk to Sergeant Sharpe and see if he would be willing to hire you. We have about ten men working that require cooked meals daily, plus other work you could do."

"Who is cooking for you now?"

"A young Indian lassie the sergeant hired."

"What would happen to her job?"

"There might be enough work for both. In fact, since John Rolfe married Pocahontas, Sharpe has been almost courting this lassie."

"Why haven't you told me about this cute young lassie before now, John? Here I have been thinking you had no contact with women, and now you tell me about her."

"I didn't think it was that important. Besides, she doesn't interest me in that way. We tease her a little, as men will. But none of the men, much less myself, get out of hand. We know how the sergeant feels about her. I would not be too surprised if he marries her. Besides, I love you, Rachel."

This was the first time John had actually used that magical word "love" with Rachel. She had, of course, intuited it; John had all the symptoms of love for her. However, she was very pleased and comforted to hear it finally coming from his lips. How she longed to pour out her passions and affections upon him. If only he could make the leap into marriage.

She was willing to suffer privations for him, but she sensed he had too much pride to ask her to forego the basic necessities and endure hardships. Colonial living was difficult enough. John was too thoughtful to make it more difficult for either of them. By waiting a bit longer, they could begin their married life with enough of the basic necessities for a home and family.

Rachel knew all this in her heart, but that didn't make waiting for John any easier. She would try to be patient and not put any more stress or pressure upon him. Still, they were both under stress. How they would manage this over the next year or more, only time would reveal.

The room began to grow colder as the logs slowly turned into red coals and ashes. Outside, a snowstorm was swirling and howling about the log cabin. John was thankful the doctor had insisted upon him staying overnight and sleeping on his office couch.

John stretched, then, quite suddenly, took Rachel in his arms and kissed her passionately. She returned his kiss just as fervently.

"Rachel, I do want to marry you and will ask for your hand just as soon as I think I can support us. If you choose to marry me, can you wait?"

"Yes, I can wait. But will you write me just as soon as you talk to Sergeant Sharpe about the job? I do feel it would be wise to change employment as soon as possible."

"Yes, I will talk with him as soon as I reach the plantation, and I will write you." They held each other for a few more moments, then Rachel said, "I think we both had better retire to our own beds before…."

She didn't have to finish her words. John was also thinking, "How much longer can I wait?"

All the way downriver, John dwelt on the thought of Rachel working close by where he could see her each day. He reminded himself it would be difficult for both to keep their emotions in check. He recalled the last day he had spent with Dorothy before leaving home. They had gone too far, and John blamed himself for what had happened. He had gone against his Christian conscience and his better judgment.

CHAPTER 43

POCAHONTAS

JOHN WASTED LITTLE time in discussing a possible job for Rachel with Sharpe. He even went so far as to say he would help support her financially with part of his pay from his position with the sergeant.

The sergeant didn't need much persuasion. He offered Rachel a job as cook and housekeeper. So a few weeks later, Rachel reluctantly informed her mistress, who had become more like a mother than an employer. Mrs. Bohune suspected most of the reason for Rachel's desired move was to be near John. She didn't suspect that another motive might lie behind Rachel's termination. Thus, she readily gave her assent and blessing. By the first of February, Rachel had moved to the Sharpe plantation across from Jamestown.

Early in May, the news of the death of Pocahontas arrived by a ship from London. She had died seven months after the

Rolfes arrived in England, leaving her husband a widower and her young son motherless.

Later in May, John Rolfe, along with a new governor, was back in the colony. He stopped on his way to Henrico to see Sergeant Sharpe. The two men spent the better part of the morning seated at the kitchen table, talking.

"This is the second wife I have lost since coming to the colony."

"Yes, I remember. First it was your baby girl in Devil's Islands, then your wife shortly after we arrived in Jamestown."

"Yes, and I still feel the loss of both of them, and now, Pocahontas."

"How can you stand it?"

"Prayer, and more prayer, and then somehow God gives me the will and courage to go on."

"What are your plans now?"

"I'm going to keep raising and promoting the planting of tobacco for the colony. I think it is the only way for the Virginia Company to survive. It is also one of the best ways for settlers to get a new start in life. Governor Dale's plan for the Virginia Company to give small plots of land attracted new immigrants and it helped your men, right? Now, the new governor must support it. Perhaps he will even expand it. Then, when farmers plant this "Virginia Gold" and we ship it to England, and eventually other countries, we can begin to compete with Spain, which now has a monopoly on the continent."

"I believe you are right. I have one hundred acres planted now, and if I can get more hired help, I will plant more. I want to thank you again for all the help you have given me and my foreman, John Thomas."

"Thomas is a good man. I watched him work with my foreman last year up at Henrico. He is worth several men. There is more good land near here on this side of the James. I plan to get another patent from Deputy Governor Argall, who came back with me and relieved George Yeardley."

"What are your immediate plans?"

"I am going up to Henrico to try and set up an Indian boys' school. I want to do this in honor and memory of Pocahontas and for our son. I believe the Lord has given me a special mission for this. I learned a lot more about my dead wife's past and her role in helping to save our colony in its early days before you and I came. She was an angel of mercy. The colony may not have survived without her help. I also believe God was in all this, and wants us to share the Christian faith with these native people."

"I am not a religious person, just an old soldier, but you have my best wishes and prayers, and if I can help you, just let me know."

"Thanks, I will."

Rachel's new position at the plantation enabled John to see her almost every day, except when he was traveling across the James or upriver to Henrico. Another room was added to the plantation house for Rachel and the Indian lassie.

They seemed to enjoy each other's company, and Rachel began to teach her friend more English. Sergeant Sharpe called her by her Indian name, Morning Dove. Most of the time, he just called her Dovie. Everyone could see that Dovie meant more to the sergeant than just an employee.

The other men warmed quickly to Rachel, but sensing that she and John were more than just good friends, they also quickly learned to respect that relationship. John tried to keep his true feelings for Rachel subdued around the other men, but this was more difficult than he had imagined.

Once in a while, he would catch her eyes on him and give her a quick wink and smile. Keeping their emotions in check was almost more than they could do, until the others in the room left to resume their duties. Then, making sure no one was nearby, John would take Rachel in his arms and kiss her gently. Usually, he would then tell her he had some task to finish and would leave the room quickly, knowing he had to be the stronger of the two.

John kept to a minimum the amount of time spent with her during evening hours. The hired men rose early and worked late. John had to keep watch of his time visiting with Rachel in order to be able to rise at dawn with his men.

Rachel, likewise, filled her days with her chores. Thus, their work schedules helped keep in check their passions for one another. John noted that the sergeant also had a little trouble keeping his feelings for his Indian maid under control.

In fact, one day, the sergeant and John were alone discussing their tobacco crops when his boss brought up the subject of his relationship with Dovie.

"John, I'm sure you have noticed my feelings for Dovie."

"Yes, I've noticed she means more to you than just a cook and housekeeper."

"You are right. Ever since John Rolfe fell in love and married Pocahontas, I have wondered why more of our settlers have not asked to do the same."

"I hear some of the men have run away to the Indian villages for that reason. Rumor has it the reason for the desertions is not only hunger and lack of good food, but loneliness for female companionship."

"I believe you are right. The Virginia Company has been trying to recruit more women to come over, but hasn't been too successful, as yet. The company also had a policy that prevented much contact with the Indians, except to trade for food. They said we must be careful to respect the Indian women, and not treat them as the Spanish did in planting their colonies and plantations."

"Do you think Rolfe's marriage to Pocahontas has given the company a reason to relax its policy about our men and Indian women?" asked John.

"For myself, I would like to see some change. I believe each request for an Indian wife should be handled on its merits. If it will further the building of better relationships between us and them, then I think that should be justification enough."

"Are you planning on making such a request?"

"Yes. She is a very special woman to me. I never had much of a marriage in my earlier days. I certainly hanker for a wife to share this plantation with me. I have talked with Rolfe about this, and he said each case must be looked at carefully, and if based on good motives should be given every consideration by the authorities."

"What if you petitioned and were turned down?"

"I don't know what I would do. I wouldn't want just to live with her out of wedlock. That would probably be grounds for canceling my land patent. Plus, if she became with child, that would not be fair to her or a child of mine. No, I think too much of her and what I would stand to lose to give in to mere lust. What about you, John? How long are you able to wait before asking Rachel? You both look like lovesick calves wanting their mother."

"I want to be able to support us both and provide for a family, should we have one."

"That's wise, John. I would like to help you achieve this goal, and I will increase your wages as soon as I can."

"Thank you. Rachel understands and doesn't want to proceed until we both are ready."

Summer slipped into fall and brought a bumper crop of tobacco. Fall ebbed into winter and finally into spring with more acreage planted in "Virginia Gold" than the previous year.

John had worked hard, cleared his plot of land, and was able to plant his first crop of tobacco. A one-room log cabin with a fireplace was constructed next to the creek that flowed into the James and served as the boundary between his and the sergeant's plantations. A small, wooden footbridge spanned the twenty-foot-wide stream that was dry much of the year. A taut rope strung between two trees served as a handrail. The main buildings of the plantation and John's cabin were less than a quarter mile apart.

Most of the time, John slept in his cabin rather than the cabin that housed the hired hands. John had slept in the extra room of the crew's cabin until his cabin was completed. He enjoyed coming to his own house and property late, after supper and some few minutes with Rachel. Some nights, he just told her goodbye and then went to his bed, worn out from a day's work. His one-room abode was sparsely furnished with a cot, a table, two chairs, a rocker, and a small rug in front of the fireplace. No pictures or window coverings graced the new cabin. John had managed to obtain glass windows inside wooden shutters, which kept out the worst of the cold and wet weather.

He invited Rachel over to see his handiwork soon after its completion. Upon entering, she exclaimed, "Oh John, how cozy and neat. Now all you need is a woman's touch."

"I agree fully, Rachel, and that is my next project."

"And when might that be, my love?"

"Patience," he whispered.

CHAPTER 44 ❧

A LONG, LONG TRIP

BY THE FALL of 1618, Rachel had worked for Sergeant Sharpe well over a year. One day, Mrs. Bohune unexpectedly paid her a visit. The two ladies were happy to see each other. Rachel had invited her former mistress, on one of her visits to Jamestown, to cross the river and see her. Her former mistress had promised that she would surprise her some day. Surprise Rachel she did. Rachel offered her a biscuit and tea in the sergeant's best dishes.

When seated and while still breathless, Rachel exclaimed, "Mistress Bohune, you have really surprised me. I have missed you so much and longed to have someone like you to talk with. Remember how we used to talk way into the nights before the nice doctor and you married?"

"Yes, child," the woman said affectionately. "Well, I must tell you that I, too, have missed the daughter I never had."

"How are you and the fine doctor?"

"We are fine, but I want to take a short trip back to London, and I wondered if you might like to accompany me."

"When would you be leaving, and for how long? I don't have the money for such a trip, and I was saving what I have for the day when John and I might be married."

"Yes, I know, dear, and it would cost you nothing but just your company to me."

"Well, I would have to ask the sergeant if I could have the time off, and if my job would be here when I return."

"If not, you could always have a job with me again."

"Thanks, but I like working close to John, and the men all treat me with respect."

"Talk it over with your employer and with John. I'm sure he would not like to be away from you for very long. We would be gone about five months, until the end of this year or early next."

"I will think it over and talk to both men; then I will write you and let you know. How soon were you planning to leave?"

"By the end of this month, depending on when the next ship sails."

Both ladies spent the next hour visiting. Then, rising from her chair, Mrs. Bohune signaled the two men who had brought her over. Promising to write, Rachel walked her former mistress down to the boat dock and waved her off. She waved until the boat was well out of earshot.

Walking back slowly up the path, she wondered how the sergeant and John would react to her potential trip to London. She was filled with excitement and apprehension.

It had been almost ten years since she had been in London. She would have to let her brother know. What would he think? Most of all, she was concerned about leaving John for the five months or more the trip would take.

Sergeant Sharpe was surprised at her request to be gone for half a year, and John, as she expected, was at a loss for words. His silence made her apprehensive, but finally he spoke.

"If this is something you want to do, I am for it. But you know I will miss you and count the days until you are back with me."

"John, it is not my job here that concerns me. It is the thought of leaving you that hurts. I, too, will count the days, and will be back within about five months. Going over and returning will take four months. Mrs. Bohune thinks she will have her business finished within a month."

"Will you be visiting your family, or staying with Mrs. Bohune?"

"I will be accompanying her and assisting in whatever ways I can. Since she is paying all expenses, I feel I must repay her by helping in whatever ways she wishes. I will try to see my family briefly. My parents are both elderly."

"How soon will you be leaving?"

"Before the end of this month. Two ships are sailing after Christmas."

"That means you will probably return after the crops are in and the work eases up."

"Yes, then you and I can spend some time together."

"Yes, we will. I am planning to add a couple of rooms to my cabin while you are away. Perhaps we can begin to make definite plans for a marriage, if you are still interested."

"You know the answer to that, John Thomas."

Sergeant Sharpe told Rachel her job would be waiting for her and to enjoy herself. The balance of the month of December passed too quickly for John as he thought about Rachel's trip.

Christmas celebrations were not quite as joyous as in past years. The day came too quickly for Rachel to leave. John accompanied her to Jamestown where Mrs. Bohune and her husband were waiting to board the *Elizabeth*.

Doctor Bohune and John accompanied the ladies to their cabin, and then stayed aboard until the ship's cannon boomed a farewell. As the ship pulled away from the dock, John and the doctor waved goodbye to their women standing at the rail. John prayed silently for Rachel's safe journey.

PART FIVE

CHAPTER 45 ❧

UNDER NEW
MANAGEMENT

IN NOVEMBER, PRIOR to Rachel's trip, the colony's governor, Sir Samuel Argall, was summoned to London by the Virginia Company to explain his poor leadership of the colony. Some of the board of directors of the Virginia Company believed the real problems with the colony were due to mismanagement by the president of the board. Sir Thomas Smith, and his team, was the king's favorite to control the Virginia Company's venture. However, he had not produced the desired wealth from the enterprise. A power struggle ensued within the board of directors, and a new team headed by Sir Edwin Sandys was elected.

This new team was against the harsh code of the previous administration and began to make more liberal changes to the company's charter. Sir George Yeardley arrived in April of 1619 as the new governor. Then, in July, a very novel change took place in managing the colony.

The first assembly in the colony representing the Virginia planters was authorized and elected. Twenty-two burgesses were chosen, two from each of the eleven plantations. They were installed in Jamestown in July and held sessions in the church.

The House of Burgesses, as it was named, met with the governor and his council and acted in a law-making capacity. Its laws were enforced unless overruled by the Virginia Company in London.

John Rolfe's new plantation across the James, next to Sergeant Sharpe's, furnished two representatives to the House of Burgesses—himself and Sharpe.

Rachel had returned shortly before the burgesses had their first session in the summer in Jamestown. She was brim-full of things to share with John, and could barely wait. He met her ship as it docked at Jamestown. A long glass had kept him informed when the ship was about to arrive.

They decided to stay overnight in Jamestown at the town's tavern. Mrs. Bohune had to wait an extra day for her husband to arrive to accompany her up to Henrico, so Rachel asked John to stay until the doctor arrived. The tavern had several small bedrooms for people in transit.

As soon as they had secured overnight arrangements, with John in a separate room and Rachel staying with Mrs. Bohune, John suggested he and Rachel walk about the island and visit some of the familiar places.

Rachel was delighted. She was glad to be back on land and able to walk on solid ground. They walked along the river path, past the cemetery, and past Rolfe's first tobacco field, to the small land bridge connecting the island to the mainland. A blockhouse nearby offered some shade from the heat on its leeward side. They found a bench and sat down.

"Tell me about your voyage and London after all these years."

"It was nice sailing, but cold. We encountered no storms at sea, for which I was glad. I stayed with Mrs. Bohune all the time I was there. She went with me to see my parents. My father had died, and Mother was being cared for by my sister-in-law."

"I'm sorry to hear about your father. Was James's wife caring for your mother?"

"Yes, and he is going to send for her as soon as he can. When he does, Mother will be taken care of by her grandson."

"How did you feel being back in London? Did you wish you could live there again?"

"No, John. I missed you and could barely wait to return."

"Did Mrs. Bohune get her business done?"

"Yes, and she felt the same as I. She is happy with her marriage to the doctor and was anxious to come home."

"Needless to say, I missed you a great deal. I missed our evening walks, and just being able to see you each morning before beginning my day's work."

"I missed you too. How are your crops doing, and your work as foreman?"

"The tobacco crops are doing fine, and Sergeant Sharpe is happy with my work with his men. He is hiring two black men from the Spanish plantations in the South Seas. He will receive them next month. One of the Dutch traders paid for their freedom. The sergeant will pay him for that. These men will be indentured like the other men we have."

"Have you had any trouble selling your tobacco crop?"

"No, I market mine each year along with the sergeant's and Rolfe's."

"Can you get more land?"

"I heard that the company is going to give one hundred acres to any planter who came here before 1616. I am going to request that later this year. The Virginia Company wants us planters to produce as much tobacco as we can. The big problem we have in doing that is lack of farm labor. If I can pay the fare for a settler coming over, I can also get fifty acres per settler. I am planning to put some of my earnings into doing that."

"How many do you think you can finance?"

"Three or four at first. They will then owe me a couple of years' wages for their fare, plus giving them room and board. After that, they can begin to earn their own wages."

"Is this why it is taking you the extra years before we can be married?"

"Yes. However, I believe I may be able to shorten that time. I hate to have to wait, but perhaps we can set a date for our wedding in a couple of years. Can you give me that much more time, Rachel?"

"If I can stay and work by your side and have you close by to be with, I can wait. Mrs. Bohune keeps asking when we are going to get married. I explain the reasons, and she thinks you are very thoughtful to want to have enough to give us a good start in our marriage."

John had his arm about Rachel and gave her a big hug. Due to other settlers walking past, he refrained from kissing her. They stood, stretched, and began to walk toward the fort. John was surprised at the number of Indians walking about, almost as if they lived on the island. He made a mental note to ask the sergeant, or some of the residents of James City, if this was routine or due to a special peace treaty with the Indians. On their plantation across the James, they seldom had an Indian visitor.

Over the next two planting seasons, John's small plantation grew to three hundred acres. The profit from his increased plantings enabled him to sponsor three settlers. He received fifty acres of land for each of these, plus the one hundred acres for arriving before 1616.

His original plot of fifty acres gave him enough room to build several curing barns and enlarge his log home. His plantation, about half the size of Sergeant Sharpe's, ran east and south along the creek that ran between planters.

Rolfe's second plantation was west of the sergeant's and was five hundred acres in size. John noticed the effects of the more liberal policies of Sir Edwin Sandys' new administration of the Virginia Company.

More women were sent over to become wives for the planters. More young children also were sent by the Virginia Company in London to provide apprenticeships for the increasing number of trades being practiced in the colony. Tobacco production of the superior brand Rolfe had introduced increased each year.

Since tobacco planting and production was prohibited in England, the colony had a virtual monopoly. A small tax was paid to the Crown for this privilege. Tobacco had become the chief export and currency for the plantations.

The planters, through their House of Burgesses, were beginning to plant the idea among the colonists of a self-representative government, not too different than England's Parliament. The big difference was this: It was all made possible through a charter granted by King James. If the king dissolved the charter establishing the Virginia Company, what would happen to this local authority?

"What the Lord giveth, the Lord can take away," thought John.

However, John was not much concerned about the king's authority. John was just a planter slowly working toward the day he would have enough resources to take a wife, raise a family, and enjoy his status as a country gentleman, if not one of England's landed gentry.

He had to pinch himself at times to see that it was not all one big dream. By hard work and the grace of God, this goal, this dream of his, was slowly being realized. Even these native

Americans, the Indians, appeared content to see the colony prosper and expand. They offered more land for development than the colony could quickly use. John had never seen such an apparent good will between the colonists and the Indians. The father of Pocahontas had died, and his brother, Opechancanough, had become chief of the Powhatans.

He appeared to want to continue the peaceful relations his father had finally decided to follow with the colony. All these things were on John's mind as he wrapped up his harvesting season in the fall of 1621.

CHAPTER 46 ❧

MARRIAGE PLANS

AFTER THE HARVESTING of this year's crop of tobacco and sale of the previous year's crop, John's work schedule slowed to a crawl. It took almost a year to cure the previous year's crop and prepare it for shipment to the London markets.

By the end of his second year of planting, John was receiving profits from his plantation. Now into his sixth year as a planter, he had accumulated enough to make plans for his marriage, following the planting season next spring.

John would be thirty years old and Rachel twenty-nine. He had been seventeen when he signed his indenture contract, and Rachel had been sixteen when she began her trip. Quite young, he had thought when they first met, to be making the trip alone. Still, her brother had invited her. However, when she had become the maidservant to Mistress Horton, John had felt relieved that Rachel would be well looked after by such a mature and dignified woman.

He asked himself, "Why was I worried about her well-being and safety, even back then? Was I beginning to fall in love with her and didn't recognize it?"

Now he knew his heart and wanted nothing more than to settle down with Rachel and raise a family in this wild and untamed land. They needed to finish making their plans, set the date, and finish expanding his log house by three more rooms.

The logs for the additions had been cut and were stacked nearby, waiting for John and the hired men to notch and assemble into walls and roof. The work could easily be done in a couple of months, prior to the planting season.

Rachel had written Mrs. Bohune for advice on her wedding dress. John had consulted Reverend Bucke, chaplain of Jamestown, to perform the wedding. The reverend had agreed. Chaplain Bucke had married four years earlier and now had a couple of children.

Now that Christmas was fast approaching, John would accompany Rachel up to Henrico to see Mrs. Bohune. He would use the occasion to consult with John Rolfe on the latest in tobacco curing and his Indian boys' school.

John and Rachel boarded the small pinnace that made regular voyages up and down the James, stopping at each of the eleven main towns and plantations. Supplies, mail, and passengers kept the boats filled. Business and trade within the colony were beginning to grow.

The vessel could carry forty passengers, a crew of three, and cargo of about thirty tons. A small cannon provided protection, if needed, from occasional bands of Indians that might try to board the ship. John and Rachel sat on a hatch cover in the bow of the ship, enjoying the morning sun.

The trip to Henrico was uneventful. The weather was pleasantly warm for the middle of December. The birch trees on the riverbanks had shed most of their leaves. White, fluffy clouds floated overhead, as if accompanying the ship.

"What a beautiful day," said Rachel. "I hope our weather stays this way until Christmas is past and the New Year comes."

"Me too," responded John. "My hired men are at work on the rooms of our new home."

"When will it be finished?"

"In about two months or sooner."

"John, I can barely wait until next May and our wedding. Can you?"

"Well, we have waited this long, and four more months will pass quickly. We both have a lot to do. I have to get the house finished and the crops planted."

"It will help if we stay busy."

They continued to discuss their wedding plans as the ship meandered up the James, making only one stop before dusk set in. They stopped at a small fort, built for overnight safety. They would finish the run to Henrico and the surrounding plantations by afternoon the next day.

In two days, with their visit over, they returned to Sharpe's plantation and begin to plan for end-of-the-year festivities. Rachel and Dove prepared extra pies of mincemeat and apple. They made candies from recipes Rachel had brought back from her trip to London. The Christmas meal would have a table graced with roasted wild turkey, venison, and roast pork from hogs previously purchased by the sergeant. A small orchard of fruit trees provided enough apples for special occasions.

Three days before Christmas, a large snowstorm began that lasted two days. All work on John's room additions was halted. The hired men of both plantations were given rest and went to Jamestown. Some of the men needed warm clothing for the winter. John and the sergeant had accounts with the general store that allowed the men to charge up to two pounds per year for personal needs.

Secretly, the men had decided to buy Rachel and Dove a present for Christmas Day from their meager charge accounts. They selected the gifts and had the wife of the store-owner wrap them to hide their contents.

Christmas Day arrived, and a long table that could seat everyone was spread with candles, mistletoe, and boughs of holly. Platters of pewter were loaded with their respective meat dishes. Cornmeal dressing, pies, and candies completed this bountiful meal.

A special guest had been invited by Sergeant Sharpe to share the day. The sergeant met John Rolfe's boat earlier that day and spent the morning in his curing barns discussing the tobacco market and Rolfe's future plans for his nearby plantation.

The dinner bell rang, and Sergeant Sharpe said, "It's time to eat. Shall we go in?"

"I'm ready. I understand you hired Mrs. Bohune's maid as your chief cook."

"Yes, and I may lose her next spring to John Thomas."

"Oh? For what reason?"

"They are planning to be married."

"Wonderful. I have dinner with the Bohunes occasionally, and they hated to lose her."

They entered the large dining room filled with tantalizing odors of food and burning pine logs from a huge fireplace. After all were seated, including Rachel and Dove, the sergeant asked John Rolfe to offer the Christmas blessing.

He prayed, "Our Father and God, we are grateful for another year of Your blessings and protection upon this colony and our plantations. We believe we are all under Your providential care and are grateful. We pray that as this year closes, and the New Year begins, You will guide us in all our decisions. Bless Sergeant Sharpe and his plantation, and John Thomas's plantation. Help me to accomplish my mission among the Indian boys to bring them the gospel of our Lord Jesus Christ. And, finally, may God save the king. Amen."

They all said, "Amen," and then the food was passed, plates were filled, and the buzz of conversation filled the room, until Joseph, one of the sergeant's men, stood and asked for a moment to say something.

Reaching under the table, he brought out two packages and gave one to Rachel, seated next to John, and one to Dove, on the sergeant's left. All stopped eating and watched both unwrap their gifts. Rachel's wool blanket was red, and Dove's was blue. Then Joseph said, "We men wanted to show our appreciation for all the fine cooking, clothes washing, and cleaning you two do for us. You are the best."

All applauded, and both ladies smiled their thanks.

"Thank you," Dove said.

"I, too, thank you," Rachel then added. "You men work hard, and your smiles as you eat our food tell us how much you do appreciate us. Thanks again from both of us."

Another snowstorm blew in from the northwest on New Year's Day and blanketed the countryside. Work on John's cabin additions was halted for several days, during which he decided to write another letter to his parents. John had tried to write at least once or twice a year since arriving in Jamestown. However, it took so long for a letter to reach his parents and a response to arrive back, that he never bothered to ask questions. He just tried to keep his parents informed on what had happened since his last correspondence. Sitting at his kitchen table by candlelight, he wrote:

Dear Mother and Father,   5 January, 1622

It has been snowing here for the last week, and the most I can do is keep a fire going in our curing barns. Wood is plentiful, so that is no problem. My men and I have been busy up until now expanding my cabin. I am adding three more rooms, so it will be large enough for my wife and me. I am planning to be married in May, after spring planting season, to Miss Rachel Jones. She has a brother here, and they are both from London. Rachel and I plan to be married in Jamestown Chapel by Chaplain Bucke. I wish you both could be here, and I trust you both are well.

From your loving son,
John

John folded the letter, sealed it with wax, addressed it, and placed it in a leather packet. The packet already had his parents' name and address burned in black letters on the outside. It would go from Jamestown by ship to Plymouth, then stagecoach to towns and villages in that section of Wales. John would be fortunate to get a reply by his wedding date.

It quit snowing the next day. This allowed John and his three hired men to resume work on the cabin. One of his men had some experience in building and carpentry. By the first week in February, they had finished two bedrooms and were working on a large dining room. When completed, it would be a cabin of five rooms: two bedrooms, a living room, a dining room, and a small kitchen.

Rachel was pleased with the size of John's new home. She could barely wait to become its new mistress. She had promised the sergeant she would continue to work for him until he could find a suitable replacement.

Sharpe had hired two more men, bringing his total to ten. Thus, he needed extra help for his Dovie. He had been consulting with Rolfe regarding the best way to petition the governor to allow him to marry his Indian lady.

Even though the colony was under more liberal management, and more social intercourse was taking place between the settlers and the natives, marriage between the two races was deemed risky, and perhaps not in the best interests of the Virginia Company, nor the Native Americans. In addition, the company had been pursuing a policy of enticing more women to come to the colony and become wives for the planters and other tradesmen. This made it more difficult for a waiver to be granted the sergeant.

However, this did not prevent Sharpe from securing letters from Rolfe and other gentlemen requesting a special waiver for himself in view of his membership in the House of Burgesses and the fact that John Rolfe's example with Pocahontas had helped the colony. Sharpe secured his letters of reference and submitted his petition for a waiver from the company policy. He was promised an answer within a couple of months. This was enough encouragement for him and Dove to begin discussions with Chaplain Bucke regarding a marriage.

The chaplain had been one of those who had furnished a letter of reference favorable to the sergeant's request. In the meantime, Dove's younger sister, Morning Swan, had come to work with her sister at Sharpe's plantation.

This allowed Rachel to take time off and begin the preparations for her own wedding. Mrs. Bohune had promised her assistance and advice when it came time to prepare her wedding dress. While in London, they had visited some of the dress shops for ideas and material.

CHAPTER 47 ❧

SPRING PLANTING

PREPARATIONS FOR SPRING planting of tobacco and other crops began as early as March in years when the winter was mild and there was promise of an early spring. Though winter was officially not over for three more weeks, the weather had been very mild for much of the season.

There had been only two big snows since the first of February. John began his final preparations for planting near the end of that month. Work on the enlargement of his cabin had been completed, and John had hired a more experienced carpenter to build several pieces of furniture for the additional rooms.

His men were anxious to get started doing the final work on the land prior to depositing the seeds into the rich, black soil. John had began farming tobacco with just three acres, then fifteen, twenty-five, and now fifty. Next year, he hoped to clear and plant another fifty acres of his three-hundred-acre plantation.

In less than two weeks, the men had planted all fifty acres of tobacco. He also planted about five acres of corn and added a few more seedlings to his apple orchard. Some of the farmers were even growing grapes for producing wine. John had given that venture more thought. At present, he had enough on his plate.

Rachel planned one more trip up to Henrico, where Mrs. Bohune, with her tailor, was making Rachel's wedding dress. It would be a gift from her former mistress. Rachel was overjoyed, knowing that within less than two months she would be Mrs. John Thomas.

Doctor Bohune and his wife would be guests of honor at the wedding in Jamestown. Rachel's brother, James, would be giving her away at the wedding. And, of course, Chaplain Bucke already had agreed to officiate.

On March 19, Rachel kissed John goodbye and boarded the river pinnace for Henrico. She planned to return in four or five days. Mrs. Bohune had asked Rachel on a previous visit to plan to stay a day or two longer with her on this visit.

John stood at the loading dock and waved until the vessel had rounded a bend. Their last few minutes together at the river's edge had left them both quite speechless. Rachel, usually never at a loss for words, just smiled and held onto John as if she didn't want to let him go.

He recalled their final conversation. "I wish you were going with me," Rachel had said. "I hate to travel alone even though I know it is safe."

"It is safe," said John, trying to reassure her. "I need to press on in the clearing of the other fifty acres if I hope to have one hundred acres in production by next year."

"I know. It is selfish of me to take you away from your work, and the sergeant still needs your supervision of his men, since he has more planting to get done."

"You are right. I keep forgetting I have two jobs to hold down. Perhaps, when I get more tobacco in production, I can give up my job with Sergeant Sharpe."

"That would give you more time for your own work, plus more time we could be together."

"Maybe in another two years I can do that, dearest."

As the small ship approached, Rachel clung even tighter to John's waist. He sensed a nervousness and anxiety in her that he had never seen before. It tugged at his heart and almost made him wish he had taken the days off and gone with her.

Finally, she was aboard with her bag, and the boat clanged its warning bell. He prayed she would be safe and come back quickly to him. It seemed the closer to their wedding date, the more nervous Rachel became.

CHAPTER 48 ❧

A STAB IN THE BACK

DOVE, SERGEANT SHARPE'S Indian maid, came from a tribe on the southern side of the James, not far up a tributary. They were one of the tribes of the Powhatan Confederacy. The peaceful relations with the Indians, largely through the marriage of Pocahontas to John Rolfe, were weakened somewhat by her death and the death of her father. Opechancanough, her uncle, appeared to want that peace to continue. There had been occasional killings by the Indians and retributive killings by the colonial authorities almost from the beginning of the colony, but for the most part, it had never turned into open warfare.

To most of the colonists, it seemed that peaceful relations were fairly solid with the Indians. The Indians and the settlers comingled in the towns and on the plantations quite freely.

Dove's sister, and occasionally her brother, could be seen in the Sharpe house or at the curing barns seeking work from the sergeant or John Thomas. Sometimes they would spend the night at the plantation before returning to their tribe a few miles away.

Three days after Rachel left, Dove's brother, Pohotunuk, arrived at the Sharpe plantation to go to work the next morning, the first day of spring. Rising at daybreak, Dove was in the kitchen preparing the breakfast meal when Pohotunuk motioned for her to come to the door. He whispered in her ear, then turned and ran in the direction of his village. The sergeant noted this and said to Dove, "Isn't your brother going to stay and work today?"

Visibly shaken, Dove answered, "My brother has brought bad news. He said the Indians have planned to attack all the settlers and plantations today. It will be this morning. He risked his life to warn me. He didn't want to be found here."

Speechless, Sharpe walked quickly to the dangling rope of the dinner bell and pulled it quickly and continuously for a minute. Within a short time, the hired men came running, sensing an emergency. By now, the sergeant, with his own musket in hand, told the men to arm themselves. He sent one of his men to warn John Thomas and his crew. Another, he dispatched across the river to warn the Jamestown settlement.

When John heard the bell ringing continuously, he barely had his clothes on. He ran to the crew's house and roused his men. They quickly dressed and followed him into his house with weapons drawn. Together, they ran quickly to the Sharpe plantation and found the sergeant with his men.

The sergeant told of the impending attack on the plantations.

"Where do you think they will attack?" asked John.

"I believe we can hold off a raiding party from my place when they come."

"Any idea when that might be?"

"No, I don't. Dove's brother said sometime this morning. I sent one of my men to warn Jamestown."

John felt a sinking feeling in his gut. What would happen to Rachel? Would Henrico get any warning? If not, he didn't want to contemplate the consequences. Everything seemed to be peaceful with the Powhatans. Why this? Why now?

"John," said the sergeant, "we've got to be ready for them. I believe you and your men can save the barns, and my men and I will protect the house. By firing from both places, we can hit them in our crossfire and make it more difficult for them to attack either place with any chance of success."

"I agree. I will station one of my men as high up in the barns as possible so as to get a good view. Whoever sees them first should fire a warning shot."

"I agree."

John and his men left for the two curing barns. John didn't wish to think of what would have happened if there had been no warning. It reminded him of the words of Jesus he had memorized as a child: "But know this, that if the Goodman of the house had known in what watch the thief would come, he would have watched, and would not have suffered his house to be broken up" (Matthew 24:43).

It appeared obvious to John that the colony had been lulled to sleep by the Indians. Chief Opechancanough must have been planning this for some time and just outsmarted the governor and the House of Burgesses.

No one had even mentioned the possibility of such a thing happening. Didn't the chief of the Powhatans know that even with the element of surprise this attack could not succeed in driving out the settlers?

He wondered how many innocent men, women, boys, and girls would be slaughtered. This was his last thought before a shot rang out in the direction of the sergeant's house.

He looked out the partly open barn door and saw a red man go down. This was it!

Overhead, one of John's men yelled and fired his piece at several attackers coming from the west side of the barns. Soon the firing got heavier from the house and inside the barn. The men were hitting their marks.

The fight was soon over when the Indians realized their game of surprise was up. They began to melt back into the forest beyond the planting fields. It was probably over for now. But for some time no one from the house or barns ventured out to test their attackers.

When the sergeant's man returned from Jamestown two days later, he said the warning was in time for Jamestown and most, if not all, the plantations and settlements downriver.

However, he had no reassurance about those upriver, such as Henrico and its surrounding plantations. John had that same sinking feeling in his gut.

"What is the governor doing about all this? Is he sending out a relief force to find out how bad it might be upriver?" he asked.

"I believe he is, but it may take several days to find out."

John knew it would take time, at least a day or two for a ship to sail down from Henrico. All he could do now was wait and pray. He had been doing that since their fight two days ago. His house had escaped damage, as had his barns.

Sharpe's plantation was now like a small fort. Guards were stationed night and day at the perimeters of the buildings. No one slept soundly. All were ready with weapons to defend one another.

Dove and her sister were at a loss for words about the attack. Of course, had it not been for her love and loyalty to Sergeant Sharpe, all of them might have lost their lives. Whether she and her sister could return to their village was questionable.

Sergeant Sharpe appeared no different in his feelings for her, or her young sister. He did wonder now if his request for a waiver to marry her would be turned down. If so, he would have to face that with Dovie when the time came.

Three days after the vicious attack, John still had no word about the fate of Rachel or Henrico. He tried to comfort himself with the old saying "No news is good news." However, he could not shake the feeling that things were not good upriver.

Finally, on the fifth day, news of the fate of those upriver from Jamestown began to trickle in. It appeared that Henrico had been all but destroyed. John made a trip across the river and soaked up every bit of word or rumor by any survivor.

The governor announced that an armed force of soldiers would be dispatched the next day to the areas of worst carnage. John asked if he could volunteer. Other groups of volunteers were being assembled to go to other areas to seek friends and relatives, and no doubt to take swift retaliation against the Indians for their cowardly acts.

John's group left the following morning. They reached what was left of Henrico around noon the following day. No Indians were encountered. Fires from burning cabins were still smoldering one week after the attacks. Hacked and mutilated bodies were everywhere.

Rolfe's plantation and barns were in ashes. The Bohunes' home, like all the stores and houses, had been burnt to the ground. No sign of life was visible.

The sight made John sick. He fell to his knees, and with tears streaming down his cheeks, he cried out, "Oh God, why, why?"

A burial detail set to work and a mass grave was dug. Most of the bodies had been decapitated, dismembered, and slaughtered beyond description.

John thought, "Such anger and hate must have seethed in the minds of these savages to have done these horrible things." At one point, he gagged and vomited. He looked in vain for any sign that he might connect with Rachel. It was as if she had vanished off the face of the earth. "They may have burned up in the house," he thought.

He didn't know what he would do if he found something of hers. Perhaps this was God's way of helping to ease the sorrow of her death. Perhaps her death was better than capture and becoming a slave, tortured by an unfeeling captor.

John worked with the other men until their captain said they must leave and search other plantation sites. Unashamedly, with tears streaming down his face, his hands black with soot and ashes, he turned his back on the remains of a once-growing village. He and Rachel had spent many precious and happy moments here. His lassie, his beautiful one, whom he had come to love as none other, was now gone.

Pangs of remorse, guilt, and regret swept over him as he cried silently. "If only I had married Rachel, instead of waiting first to build my plantation. She might be alive today. All I have now is land and Virginia Gold."

At that moment he heard an inner voice whisper, "What if a man should gain the whole world and lose his soul?" John recognized these as Jesus' words. He had heard them more than once from his old rector back home in Wales. With Rachel gone, lost forever, he felt like he had just lost his soul. Would this hole in his heart ever be filled?

CHAPTER 49 ∾

BROKEN DREAMS

A WEEK LATER, John was back in his cabin, sitting at his kitchen table, writing a letter to his mother in Wales. His rescue party of soldiers had found no survivors, only more burned-up plantations and more decapitated bodies that were quickly buried. A careful count of bodies and identifications were made at each grisly site.

They had killed a few wandering Indians and sunk several canoes after slaying the red men who tried to paddle out of range of the soldiers' muskets. When they reached Jamestown and reported their findings to the governor, the known dead were tallied at over three hundred, with some plantations and farms not yet included.

Each night of the trip, aboard the pinnace, John's sleep was fitful and troubled. He dreamed of Rachel and their last conversation while waiting for the boat to take her upriver. He awoke with his face wet from tears, crying in his dream. The dreams fed his guilt, which seemed to grow a little each day. His self-blame made him sick and depressed. He barely ate enough to keep going. "Maybe writing Mother and telling her how I feel would bring some relief," he said to himself.

After laying down the quill pen, another thought came to him. "I will go see Chaplain Bucke and share my guilt at the loss of Rachel with him. Perhaps that will bring some relief. I can't go on like this."

Picking up the pen again, he quickly wrote his mother, telling her about the massacre and the loss of Rachel. After finishing the letter and placing it in the leather address packet, he decided to take their small skiff and row over the James to see Chaplain Bucke. He would mail his letter while there.

Chaplain Bucke had just finished his noon meal with his wife and two small children when John knocked at his cabin. He invited John in and said he could see him.

After both were seated, John said, "Chaplain Bucke, I have a terrible burden I am carrying that is weighing me down. My fiancé, Rachel, whom you met, went to Henrico to visit Mrs. Bohune, and she was there when the awful attacks took place. She was killed, and I feel I am mostly to blame because I kept delaying the wedding until I finished some work on my plantation." John continued with tears streaming down his face. "If I had not put my plantation first, Rachel more than likely would be alive today, and I would not be here talking to you."

"I see," said Chaplain Bucke. "You are blaming yourself for her death."

"Yes, and it is tearing me up inside."

"I take it that Rachel was in agreement with your need to get the plantation out of the way first. Is that correct?"

"Yes. She was patient with me and wanted me to be happy and ready for the marriage."

"John, I understand your guilt, and God knows of your pain and regrets. But you are not responsible for the terrible and sin-filled hate that caused those Powhatans to murder the innocent, including your Rachel. God will punish them for their crimes."

"I understand that, Chaplain Bucke, but that doesn't excuse my selfishness for putting a material possession ahead of Rachel and our marriage."

"Right, John. But one thing we learn as we mature and grow in our relationship with God is that we, too, must accept the responsibility and the consequences for our choices in life. Even for those that bring us pain and suffering."

"But how do you stop hating and blaming yourself when you have made a stupid choice that caused another's death, the death of the one you loved so much?"

"First, you ask God to forgive you. Then you forgive yourself, and finally, you begin again to live each day and not look back on your past sins and poor choices. You live each day asking for God's grace to make the best decisions and avoid poor choices that might hurt others. Finally, John, one more bit of advice. If you could turn over the care of your plantation to Sergeant Sharpe for a few months and take a long trip, maybe back home, I believe that would help somewhat."

John was quiet for a moment, letting the chaplain's words sink in. "What good would it do to go home?" he thought.

"I thank you, Chaplain Bucke, for your advice and the help you have given me. I will keep in touch and let you know how I am doing from time to time."

"Let's pray, John. Father, help my friend John to reach up to You and forgive himself. You will forgive him when he asks. Help him to see a bit further down the road of this life and know that You will help him as he puts Your truth and values and others before self. Amen."

"Amen," John echoed.

CHAPTER 50 ❧

GOING HOME

ALL THE WAY back across the James, as he rowed, John remembered the chaplain's counsel and prayed not only a prayer asking God's forgiveness, but one to the spirit of Rachel, asking her to forgive him. Then, he said, "Lord, I will forgive myself. Help me to do this each time I slip into the past and relive my yesterdays."

When he reached the south shore, he looked up Sergeant Sharpe and told him of his talk with Chaplain Bucke. When he mentioned the chaplain's advice regarding taking a trip, and the possibility of Sergeant Sharpe managing his plantation for awhile, the sergeant was quiet for a moment.

"John, you have been like a son to me," he then said. "I have watched you grow, and I know how much you wanted to fulfill your and Rachel's dreams. It has hurt me almost as much as you to hear of Rachel's death. She was a wonderful lassie and friend. So yes, I will be happy to look after your plantation until you get back. Then, maybe I can take a little trip and you can return the favor. How does that sound?"

"It sounds great, William," he returned, using the sergeant's first name for the first time. "I think I will go back home to Wales and see my family. I should be back within six months or less. I will try to return in time for the fall harvest."

Ten days later, John was aboard the *Sea Venture* headed for England. He thought it ironic that this was the same name of the ship on which he had originally sailed in 1609. Its remains were at the bottom of the sea at the eastern end of Devil's Islands, now renamed Somers Islands, after Sir George Somers.

This new *Sea Venture* had other passengers returning to England following the Indian uprising. They were fleeing from the chaos and effects of the massacre. The voyage took a little over six weeks.

The ship docked at Plymouth before proceeding on to London. John felt strange to be setting foot on his native soil for the first time in thirteen years. Several others disembarked with John, and one gentleman said he was catching a coach to a town in Wales, close to Carmarthen. John arranged fare, and was soon traveling along for the two-day journey. What would it be like to see his mother and father? And what had happened to Dorothy? His mother had never mentioned her. She was probably married and with family by now, he thought.

Though John now had some wealth, some land, and could be called a gentleman farmer, his dream of returning with enough wealth to become a landed gentleman was not possible. That memory was barely a passing thought as the coach rolled into his home village.

His parents' home was a quaint little cottage at the end of a lane on the edge of the village. As he walked along, carrying his bags, he tried to resurrect his memories of his hometown: the location of the old church, the lane where Dorothy had lived. Within a few minutes, John stood in front of his parents' small house and was rapping on the door. John barely recognized the gray-haired, wrinkled woman who opened the door to him.

"John, son," she sobbed. "Is it really you?"

Standing behind her, stooped, gray-headed, and showing his age of fifty-two, smiled his father. He was missing several teeth, as was John's mother. He gathered both in his arms and began to cry with joy.

"Yes, it's me. I am so happy to see you." They held each other for a few moments, drinking in the sight and touch of one another.

"We just received your letter yesterday, saying you were coming. We didn't know when that might happen. We were saddened to hear of Rachel's death. It must have hurt you deeply."

"Yes, Mother. I could barely stand the pain when I went to the town where she had gone and discovered no sign or trace of her. We believe she must have been killed and burned up in the house where she was visiting."

"What are you going to do now, son?" asked his father.

"I am not sure. I have a tobacco plantation of three hundred acres and a house and some savings, so I will probably return and build on that. Are you still working for Mr. Wooley?"

"No, John. His son returned, as you know. Shortly after that, the elder Mr. Wooley died, and William took over the business and made some changes."

"Where are you working now?"

"I'm not. Work is still as scarce as when you left. But I help the new vicar keep up the church work, and that gives your mother and me enough to buy food, if we are careful."

Now John realized all over again why he had felt so compelled to seek a future in another land. He wished his parents might go back with him where he could take care of them in their waning years of life.

"Aren't you going to ask about Dorothy?" his mother suddenly asked.

"Yes. I suppose she is married and has a family."

"Yes and no. She did marry a couple of years after you left, but her husband left for some far-off place and hasn't been heard from in over ten years."

"How big a family does she have?"

"One youngster, a boy. They moved in with her parents, and they have tried to survive as one family. She works some at the local pub as a cook, but that barely pays enough to buy food." Noting a new light in John's eyes, she added, "Wouldn't you like to see her?"

"Yes, I think I would. I will visit the pub tomorrow."

John's mother smiled and led the way to the kitchen, where a meal was under preparation. John hadn't felt this hungry for some time.

CHAPTER 51 ❧

DOROTHY

JOHN HADN'T SLEPT this soundly in several months. He awoke in his old bed in a small, barren room at the rear of his parents' cottage. Coming back home again had given him time to deal somewhat with the tragedy of Rachel's loss.

He was aware that one may never go back, for the direction of life is ever forward. Saying a quick prayer of thankfulness for the new day, he arose, dressed, and had something to eat with his mother. His father had left for the rectory.

"Mother, when is the pub open for business?"

"They serve breakfast for overnight guests and a few old men who never learned to cook."

"Do you think Dorothy is their morning cook?"

"I'm not sure. Why don't you go see."

"I think I will, though she may not want to see me."

"Son, you at least were honest with her. A woman admires that in a man."

"I didn't quickly break off the vow I made with her. It took me over a year."

"Well, son, just go see her, and maybe you can both move on with your lives."

John made his way to the pub and entered its dark interior. Three men were gathered around a table, finishing their breakfast. The bartender was talking to a customer sitting on a stool at the end of an oak counter. He looked up and moved toward John, who took a stool near the customer.

"What will you have, friend?"

John didn't remember this pub owner. It had been years since he had been inside the pub.

"I'm looking for a friend of mine who works for you. Her name is Dorothy."

"Yeah, she works here, but she is not here today. She only works a few mornings a week."

"Oh! Well, thank you."

"And who might you be, stranger?"

"I'm John Thomas. I'm William Thomas's son."

"You are Bill Thomas's son? I know your father, but I didn't know he had a son."

"I have been in the colony of Virginia. I left here thirteen years ago as a lad."

"Well, well. What brings you back home?"

"Just wanted to come home again and see my folks."

"What's going on over there?"

"We had an Indian uprising. A lot of settlers killed. My lassie was one of them."

The bartender expressed his sorrow, which John acknowledged as he got up to leave. As he left, he remembered where Dorothy had lived, but didn't know if her folks still lived there. He walked to the village church and found his father cleaning the building. The rector, John remembered, had died, and a young pastor had taken his place. He was nowhere to be seen.

John asked his father if Dorothy's parents still lived in the same place.

"Yes, John, the same place you used to visit quite often, as I recall. Was she at the pub?"

"No. I'm going to walk over and see if she is at home."

"I think that would be nice of you. After all, she might have been your wife back then."

"Yes, I know. I just want to see her again, and see how she has survived with a missing husband."

"I believe she has taken it all fairly well. When I see her at church, she is friendly with your mother and me."

"I'll be back soon. I may come back and meet your rector if he is here by then."

John headed toward Dorothy's home on the opposite end of the village. He met a few people who spoke but didn't recognize him. He was a stranger in the town where he had grown up. John recognized some of them, but thirteen years, and his beard, shrouded his identity.

The home of Dorothy's parents stood at the end of a shady lane. A rope swing hung from a large limb in the yard. John cleared his throat and knocked on the door. A woman's voice rang out.

"Who is it?"

"John Thomas."

Dorothy slowly opened the door. She was barefoot, not fully dressed, and her hair uncombed. Peering up sleepily at his bearded face, she slowly began to smile as she recognized John through his beard and the extra weight added over the years.

She, too, had changed. She was heavier, and appeared shorter than he remembered. "Yes, Dorothy, I'm John."

"John, you have changed. I barely recognized you with your beard."

"We both have changed."

"Yes, I am afraid so. What brings you back home? Your mother told me you were getting married."

"Yes, I was, but Rachel died in an Indian massacre. Our chaplain suggested I take a trip back home to help me get over my loss."

"I know the feeling. My husband, Benjamin, left me ten years ago for a sailing job with the Far East Trading Company, and I haven't heard from him since. Give me a few minutes to get dressed."

When Dorothy finally joined John outside, a bench beneath a shade tree beckoned them, so Dorothy led the way toward it, inviting John to be seated. It was long enough for four people. She sat on one end and turned to face John, smoothing out her hair.

"Do you believe your husband is alive, Dorothy?"

"No. The trading company lost some ships in a typhoon several years ago, so I believe he may have perished at sea."

"Mother told me you have a child."

"Yes, a boy named John. He is twelve now, and he reminds me of you." Seeing his expression, she said softly, "John?"

"Oh," he said, smiling. Changing the subject for now, he continued. "I went to the pub, and they told me you only worked a few mornings per week."

"Yes, it helps to buy food, and my folks provide most other necessities."

Even though Dorothy was now twenty-nine, and a few pounds heavier, she still had a girlish charm about her, the same beauty that had attracted John some thirteen years ago. He felt some of those old emotions again as they began to recall their past.

John spent the better part of the morning in Dorothy's garden, until the hard bench reminded them it was approaching the dinner hour. Her son came out and asked about some food.

Dorothy introduced him to John, who said, "I like your name, young man. A lot of good men are named John. One even wrote part of the Bible."

Noting young John's hunger, he turned to Dorothy and said, "If you are working in the morning, I will come to the pub for breakfast. Perhaps we can see each other later in the day after you are finished with your work."

"I would like that, John. Maybe we could walk to the lake where we used to spend a lot of free time."

"I would love that. I'll sample your cooking in the morning."

As John walked to his parents' home, he wondered if it were possible to replace his love for Rachel with a love for Dorothy, even the lassie he had once cared so deeply about. Then he recalled seeing a beautiful diamond on Mrs. Bohune's finger.

The bright sun had created a myriad of dazzling lights from that single diamond. "Can love be like a diamond with its many points of light?" he mused. "And, if love comes closest to describing who God is in His being, then maybe God can give us a different point of light, or love, for each person who comes into our life."

His love for Rachel could never be erased. It was as unique as she. But God could give him another unique love for Dorothy. She had changed. She was no longer the lassie he once knew. She was now a grown woman, with a child, no doubt a widow. She was different, unique, and beautiful in a different way than Rachel.

If God rekindled that love he once had for Dorothy, it would not be the same. It would be a more mature, settled, knowledgeable, and understanding love. After all, both had suffered deep losses, pain, and hurt. And both of them would be cautious and even somewhat fearful of investing their feelings in a new relationship.

Over the next three weeks, John and Dorothy plumbed the depths of their doubts, fears, and pain. They talked of renewing their feelings for each other. Dorothy did not blame John for the decisions he made with Rachel, and John did not blame Dorothy for getting married and wanting a family. They forgave each other.

Then one evening, John asked Dorothy if she would marry him and take herself and her son back to Virginia with him.

"I would hate to move so far away from my parents, but my brother and sister could take care of them when the time came. Would it be safe for me and John since the Indian uprising?"

"Despite appearances, only a tenth of the residents of the colony perished. I don't think we will ever be caught by surprise as before. So, to answer your question, I believe it would be safe. Our plantations across the river from Jamestown escaped harm."

"John, I never stopped loving you, even after I married. I named John after you to hold on to the memory of you. Have you noticed my son's age? He was born nine months after you left for Jamestown. Benny was not his father. You were. Remember our last day together? I didn't marry Benny until a year after John was born. When I discovered I was going to have a baby, I kept the secret and went to live with my aunt and uncle in Plymouth. That is where I met Benny and got married. Benny was a good husband, but he couldn't get over his love for the sea."

Pausing to catch her breath, she quietly asked, "Do you still want me for your wife?"

John was quiet for a moment, then almost shouted, "Yes, Dorothy, now more than ever. I never dreamed I had a son here. He really is my boy, John Jr. How soon can we get married?"

I will have to file papers of annulment. After ten years, and no word from Benjamin, it is automatically granted."

"How long would that take?"

"Perhaps a week. I would like to be married here."

"I would love that. Our parents could be present. The vicar here could perform the ceremony."

"Oh, I'm beginning to feel like a bride again, your bride, at last."

John just smiled, and gathering Dorothy in his arms, he kissed her almost as passionately as he remembered when leaving for Jamestown. She filed papers of annulment that same day, and they began to prepare for their wedding.

Two weeks later, they were married in the village church, to the cheers and tears of both families and friends. John was nervous on their wedding night. Dorothy's boss gave them his best room for sleeping arrangements until they left for Jamestown.

His knowledge that Dorothy was not a virgin made John apprehensive as to how she would react to his inexperience. She had been his first, and only. After undressing by the light of a candle, Dorothy disrobed completely and lay beside him.

"John, I don't know if you have ever had any woman to sleep with, and I don't care, because now we have each other. I have not been with any other man since my former husband, Ben. Just hold me in your arms and love me as you wish. I am so excited to lie here beside you, my precious husband."

John felt less nervous as he began to kiss and hold Dorothy in his arms. For the next hour or two, they explored each other's bodies as Dorothy guided John to the joys of sexual bliss without guilt or shame. He returned again and again to drink at her well of love as they passionately gave themselves to each other. John didn't realize marital love could be so blissful.

He recalled reading in the Bible the Song of Solomon, where it described this marital bliss in these words:

> Thy lips are like a thread of scarlet, and thy speech is comely; thy temples are like a piece of a pomegranate within thy locks…. Thy two breasts are like two young roes that are twins, which feed among the lilies. Until the day breaks and the shadows flee away, I will get me to the mountain of myrrh, and to the hill of frankincense. Thou art all fair, my love; there is no spot in thee. (Song of Solomon 4:3–6)

One week later, John made plans for passage of his new family back to Jamestown. They would leave from Plymouth on the new *Sea Venture* the first of August.

CHAPTER 52

REBOUNDING

AS THE *SEA Venture* loped along across the swells of the north Atlantic, John felt like a kid again running alongside a cantering horse. He remembered the farm of a landed gentleman where he worked as a stable boy for a few years.

This was where he got his dream of becoming one of the landed gentry, if and when he ever earned enough wealth. This dream had fostered his decision to indenture himself to leave parents, sweetheart, and homeland in search of gold in Jamestown. The "gold" he found was brown, smoke-cured leaves of tobacco, the currency of colonial Virginia.

Gold, like love, came in many different forms, products, and ways. Gold could buy many things, but it could not buy love of the genuine kind, peace, or contentment.

John had some Virginia Gold, some land, and a plantation, but it was not enough to fill the void in his life when he lost Rachel. Now, it was not gold, not Virginia Gold, that had persuaded Dorothy to renew her life with John. It was just plain love. Their kind of relationship could not be bought.

This *Sea Venture* ate up the leagues of the sea more quickly than its namesake in 1609. By the middle of September, John and his family were in Jamestown.

The plantations were suffering from an extreme food shortage. This was brought on by the massacre and subsequent retaliation against the Indians, who were the source of most of their corn and other food supplies. In addition, the Virginia Company had a virtual monopoly and stranglehold on imports, not only of food, but other equipment and supplies. The imports could only be paid for in Virginia Gold, but the company had inflated the cost of all supplies so much that the planters could barely make a profit from their tobacco, on which they had to pay a tax to the Crown.

King James personally detested the use of tobacco and forbade its planting in England. Yet he allowed its growth through the Virginia Company in the colony, as long as it brought wealth to him.

Sergeant Sharpe met John and his new family soon after they docked. He had two of his men and his personal boat on hand to ferry them all over to the plantations. On the trip over the James, he spoke to John about the hard times in which the colony found itself.

"John, remember the land you planted in corn? I doubled that acreage, and it is bringing almost as much as tobacco due to the food shortage."

"Did my men harvest my crop of corn?"

"Yes, and it's worth almost its weight in gold, the metallic kind."

"Do we still have time for a fall planting of more corn?"

"Yes, I believe we do, and I think it would be wise, not only for our survival but to help out the shortage over in Jamestown."

"What is the House of Burgesses doing about these problems?"

"They are petitioning the king for a new charter and new management by the Virginia Company."

"Will it happen?"

"It will take a year at least, maybe more, for things to get better."

They talked on for a while until the boat reached the landing. John's men were waiting to transport trunks and other belongings of John's new family to his plantation. John carried Dorothy over the threshold, with John Jr. following close behind.

Dove's sister, Morning Swan, greeted them. Sergeant Sharpe explained her presence as his gift of welcome to Dorothy and John until other arrangements could be made. Dorothy was very thankful to the sergeant. Morning Swan was about sixteen, and almost as attractive as her sister. John thanked his friend for Swan's help, and then asked if there had been any more trouble with the Indians, and if he had heard from John Rolfe.

"No word about Rolfe. The president of the burgesses thinks he perished in the Henrico massacre. They are planning to replace him on that body. They are giving it a little more time, just in case he was taken captive."

"As for the Indians, Sir Francis Wyatt has been keeping them on the defensive, and very few attacks have been reported. I think they have learned their lesson."

"Let's hope so. Have any of the tribes requested peace settlements with us?"

"Some, mostly on our side of the James."

"Good. I would hate to have to farm with a rifle in one hand and a hoe in the other."

"I think we are going to see things get back to normal, John. It may take a year or two. Come over tomorrow, or whenever you can. I have some more things to tell you."

"I will, William, and thanks again for bringing Swan. Also, thanks for looking after my plantation while I was gone. I'll do the same for you if you ever need it."

"Glad to help you out. I'm also glad to see you at peace again after losing Rachel."

"Dorothy and John Jr. are a godsend."

CHAPTER 53

A DREAM FULFILLED

AT A MEETING of the House of Burgesses, following John and Dorothy's arrival, John was elected to fill the vacancy of John Rolfe's term of office. This was a temporary appointment by the house in case John Rolfe was found or his death established.

Adjusting to the life of farming was not easy for Dorothy and John Jr. The lack of other people nearby with which to visit and the distance across the river to Jamestown were handicaps that took time to overcome.

Having Dove and her sister Swan nearby, even though a different race, helped somewhat. John Jr. and his father became better acquainted. John had no experience as a father. John Jr. had mostly interacted with his mother and grandparents since infancy. So it took John and his new son some months to grow into their new roles and relationship with each other. Dorothy's firm love and discipline made the transition easier. John's expressive love for Dorothy gave their son a new sense of security.

John took John Jr. with him to his work whenever possible to foster the relationship as father and son. Thus John and his new family spent their first Christmas Eve thanking God for their love for each other and their blessings of health and prosperity in their new land.

On Christmas Day, Dorothy hosted a dinner for Sergeant Sharpe, his men, and Dove and Swan. It required two long tables to seat all. Dorothy showed her skill as a cook in her tasty recipes that graced the heavily laden tables.

After dinner, John and the sergeant took a short walk to one of John's curing barns. "Whatever became of your special request for a waiver to marry Dove?" John asked.

"After the attacks, I asked the governor to put it on hold."

"Do you still want to marry her?"

"I'm not sure. The feelings in the colony have so turned against the Indians that I think it would be hard for Dove or me to have a normal, happy marriage. I counseled with Chaplain Bucke, and he suggested I withdraw the request."

"How did Dove react to that?"

"She said she understood and would be willing to wait to see if a peace treaty with her people would make any difference. That's where it stands for now."

"I see," replied John.

Gradually, during the next two years, John and his additional hired men were able to clear and plant most of his three-hundred-acre plantation in tobacco and corn. Food was scarce in the colony, so John was able to sell his surplus corn for a good price.

By agreeing to grow corn for Jamestown's consumption, John was able to add another two hundred acres to the size of his plantation. Now, his and Sergeant William Sharpe's plantations were approximately the same size.

In London, the management of the Virginia Company increasingly was unable to finance itself. Facing bankruptcy in the summer of 1623, the king's privy council took control. This led to its charter being revoked by the Crown the following summer, and Virginia became a royal colony.

CHAPTER 54

THE REAL GOLD

THURSDAY, NOVEMBER 3, 1625, dawned clear and crisp at John's plantation. It was his thirty-fourth birthday. He awoke before the sun was up, dressed quietly without disturbing Dorothy and the kids, and tiptoed quietly downstairs.

John unbolted the front door to their comfortable log cabin home and walked out, closing the door softly behind him. His two foxhounds nudged him. Tails wagging, they waited expectantly for him to stroke their velvety ears.

A squirrel and a magpie were squawking at each other from a black walnut tree near the house. John strode down a winding path to a large open building. Rows of brown tobacco leaves filled this curing barn with a heavy aroma. His eyes caressed this latest bumper crop from his five-hundred-acre plantation.

"These leaves are almost ready for shipment to London," John muttered. However, this was only the nearest of several curing barns filled with this year's crop. The others were located strategically near plots of land carved out of the forest. Tobacco plants took a lot out of the soil. This required more land to be cleared every few years to maintain his level of shipments.

As he stroked the golden brown leaves and smelled their scent, he thought back over his years of good fortune and hard labor. He had come a long way from his native Wales over the last seventeen years. "Not bad for beginning as an indentured servant," he thought.

True, he had been blessed by his God. Also, he had held onto his original faith in his vision to become a landed gentleman. Rising from his roots of poverty, he had realized his dream that someday he would own land, create wealth, and raise a family.

Could he have ever done it in Wales? Could this ever have happened if he had not ventured forth to this faraway colony of Virginia? He doubted it. That he could rise above the rank of a nobody to a plantation owner by means of this Virginia Gold was indeed amazing

In his native Wales, he would have to be born with rank or wealth in order to achieve status as a gentleman. Here, all he needed was a vision, hard work, and faith in God. Of course, it helped if one had a good supply of tobacco leaves to sell.

This tobacco, this currency of the colony, was indeed the gold that allowed Virginia to grow and expand so quickly as a colony of plantations. "But even more important," thought John, "is the freedom and opportunity to exploit and export this Virginia Gold."

After tobacco, would some other product become the currency? Would it, as tobacco, allow other immigrants the freedom and opportunity to move above poverty to become landed gentlemen?

For several minutes, John let the thoughts of his wealth and achievements sweep over him. Then other questions began to seep into his consciousness. "Did I really accomplish all of this by myself? To be honest, I had lots of help along the way," he told himself.

This self-examination of himself continued. "If I have achieved all this wealth and Virginia gold, why don't I feel satisfied?" Just below the surface of his conscious mind, John felt something akin to an inner conflict. He couldn't quite put his finger on it. It was a nagging feeling of discontentment. After all this success, why was he feeling this way? Only a few minutes ago, he was congratulating himself. Now, he had a feeling of unease, of something almost akin to guilt. Why? All at once, he remembered something his mother had given him in answer to a question.

"Mother, how can you and Father be so content and happy with your lot and status in life?"

"Son," she had said, "happiness and peace in life are not dependent on your wealth, but rather on your relationship with God. Contentment with godliness is the real wealth."

John had argued with her over this and made it clear he was going to set his sights higher than both of them, and he had, but even now, with all his wealth, when he should have been most at peace with himself, he felt something was missing.

All at once, it hit him. He had set his first priority on his dream of material wealth. And it had cost him. He could have married Rachel sooner and saved her life, no doubt. His dream of reaching his material goals could have waited a few more years. Tears began to flow as he remembered Rachel and her death, her love, and prayers for him.

The voice of John Jr. shouting, "Father!" brought John back to himself.

Today was his birthday, and God's goodness had given him a second chance at love with Dorothy and their growing family of three sons. Now John had his answer as to why he had felt a nagging, negative feeling of discontent and a lack of peace with himself.

Mother was right, after all. The true wealth was not the Virginia Gold he had focused on for the past seventeen years, but rather his relationship with his Lord and Christ and the love of his wife and children.

What was that other scripture Mother would quote to him? "Seek ye first the Kingdom of God, and His righteousness, then all these other things shall be added unto you as well."

"Thank God for mothers," he muttered. "Yes, and fathers also," he added.

John had gotten it backwards for seventeen years, but now he believed he had his priorities straight. He raced his two hounds up the path to home, to his kids, and to his loving Dorothy.

THE ISLANDS OF BERMUDA

JUAN BERMUDEZ, A Spanish explorer, discovered this chain of small islands as early as 1505. Their location is approximately seven hundred miles southeast of New York City. They were first called "Devil's Islands" due to the weird sounds emanating from them. They were later called "Somers Islands" after Sir George Somers, a British admiral.

Somers' ship, the *Sea Venture*, carrying colonists to Virginia, was damaged by a hurricane and landed here in 1609. Later, Somers Islands became a British colony. Today, it is mostly called Bermuda after the name of its discoverer.

The map of the islands below shows the locations of the few towns and points of interest today in Bermuda. The islands are made up of seven main islands, close to each other and connected by bridges. From the air, Bermuda appears in the shape of a fishhook. The land area is approximately twenty-one square miles, and the islands run from east to west.

Most historians agree that Shakespeare used the account of the tempest that Sir George Somers' fleet of ships encountered as part of his plot for his final play, *The Tempest*.

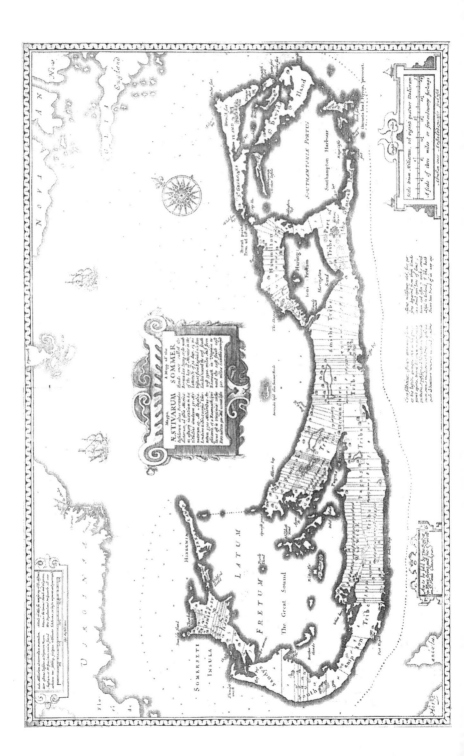

BIBLIOGRAPHY

Americana Encyclopedia. Americana Corporation Publishers. 1969.

Chandler, Jane Thomas. *The Thomas Tree.* Skullbone Printers Publishers. 1982.

Deans, Bob. *The River Where America Began.* Roman and Littlefield Publishers, Inc. 2007.

Doherty, Kieran. *Sea Venture.* St. Martin's Press. 2007.

Haile, Edward Wright, ed. *Jamestown Narratives.* Round House Publishers. 1998.

Hume, Ivor Noel. *The Virginia Adventure.* Alfred A. Knopf, Inc. 1994.

Kelso, William M. *Jamestown, The Buried Truth.* University of Virginia Press. 2006.

Kemp, Peter. *The Oxford Companion to Ships and the Sea.* Oxford University Press. 1976.

Peden, William. *Notes on the State of Virginia.* University of North Carolina Press. 1954.

Polk, William R. *The Birth of America.* HarperCollins. 2006.

Quinn, Arthur. *A New World*. Berkley Publishing Group. 1994.

Raine, David F. *Sir George Somers*. Pompano Publications, 1984.

Schleienger Jr., Arthur M. *The Almanac of American History*. Brompton Books Corporation. 1993.

Taylor, Alan. *American Colonies*. Penguin Books. 2001.

The Holy Bible. The Geneva Version

Wooley, Benjamin. *Savage Kingdom*. HarperCollins. 2007.

WinePressPublishing
Your Book, Defined.
Since 1991.

To order additional copies of this book call:
1-877-421-READ (7323)
or please visit our website at
www.WinePressbooks.com

If you enjoyed this quality custom-published book,
drop by our website for more books and information.

www.winepresspublishing.com

"Your partner in custom publishing."

CPSIA information can be obtained at www.ICGtesting.com
Printed in the USA
242543LV00002B/1/P

9 781414 117072